John Francis Hunter, author of THE GAY INSIDER, says:

"*All Is Well* is, to date, the best work of fiction of the new gay literature. Its theme is liberation, played with deceptive simplicity and not a trace of political bombast. Yet it *is* political, in that it is a paean to a way of life that is counter-culture all the way. Suspenseful and phantasmagoric, swift-moving yet entirely thorough in all its revelation of a metamorphosis that could be Everyman's, *All Is Well* grabs you and keeps you—and if you dig its message will never let you go. The captive gay, or even part-captive, who carefully reads and really understands and actually applies the wisdom of this novel won't need a shrink and can get by without an organization or any formal experiment in consciousness-raising.... What's more, *All Is Well* is a novel of, for and about sex, with some astoundingly erotic scenes that are as profound a manifesto of the right to discover and be one's total self as any rhetoric on the essential subject that I've heard or read. I recommend it wholeheartedly as a must to today's—or tomorrow's—American male homosexual."

NOTE: *All Is Well* is the third of the "All" books, a sequel to the bestselling *All Or Nothing* and *I Want It All.* An expanded and rewritten version of *All Or Nothing* is currently in preparation, and will be published soon by The Other Traveller.

DEDICATION:

This book is for all those who have been there—and for all those who are only beginning to realize that's where they are going—with a special note of gratitude and love to The Stoned Freak Typing Company's Brother Jack.

But most of all, this book is for Herb.

ALL IS WELL

Dírk Vanden

THE OLYMPIA PRESS

First published in Great Britain in 1972 by
The Olympia Press Limited,
20 Rupert Street, London W1

Printed in Great Britain by Oxley Press Ltd

ISBN 700 414 30 4

AUTHOR'S NOTE

In all of my previous books, sex has necessarily been the predominant theme, because whether or not their assumptions were correct, my publishers insisted on "hot sex" and lots of it, the kinkier the better, with a little plot and characterization tossed in here and there for good measure. Olympia has allowed me far more freedom in writing *All Is Well;* the sex is still there (as it must be in gay novels as well as gay lives) but only as one of many aspects of the story. Some readers may find the sex scenes less masturbatory as a result. I've had to make a decision—to write "just another sex book" or to test my convictions that gay people want to understand themselves and one another more than they want to jack off. After all, there are thousands of books which supply masturbatory fantasies for those who want them; there are very few books which advance the idea that being gay isn't as wretched and sinful as we've all been taught to believe it is.

There is a tremendously exciting reformation going on, all over the world, and I feel that gay people are going to wake up and find themselves in the vanguard of that reformation. But in order to "wake up" we must first understand ourselves—and that, more than anything else, is what *All Is Well* is all about.

Dirk Vanden

PART 1

Chapter 1

The note was creased and worn from many openings and refoldings. The printing was childish and the spelling atrocious, but I knew that no child had conceived such a frightening thing:

DERE ROBBER. THIS HERE IS A WARNING. YOU ARE GOING TO DIE. YOR A WIKID AND TERIBEL MAN. YOU HURT PEEPLE. YOR WIFE HATES YOR GUTS AND THE GIRLS AND YOR SUN ALSO. BUT I HATE YOR MORE. YOU DESERV TO DIE AND IF GOD DONT GIT YOU I WIL.

PS. YOR SUN IS A QUEER IF YOU DONT NO THAT ALL READY. IF YOU THING I AM FOOLING ASK JERY ASHBY. SO HA HA. THE JOKE IS ON YOU.

SINED YOU NO WHO

My hands were shaking as I angrily folded the note. I wanted to rip it to shreds, or crumple and burn it—get rid of it, forget it! What a blessed relief it would be just to get it out of my mind, if only for a couple of hours, or even a few minutes! Instead, I opened and read it again. The action had become a new habit—reading it, refolding it, unfolding it to read it again....

Just two weeks ago it had come in the mail—two weeks that were now beginning to seem like two years. It had been lying innocently on my bed (where Kate always put the mail addressed specifically to me—fortunately) along with the telephone bill and a real estate brochure, addressed to *MR ROBBER THORNE.* I'd laughed at first, muttering, "Some idiot doesn't know how to spell Robert." Then I'd opened the evil thing!

PS. YOR SUN IS A QUEER....

I pressed my hands hard against my legs, trying to stop them from trembling.

I needed a drink.

I looked at my watch; my plane wasn't due to start loading for another ten minutes or so. I shuddered at the thought of taking that flight, but it had to be done. And I knew I could face it a lot more easily with a good stiff drink in my stomach.

I put the note and envelope into my briefcase, then stood wearily, glancing toward the huge front windows of the San Francisco airport. With the late afternoon sun slanting across the glass, the windows had become partly opaque, and for a few moments I studied my transparent reflection. At least I didn't look as bad as I felt. The new clothes helped. I nodded to myself, thinking that Virginia, my secretary, would be delighted when I came in Monday morning: "Oh, wow, you did it! Oh, Mr. Thorne, now you really *do* look like him!" She insisted that I looked like her "very most favorite" movie star, Sean Connery, and although I couldn't quite see the resemblance, I'd kept his James Bond image in mind, buying the new jacket and trousers. I still wasn't sure that I liked the snug-fitting bellbottoms, but maybe that was simply because I wasn't used to them. Or maybe it was because I felt foolish for spending almost a hundred dollars just to please my secretary—but, dammit, a man needed to please *somebody* once in a while.

What the hell? Other men my age were wearing

bellbottoms, some of them a lot tighter and gaudier than these; the young man who'd sold them to me had insisted, "Oh, yes, sir, I'd say these were *super-conservative*. I mean, no one's going to think you're a hippie or anything like that."

I was distracted from my thoughts by a growing uneasiness, sensing that someone was watching me. I tried to see who it might be by looking at the other reflections in the window, but the images were too hazy, and the glass kept wavering, each time someone came through the doors from outside.

I sat down again, trying to look casual—but my heart was starting to beat faster and the muscles in my stomach were tensing almost painfully: it wasn't the first time today that I'd felt someone was watching me.

I'd awakened in my hotel room that morning with the vivid impression that someone was there in the room with me; even though that proved untrue, I couldn't get rid of the conviction that someone had been in the room sometime during the night. I'd found nothing actually missing or noticeably out of place, but somehow it had seemed that things were *not quite* as I'd left them. Then later, walking along Van Ness on my way to the American Graphic Designers' Association conference, I'd had the impression that someone was following me. Once more I'd been unable to confirm the suspicion. It had happened again in a coffee shop, just before the last session of the conference. I'd gone through the day with the increasingly uneasy premonition that something was going to happen—something bad, maybe even disastrous.

And now it was happening again!

I turned in the seat. At first there seemed to be no one the slightest bit interested in me, but as I glanced through the busy, noisy crowd, for some reason my eyes kept returning to a man standing at a bookstall about ten feet away. He was seemingly intent on reading a paperback novel, but something about him—I couldn't tell what—gave me the feeling that he wasn't reading the book at all.

He glanced up, and I turned away, but not before his gaze had met mine in a way that convinced me he'd been the one watching me. Moreover, I had a strangely uncomfortable feeling that I recognized him.

I was sure he wasn't anyone I knew well—at least not at the present; something in my mind hinted that I'd known him a long time ago, maybe in college. If that were true, it would explain why he'd been watching me; he could have been trying to remember where he'd known me before—just as I was doing.

I glanced over my shoulder again. For a moment I thought he had gone—or had realized I'd seen him and had ducked behind one of the racks—but then I saw him at the counter, buying the book he'd been looking at. Obviously he was making no attempt to hide. At the moment he was leaning on the counter, looking thoroughly unconcerned, waiting for the cashier to bring back his change, casually watching the crowd moving around him.

He was a large man and rather good-looking—or perhaps "rugged" was a better word. I guessed he would stand an inch or so taller than I—maybe six-two or six-three. Dark hair, broad shoulders, a solid, muscular body. (I decided that women would probably find him very "sexy".) There was something about him that seemed out-of-place, and it took several moments before I could decide what it was. He looked so natural and at ease in his clothing that it wasn't until I'd looked around at several other men that I realized what made him look different. Most of the men I could see were dressed like myself, in sport coats and slacks, or in business suits; he was wearing a plain white T-shirt and the tightest pair of levis I'd seen in a long time. With his faded denim jacket hanging over one muscular arm, he looked like a burly sheepherder just down from the hills, freshly scrubbed, ready for a "night out in the Big City". But a *friendly* sheepherder. He didn't look at all sinister or dangerous. I couldn't quite picture him sneaking into my room, or skulking after me in the street. He looked more like the type who would march up and say, "Hey, don't I know you from somewheres?"

The only thing that really disturbed me about him was the obscene slouch he affected, which tightened his levis even more, displaying a thick and embarrassing bulge in his crotch; even from where I was sitting, the details of his sex organs were obvious. There was no way anyone could have helped noticing.

He stood up from the slouch as the cashier said something behind him, and I looked up to his face—and found his eyes looking directly at mine. He nodded and grinned, then turned to the cashier, and I quickly looked away, embarrassed at having been caught staring.

A tinny voice startled me: "Your attention please. United Airline's flight nine-seventeen, nonstop to Salt Lake City, is now loading at gate twenty-two...."

The voice pushed all thought of the man totally out of my mind. I sat staring out of the window again, feeling numb. Now that the moment had come, I didn't want to get on that plane! I'd planned it all so carefully up to this point, but now that the end of my plan was in sight I didn't want to complete it. I wanted to rush back outside, jump into the nearest cab, and speed back into San Francisco.

But I couldn't do that and I knew it; I had to go through with it; I had to be sure.

Now it was even too late to have that drink!

The announcement came again and I reluctantly stood up and started toward the long corridor to the loading ramps.

"Hey! Hey, you! Wait!"

The voice was like a blast of icy wind. I stopped short, my back muscles tensing like fists along my spine. I wanted to turn, to glance back casually, but for a terrible moment I couldn't move. Wildly in my mind I saw several men coming toward me, guns drawn from secret holsters, handcuffs open, ready to arrest me for some dreadful crime I hadn't committed.

"Hey! Your briefcase."

I looked down at my empty hand. "Oh, God!"

The note was in that briefcase!

I spun around–and almost collided with the man who'd been watching me. He smiled as he held out the briefcase, and I forced myself to smile calmly as I took it. "Thank you," I told him. "Don't want to lose that." I added: "Nothing really valuable in it, but I wouldn't want to just leave it behind."

He nodded and smiled again. "Good thing I noticed."

"Yes. Thank you."

Now that we stood face to face, that feeling that I knew him grew even stronger. I waited before saying anything, hoping he'd ask: "Aren't you Robert Thorne? Remember me? I'm..." But he didn't. I watched his brown eyes for a flicker of recognition, but if there was any he didn't let it show.

I felt foolish asking, but I had to know. "Do I know you from someplace?"

He looked startled. "I don't think so."

"Oh." I looked down uncomfortably. "I...just thought...the way you were....staring...."

"Me?" He chuckled softly. "I thought *you* were staring."

"No," I said quickly. I could feel my face burning again. "At least, I didn't mean to. I'm sorry if... I just had this feeling I knew you. Sorry."

"Hell, that's okay. Don't apologize."

"Well, thanks for finding the briefcase." I hesitated, unsure of what to say next–he looked as if he expected me to say something.

"Are you on nine-seventeen?" he asked.

"What? Oh, yes. Yes, I am."

"Well...." He grinned. "That's a pleasant coincidence. So am I. I guess we'd better hurry." He started down the corridor, then paused to look back at me.

I laughed nervously, feeling like a flustered kid, then hurried to catch up with him. As I fell into step beside him I asked, "Do you live in Salt Lake?"

"Unfortunately."

"Oh? You don't like it?"

"Even less after spending a week here. Oh, it's okay, I guess, if you happen to be a good Mormon—which I'm not." He paused for a moment, then asked: "How about you?"

"Pardon me?"

"Are you a good Mormon?"

"No," I said. "Not a *good* one."

"Well, then, you should know what I mean. Ah, but San Francisco! Now there's a *real* city for you."

"Yes," I agreed. "I've certainly enjoyed it."

"Yeah," he said softly, as though remembering something pleasant, "it's just about the only place I know of where a guy can really find just about anything he's looking for, you know? You here on vacation?"

"No. Business."

"Oh. Did you get out at all?"

"Not too much."

"Well...." He was silent for a moment as we walked, then laughed softly. I turned to him, wondering what he had found amusing. He seemed lost in some memory, unaware I was looking at him. Even though he'd denied it, I couldn't get over the feeling that I recognized him. I guessed he was roughly the same age as I, or a year or so younger—in his early thirties at least; we were both built about the same, although his musculature was better defined than mine; both of us were dark-haired. Maybe that was it! Maybe, somehow, he reminded me of myself. To a casual stranger, seeing us walking together, we might easily have looked like brothers. Of course, I was clean-shaven, while he sported a thick moustache and bushy sideburns; and his hair was somewhat long: neatly trimmed, but definitely longer than I liked to see hair on a man. Still, I had to admit that it didn't look particularly bad. It went with that overall "sheepherder" image; it suited him.

I reminded myself that I had to get over my aversion to long hair on men. It was a lesson I'd had crammed down my throat at the Design Conference, where at least half of the men had worn long hair, moustaches, even full beards. As a matter of fact, a couple of times I'd caught myself staring into a mirror, wondering what I might look like with a nice bushy moustache—but I'd put the idea out of mind very quickly. Virginia would get a big kick out of it, but our customers wouldn't. Not in Salt Lake City, Utah. Not those straitlaced old bastards. With them, my problem was to look *more* mature, not less, and I knew they would equate even a moustache with "hippies", as I had done. At thirty-five I looked more like thirty—which was remarkable considering all I'd been through lately—and sometimes I had trouble convincing a new account that I was mature enough to have my own company, experienced enough to handle their precious advertising campaign, even though *Bogen & Thorne* was one of the better-known agencies in Salt Lake, and had been for several years.

The plane was only about three-quarters full, and we were apparently the last two passengers. There were several pairs of seats still vacant. I glanced around the cabin, about to ask the man whether he'd prefer the front or the back of the plane, when he said, "Well, good. We can both get window seats. Talk to you later."

In spite of the strange way we'd met, I'd assumed we would sit together and talk on the way home. I'd been thinking it would be a relief to talk to somebody, get my mind off my problems. But apparently my "new friend" wasn't all that interested in conversation. I shrugged off my momentary disappointment and said, "Fine. After dinner, maybe."

"Right." He nodded, then slid into a seat in front of the wings. I continued back almost to the rear. With my briefcase in the aisle seat, I strapped myself down by the window. As a stewardess came by, checking seatbelts, the jet shuddered and started away from its berth. For a few minutes I watched the airport buildings recede in the gathering twilight; then, as the plane rumbled and shuddered, waiting for clearance for takeoff, I took the note out of my briefcase and slipped it into my inside coat pocket. It wasn't too likely I'd forget it again, but I didn't want to take chances.

Even though I'd resisted the impulse to read the note again, I couldn't keep myself from thinking about it. The threat to my life didn't particularly worry me, mainly because I could not take it seriously. Nor was I shocked by the idea that Kate hated me; I'd been living with that fact for years. No, the thing which disturbed me was that PS—that supposedly tossed-in fill-up about Chuck. To me, that was the core of the message, and the rest merely windowdressing, carefully designed to confuse or frighten me, to distract me from the real threat of the thing: blackmail! Naturally I was hurt and disgusted by the accusation that my son was a homosexual—what father wouldn't be? Although I might have understood and forgiven him even that "youthful indiscretion" (after all, he was only sixteen) if he hadn't been so stupid, or so intentionally spiteful, as to let someone know about it. Because, whoever he was, that someone was obviously determined to put me through whatever hell he could devise—make me feel guilty and miserable because, supposedly, it was a father's fault when a son turned homosexual, etc., etc.—all as a buildup to another note requesting a few thousand dollars in return for his silence.

I wasn't fooled for a minute by the childish printing and spelling. I was certain the writer could spell as well as I. He'd been "mature" enough to know how to address and mail the envelope.

The more I thought about it, the more I was convinced that the clue to the culprit's identity lay in the note itself: "If you think I am fooling, ask Jerry Ashby." No matter what else might be wrong with Chuck's so-called "best friend", he wasn't stupid. He was smart enough to pretend to be stupid—if he saw something in it for him. The whole thing could easily be one of Ashby's wild schemes to make money for one of those underground groups he belonged to, that he'd talked Chuck into joining. With the morals those kids had, he wouldn't be above setting up his best-friend for something like this: getting him drunk—or worse, doped up—then seducing him, with one of his long-haired cronies in the closet taking pictures. But if I could catch him in a compromising situation himself, that would be the end of it right there. Also it would give me a legitimate reason for forbidding Chuck to ever see him again.

The big jet was moving now, faster and faster down the runway. I leaned close to the window, looking down as the ground suddenly dropped away from under us, and a bright thrill coursed through my body. I loved that moment of takeoff; it always reminded me of riding in elevators when I was a child. San Francisco grew smaller and smaller as the jet climbed over the Berkeley hills. The day had been clear and cloudless and now the sun was a flattened fiery red ball sinking into a golden ocean. The early evening sparkle of lights around the shimmering bay slowly faded in a light haze, then vanished beyond the edges of my window.

It was truly a beautiful city, I thought. Throughout both days of the AGDA conference, I'd toyed with ideas of moving there permanently, but the ideas had all been impractical, simply wishful thinking. (I couldn't move anywhere at least until Chuck was old enough to take care of himself; I had a responsibility there which I wasn't about to abandon.) I'd had to decide to be satisfied with an occasional visit whenever some artist or design or advertising group had a conference. Still, it was a pity I'd had to leave early. I could have spent all day tomorrow, Easter Sunday, just wandering around in the bright spring sunshine—through Ghiradelli Square, or in Golden Gate Park, maybe taking one of the boat tours of the bay.

Well, no use torturing myself; I'd have to spend Easter at home. I could only hope that it wouldn't turn into a sordid fight with Chuck.

Low ranges of hills passed under us, fading sunlight illuminating their western sides, darkness gathering behind them. I watched strange unfathomable light-patterns on the ground—cities, towns, freeways, airports—again very tempted to wish I hadn't taken the flight. No one expected me home until late tomorrow night.

But that, of course, was the whole point: nobody expected me. I'd arranged it that way for a definite reason, and now I had to go through with my plans.

Humorlessly I thought: *Oh, what tangled web's we weave....*

But I had to be sure—and this was the only way I could think of to be sure. I had to catch him in the act. It was a rotten thing to do, deliberately tricking my own son, but it had to be done. Any other way, he could simply deny the accusation. I had to surprise him, take him off his guard. If he knew I suspected him, I'd never find out anything.

I was tempted to confront him with the note and tell him, "You've made your bed, now lie in it!" Running around with that hippie crowd, getting involved with that underground newspaper, getting himself kicked out of school for those ridiculous protests. I'd asked him a hundred times to stop seeing that damned Jerry Ashby, but he just wouldn't listen. Constantly giving me that smug silence that said, "What do you know about anything? You're an old man!"

"Good evening...."

My heart lurched against my chest and my head jerked up, half expecting to see that man standing over me, knowing what I'd been thinking. I cursed myself for being so jumpy. I was acting as though *I* had done something wrong.

"...your captain, John Everest. Welcome aboard United's flight nine-seventeen to Salt Lake City. We are slightly behind schedule, but we've got a good tail-wind and should make it up. Our projected arrival time is nine thirty-five. We will be flying at an altitude..."

Nine thirty-five. That would put me home about ten, or a little after. If the note were true, if Chuck were having...an affair...with the Ashby kid, that would be just about the perfect time to catch them. Like Chuck, Ashby lived at home with his parents, and if I'd guessed rightly, he'd be the first to suggest that they spend the evening at our place. With Kate in Ogden—she'd have left early this morning—and me in San Francisco, they'd think they had the whole house to themselves for the night. At least that's how I'd planned it. That's why I'd decided to go to the AGDA Conference in the first place; that's why I'd suggested that Kate take the girls to spend Easter vacation with her parents in Ogden; that's why I'd made such a point of telling Chuck I wouldn't be home until Sunday night. Let Ashby hang himself with his own rope! I'd suspected the kid of being queer from the first moment I'd seen him, and if my suspicions were correct, I was sure he would jump at the bait I'd held out to him.

Of course, Ashby wasn't the only suspect. My partner, Ed Bogen, was right up there, second on the list; but before I risked making a fool of myself, confronting Ed, I had to eliminate Ashby.

"Sir?" I jerked around. A pretty blonde stewardess was leaning over the vacant seat next to mine, smiling brightly. "We'll be serving dinner in about ten minutes," she said sweetly. "Would you care for a cocktail first?"

Even though I'd been thinking about getting a drink, back in the airport, and even though I knew that I needed one to relax me and get my mind out of the rut of stewing over that damned note, still I felt a reluctance to say "yes" immediately. Old habits were hard to break. I'd been a good Mormon teetotaler up until five years ago, except for a brief lapse during high school, and I still couldn't help feeling a kind of smug hostility toward anyone offering me a drink. Even now I made it a practice to never drink liquor in a public place where any of my customers might see me. But this, I reminded myself, was not Salt Lake; there was no one on the plane who might recognize me (with the possible exception of the man who'd been watching me) so, finally, I smiled back up at the stewardess and said, "Yes, I believe I will."

I selected a miniature Smirnoff from her tray.

"Would you like a mix?" she asked. "Seven-Up? Ginger Ale?"

"Seven-Up will be fine."

She poured the beverage into a cocktail glass. "Enjoy your flight, Sir."

"Thank you."

I watched her move on to the next seats, wondering what kind of attitude a girl had to have to seem happy like that all the time? I emptied the little bottle into the glass, then raised a silent toast to the smiling hostess: *Here's to you, pretty thing. May you never get married and have children and problems.*

Kate had looked like that, once, many years ago. Not that pretty, of course, not then—Kate had been a late bloomer, and her beauty, when I'd started going with her, had been more of an inner glow, a spiritual beauty. Now that had reversed itself; now she was a physically attractive woman, with nothing but an ugly void inside.

I leaned back, sipping the cocktail. That had been so long ago. Seventeen years. How she had smiled then! How delightfully she had laughed—the laughter of innocence! How I had loved just being with her, watching her smile, hearing her laugh....

"May I?" The man who had rescued my briefcase stood in the aisle, holding his cocktail glass.

I smiled up at him and moved the briefcase under my seat, grateful that he'd stopped my dark mood before it had really taken hold of me. "Sure thing."

He sat with a loud sigh, adjusted himself (with those tight pants of his, I guessed that sitting down was something of a problem) then turned to me. He lifted his glass. "Here's to San Francisco." He took a quick sip. "God, I really hated to leave. I had one very nice thing going.... But, *c'est la vie*, as they say. 'All things must pass,' as good old George puts it." He grinned. "I'll warn you, I'm already a little bit drunk. One sweet little old lady gave me hers. Very Christian of her, wouldn't you say?"

"Very," I said, grinning back at him. He was the type who could charm little old ladies out of their gold teeth if he took the notion. His appearance was disarming; just to look at him, you'd expect him to swagger and swear like a sailor, but when he came out with something like *c'est la vie*, it took you off your guard. I decided he could be a fantastically successful salesman—or con man.

"By the way," he said, "we didn't introduce ourselves. I'm John Adams."

I reached across to shake hands. "Robert Thorne."

"Okay to call you *Bob?*"

"I'd rather you didn't," I said quickly, then added:

"I'm not being rude; I just don't care for the nick-name."

He shrugged. "So what's new and exciting in your life, Robert?"

"Not very much."

"Well, that's too bad. When I'm King, everybody will have at least one new and exciting thing happen at least once a day."

"I hope I'm around when you get to be King."

He looked at me, smiling as though we shared some kind of secret. "I hope so too." He took another sip of his drink. "How many of these things do we get?"

I shrugged. "I really don't know. One, I guess."

He patted my arm. "Not if old John has anything to say about it. When we land in good old New Jerusalem, I fully intend to be as *non compos mentis* as possible."

I laughed. "You really hate Salt Lake, don't you?"

"No, not really." He leaned out into the aisle and called, "Oh, Miss...." then sighed and settled down into the seat. He started to say something, then grimaced. He muttered, "Pardon me," and squeezed his hand under the waistband of his levis, tugged at something, then sighed again. "No," he said, "it's just that a place like San Francisco can spoil you, you know? You want something, just reach out and grab it. In Salt Lake we're still playing all the old games, and man, I'll tell you, I've had Oscar Wilde up to here, you know?"

Before I could say, "No, I don't know. What does Oscar Wilde have to do with it?" the stewardess appeared with her tray. "Yes, sir?"

"Hello again," John Adams said brightly. "My friend and I would certainly appreciate another little drink—if it's not against the rules."

She smiled like a light being turned on. "Of course." As I watched her pour the drinks, I realized why John had adjusted himself; her eyes strayed several times to his prominent crotch. As much as it annoyed—or embarrassed—me, John obviously knew how to get the best mileage out of his "physical attributes". Surprisingly enough, except for a quick glance at her bosom, John seemed not the least bit interested in his admirer. I decided he was probably so used to it, it had ceased to be a novelty to him. When she had gone, he turned to me, lifting his glass. "What shall we drink to, Robert?"

I shrugged. "You choose. I can't think of anything worth toasting."

"My God, is it that bad? Let's see.... How about sex?"

I lifted my glass. "Whatever *that* is." I finished what was left of my first drink and exchanged it for the fresh one. When I glanced up, John was staring at me, frowning dramatically, but with a mischievous sparkle in his eyes.

"Welllllll," he drawled, "if I remember what my Mommy told me... What's the matter, Robert? Aren't you getting your share of the goodies?"

I tried to think of an amusing answer, something to match his bantering tone, but he'd hit on a subject a little too close to home for me to make jokes about it. In fact I began to wonder at that point whether John Adams and I had anything in common that we could talk about. Obviously he was a real cockswain with the ladies, and no matter how I might want to, I knew I couldn't match clever sexual anecdotes with him. "I'm getting along," I said.

"Getting along? Come on. A guy like you, just *getting along?*"

"It's a long sad story, John. I could write a book." I chuckled humorlessly. "But I'm afraid it wouldn't be a very interesting book." I glanced out the window and took another drink.

"Look," he said seriously. "Am I bugging you or something? I tend to be slightly aggressive when I'm drunk."

"No," I said quickly, "of course you're not 'bugging' me. It's just...just a personal problem I've had on my mind. It's hard to shift gears."

"Oh, yeah. Yeah, I know how that is. Maybe I should go grab us another couple of drinks. I'm sure she'd let me have them."

I turned to him, grinning. "I'm sure she would, too. No, that's all right. This one will hit me in a minute or two."

"Fine." He smiled, then his gaze shifted to the window. "Beautiful, isn't it?"

For a moment I didn't turn, but looked at his face. There was something about this man that intrigued me and frightened me, both at the same time. I knew that he wasn't at all what he seemed, with his levis and T-shirt and scruffy boots. His words and the tones of his voice belied the rough, uncultured exterior. I had the feeling that John Adams wasn't like any other man I'd ever met. I had an almost overwhelming desire to touch him.

I turned quickly to the window. Outside, all traces of daylight had gone and the stars were breathtakingly brilliant—but they seemed so remote, so vastly far away. Something inside me seemed to swell and burst open and I shuddered, gritting my teeth to keep from suddenly starting to bawl like a little kid! I felt so unbearably lonely!

What the hell is the matter with me?

All day long those crazy thoughts about being watched and followed, and now... Here this guy had come back to talk to me, to offer his company, maybe even his friendship, and I couldn't even *talk* to him! I felt as though my entire body, including my brain, was trussed up with invisible cords. And that terrible feeling that something disastrous was coming closer and closer and closer!

I closed my eyes tightly, turning so he couldn't see.

Suddenly, vividly, I saw Kate, and she was laughing. I could almost hear the taunting, scathing sound of it.

Damn you, Kate Jensen! Damn the moment I ever laid eyes on you!

"...in a black mood, aren't you?"

At the sound of his voice, Kate's image vanished. I took a deep breath and turned to him. "I'm sorry, John."

"Do you feel like talking about it? I'm a very good listener."

I tried to smile. "I'm afraid it would bore you stiff. Look, I'm sorry. I really do want to talk to you, John, but..."

"I understand. You think maybe you'll feel better after dinner?"

"I'm sure I will. As soon as this damned drink gets going."

"Okay." He nodded, then stood up, tugging at his levis again. "I'll see you then." He started away, then turned and regarded me. "Robert..." He came back and stood pensively looking down at me. "Did you really think I was staring at you, back at the airport?"

The question was completely unexpected and it flustered me; I couldn't help twisting it into some kind of accusation. "Well...yes. I *thought* you were."

"Why? I mean, why did you think I'd be staring at you?"

"I told you, I thought maybe we knew one another."

"And that's all?"

I shook my head helplessly. "I don't understand what you're getting at."

"Nothing really—except a confession of sorts. I didn't think I was staring, but I had noticed you."

"Oh?"

"Should we talk about it after dinner?"

I nodded unsurely. "All right..."

"Don't look so worried, Robert. It's nothing world-shattering. I just thought you looked like somebody I'd like to know." He grinned, then winked, and then walked away, leaving me feeling as though someone had jerked a rug out from under me.

The dinner was soggy, but relatively warm and tasty, and by then the alcohol had relaxed me to where I could almost enjoy it. As I ate, I thought about John Adams' "confession of sorts". In a way, it made me feel better, because it reassured me that I hadn't been imagining things, and that let me hope I hadn't imagined the other times I'd felt I was being watched. I hoped that I hadn't put him off by being so damned gloomy. I really did want to get to know him. If he'd give me another chance, maybe I could tell him about myself. I knew that I desperately needed *someone* to talk to, someone I could confide in. These last two weeks I'd begun to realize how little I'd talked to anyone since that morning I'd walked into Kate's room in the hospital, five years ago, so proud and happy and so anxious to see my twin daughters—only to have my entire world shattered by three words: "They're not yours."

And now I was so bound up, so shut away in my own private miserable world, nothing had been able to get through to me. It seemed I'd been in some kind of emotional deep-freeze for five numb, endless years. I couldn't even remember those years! One day had followed another, and somehow five years had gone by. I could remember that morning in the hospital—and then the evening I'd come home and opened that note—but in between those two times was a vast grey void.

Perhaps, I thought, receiving that note would turn out to be a good thing. Perhaps it had jarred me enough to rouse me out of the deep-freeze. Instead of simply living with the problem, perhaps I could somehow come to terms with it, maybe even settle it. If it turned out that Jerry Ashby wasn't the culprit (and I prayed, for

Chuck's sake, that he wasn't) then I'd be forced to confront Ed Bogen; it would all have to come out then, the whole dreary, ugly mess, and perhaps that would be good.

Ed had once been my closest friend, as well as my business partner, and it was just possible that a shred of our original friendship could still function. It wasn't all that improbable that Ed had written the note to force such a confrontation. I was sure that he knew I was well aware of who the girls' father really was, and it was possible that he was as miserable about it as I was.

Maybe that was the "disastrous" change I'd felt coming.

After dinner I finished what was left of my drink, waiting for Adams to join me again. As the minutes dragged by, I leaned back in the seat and closed my eyes, thinking again about San Francisco...that bright afternoon I'd gone walking down by Ghiradelli Square ...the young, bearded artists, half-naked, in ragged faded levis, their paintings propped up along the sidewalks... bright-eyed long-long-haired girls selling strawflowers... posters of naked boys and girls, running along seashores, over grassy hills...*MAKE LOVE, NOT WAR*...musicians standing on street corners, singing songs about Love and Peace....

"...Sir?"

A hand touched my shoulder.

"Sir?"

I sat up, forcing my eyes open—and looked up at the pretty blonde stewardess. "We're beginning our approach to the Salt Lake Airport," she said. "Would you fasten your seat belt, please?" Sleepily I fumbled to fasten the clasp; she leaned over to help me, then smiled and said, "Thank you, Sir."

I felt the plane tilt into a bank, looked out the window. Salt Lake City looked like a bed of warm embers, heaped up in a dark "firepit" of the mountains.

Other embers trailed north and south, with little glowing beds marking other towns. I wanted to feel warm and happy at the sight of "home", but I couldn't. The hour was approaching when I'd have to confront Chuck, and I felt no comfort at all in that thought.

For a few moments I wondered why John Adams hadn't come back after dinner, but then I decided that, like everything and everyone else in life, he had been merely another "promise" that couldn't be fulfilled. I couldn't allow myself to be upset about it.

The plane finished its turn and the city moved to the opposite side of the plane. My window looked west toward the lake. The night was sharply clear. I could have counted the cars on the freeway.

Lucky devils, I thought. Some of those cars were going to San Francisco. How I wished I could have been in one of them.

To my amazement, John Adams was waiting at the bottom of the ramp. He fell into line beside me, putting his hand on my shoulder. "I came back to talk," he said, "but you were asleep."

"I guess I dozed off after dinner."

"Yeah. With that dinner, I don't blame you. It feels like a big lump of lead in my gut. Where you headed now?"

"Home," I said.

"How about letting me buy you a beer?"

I considered it, then shook my head. "I'd better not, John. It's sort of important that I get right home."

"Someone expecting you?"

"Well...not exactly. It's too complicated to explain, John."

"Oh, well." He shrugged and took his hand away from my shoulder. "Maybe some other time."

"Yes," I said. "Definitely."

"You mean that?"

I glanced at him, wondering why he should sound so

surprised. Had I seemed that standoffish? "Of course I mean it. I'm not always in such a lousy mood."

He smiled brightly. "Well, good." He reached into a pocket and gave me a small piece of paper; it had his name and telephone number carefully hand-printed. "I hoped you'd feel that way. Maybe dinner some night?"

"I'd like that." I put the paper into my coat pocket, next to the envelope. "Maybe some evening this week," I said. "My wife's out of town."

He turned to look at me, and for a fleeting moment there was an expression of confusion on his face. "Your wife?"

"Yes," I said. "She's in Ogden for the week. Took the girls to Grandma's for Easter."

"And what she doesn't know won't hurt her, is that it?"

I laughed. "It wouldn't hurt her even if she did know."

"I see. Well...I'm not married, Robert." He said it as though there were some kind of secret meaning in the words.

"You're lucky."

"You still want to come to dinner?"

"Of course—unless you're a lousy cook."

He laughed and gripped my shoulder again. "How old are they—your kids?"

"The girls are five; they're twins. And my boy is sixteen."

He frowned. "You're kidding. Sixteen?"

"I married young."

"Jesus, I'll say you did. How old were you, twelve?"

"No. We were both eighteen." I smiled, watching him silently adding eighteen and sixteen—plus one for the pregnancy. Most people had trouble believing that I had a sixteen-year-old son. Sometimes I had trouble believing it myself.

As we approached the baggage-return area, I spotted a Men's Room. My bladder had been uncomfortably full when I'd awakened on the plane, and I knew if I didn't go now, I'd be miserable on the drive home. I told John, "Excuse me," and turned aside into the room, assuming that we'd finish the conversation as we waited for our luggage.

I heard someone follow me into the room, but I didn't bother turning to see who it was; I stepped up to a urinal and concentrated on the splash of the stream in the cigarette shreds and filters. I was almost finished when I felt that uncomfortable awareness that someone was watching me. I glanced sideways.

John Adams stood at the next urinal; he was looking directly down at my penis.

And I couldn't help noticing that his own penis was standing out from his fly thick and half-erect. He was milking it lazily.

For a moment I was too stunned to think; all I could do was stand there and stare back at him. And in that moment, he reached out toward me—and touched me.

A chill shot through my body.

"Very nice, Robert," he whispered.

I jerked back, turning quickly away, frantically stuffing myself back into my shorts. It was all beginning to make sense to me now.

"Robert...."

I felt a hand on my shoulder. Blind fury erupted inside me and I spun around to face him, knocking his hand away. "Don't you touch me, you—" I shuddered painfully.

"Hey, now, hold on just a damn minute."

"You go straight to Hell, you filthy...*pervert!*"

Suddenly he started to laugh, and that only heightened my fury. "You sonofabitch! I'll call the police!"

"Oh?"

His pants were still open, his erection slowly drooping downward, jerking as it did.

"I'd think twice about telling anyone, Robert. Just

remember, it's your word against mine. And you really don't know who I am, do you? They might just believe me–and think *you* were the *pervert.*"

We stared at each other for a long moment; then he shook his head sadly and eased his limbering organ into his tight pants, adjusted it, then calmly zipped up. He put his hand on my shoulder and squeezed. "I'm really very sorry, Robert. It would have been fun."

He walked calmly out the door.

I stood as though frozen to the spot, staring after him, a terrible empty feeling deep in my body.

Chapter 2

The door of the Men's Room slowly eased itself closed, and I stared at it, unable to move, unable to slow down my churning mind long enough to decide what to do next. My hands had begun trembling; the muscles of my back were now tensing spasmodically; my legs felt as though they would buckle any moment.

I tried to move forward, aware that I couldn't just stand there, shaking like an idiot; someone would come in and see me! But my body lurched drunkenly sideways and I had to catch one of the pipes on the urinals just to keep from sprawling on my face.

I fumbled in my pocket for a dime and somehow managed to get into one of the toilet stalls, where I sat numbly, holding my head, trying to talk sense to myself, for what seemed like an hour. I heard the door open and close many times, watched shoes shuffle past on the dirty tile, listened to splashing and gurgling noises—until finally I felt I could walk again.

I told myself over and over that nothing disastrous had actually happened; all he had done was touch me; I hadn't asked him to touch me; there was no reason at all to blame myself for anything that had happened. There was no way I could have known why he'd been staring at me, why he'd been so "friendly", why he'd kept touching me, squeezing my shoulder.

The fact that I'd been preoccupied with a problem which concerned homosexuality was nothing but a coincidence—it had to be. Just one of those damnable ironies that Fate seemed to delight in. I was certain I'd neither done nor said anything to make him believe I had even a casual interest in the subject, let alone might be willing to subject myself to his degenerate idea of "fun"!

But then why the hell was it affecting me like this?

I could not understand why *I* was the one feeling so

helplessly wretched. It should have been just the other way around: *I* should have walked out that door, leaving *him* feeling rejected and miserable.

There was only one thing I could blame myself for, and that was for not guessing his real motives in the first place: I should have realized that normal men simply were not that friendly, that eager to get to know strangers. I should have realized he was queer just from the way he ignored that stewardess—it hadn't been for her benefit he'd adjusted his crotch; that had been strictly an attempt to intrigue me.

I felt like a complete fool. How could I have been so damned gullible, thinking we could be friends, thinking I could talk to him, tell him my troubles? Thank God I'd been in a bad mood and hadn't started babbling to him about Chuck and the note!

But I couldn't stop feeling that something beautiful had been spoiled. It seemed that a door of some sort had been opened, just slightly, and beyond that door had been something I'd wanted all my life, something warm, sincere—something beautiful—and then the door had been slammed in my face. I couldn't get his image out of my mind—so damned handsome, so very charming—standing there with his penis sticking out, telling me how sorry he was, how much "fun" it could have been.

Well, I told myself, *you've met your first real live queer.* That was certainly nothing to be ashamed of; it didn't mean there was anything wrong with me, just because I'd attracted a pervert.

When I finally came out of the Men's Room, the baggage return area was deserted; my overnighter was going around and around on the revolving table, all by itself. I picked it up and walked slowly out to the parking lot, feeling as though I'd been kicked in the head. I seemed to be walking in a dream, knowing I was dreaming but unable to wake myself up.

I located the Volkswagen, inspected it all around, then got in and took my bottle of vodka from under the back seat. The stuff burned like fury in my throat, but I forced it down, knowing I had to do something to get out of this terrible lethargy. I had to forget what had happened, put it completely out of my mind. It was only an isolated incident that could have happened to anyone. Just a couple of hours out of my life. Tomorrow, I told myself, it would seem like a dream, so why not start right now treating it as such? Just a nightmare, nothing more. I'd had plenty of nightmares before.

I chuckled, feeling slightly better: most of my life, recently, had seemed like a series of nightmares. There was no reason to let this particular one upset me any more than the others had done.

But there was a lesson to be learned, I decided: I couldn't allow myself to be gullible; I couldn't keep hoping that "beautiful doors" would miraculously open for me. Life wasn't like that. Life *was* a continuing nightmare. Hopes and promises were nothing but fantasies. The best any man could reasonably hope for was just to get by. To want anything more was to open yourself childishly to one disappointment after another—and that, when you considered it logically, was nothing more than self-torture—insanity—it was what the psychologists called "immaturity". A man had to grow up and get over his childish, idealistic notions of "friendship" and "beauty" and "love". Those were Sunday School promises. A man had to face reality and learn how to live with its ugliness, that was all.

And one of life's ugly realities still lay ahead of me. The sooner I got home and faced it, the better we'd all be for it.

I was feeling much more my old self as I drove onto the freeway and headed the car east toward the city. I'd managed to relegate John Adams to the position he richly deserved—to that of a nightmare creature. Instead of feeling threatened by the man, I could now begin to feel sorry for him. What a miserable hell his life must be, courting strange men in airports, propositioning them in restrooms.

Actually, I ought to be glad it had happened, because it gave me even more reason to try to save Chuck from that kind of life. Being forced to think it through the way I had, now maybe I could explain it to Chuck in terms he could understand.

I rolled down the window of my little bug, letting the cold tingle of wind calm me even more. The weather seemed to have changed while I'd been out of town; maybe spring had come at last. We'd had a long and cold winter, but now I could see that many of the trees were leafing out; soon the flowers would start blooming. Hopefully we'd be able to enjoy springtime for a few weeks, before the wretched heat of summer started making things miserable again.

I followed the freeway east to the Sugarhouse exit, drove past *Bogen & Thorne, Advertising* to make sure it hadn't burned down or been broken into in my absence, then followed 9th East to 13th South. I parked a block away from the house, had another quick drink, then locked the car and started the last few hundred feet of the distasteful journey on foot.

In spite of the alcohol my heart was thudding like a drum in my chest. I wanted to rehearse what I would say, but I had no idea what I would find. Would all the lights be blazing away, the stereo tuned to that damnable rock-and-roll station? Fifteen or twenty long-haired hippies doped-up in the front room, or scattered throughout the house? Would the lights all be out, with Chuck and his...whatever...sequestered in his room? This was something I hadn't been able to plan in advance. Just as long as I could get in the front door before anyone heard me, there'd be no way for them to escape without my hearing or seeing them.

What would Chuck do if he was in bed with Ashby? An image came into my mind—of Chuck standing naked at the top of the stairs, blinking down at me...but the image was hazy; what would my son look like, naked? I hadn't seen him undressed, even in a swim suit, since he was nine or ten years old.

I slowed my stride and thought about that: I really didn't know what my son looked like. He'd shot up like a weed since starting through puberty, and now he stood almost as tall as I. According to Kate, he was wearing clothes only one size smaller than mine, which meant he was going to be a very hefty guy. He had my features and coloring, and his body seemed to be large and muscular. At sixteen, he was a very handsome boy. Manly-looking....

I cringed! *Manly-looking!* Was that all it was? An appearance?

I remembered thinking how "manly-looking" John Adams had been—thinking what a cockswain he was with the ladies!

I stopped and stepped under the shadow of a freshly-leafed tree. *I did not want to find out that my son was a queer!* For at least the thousandth time I asked myself: *What will you do if he is? Throw him out? Try to talk sense to him? Quote the law, or the Bible? Plead with him to change?*

I glanced at my watch—just past ten-thirty.

I took a deep breath, squared my shoulders, started walking again. It had to be done. I had to be sure. One way or the other, like it or hate it, I had to be sure.

A dim light was burning inside; I guessed it was coming from the kitchen, or perhaps the upstairs hallway. I didn't know what kind of car Jerry Ashby drove, so I didn't bother checking the cars parked along the street. The driveway was empty. I walked very carefully up the front steps, held the keys tightly to keep them from rattling as I painstakingly opened the front door.

Silence greeted me.

I tiptoed into the kitchen. The stove light was on. The kitchen was spotlessly clean, just as I'd left it. I went up the stairs, holding tightly to the banister, stepping over the ninth tread which squeaked. The upstairs was dark. No hint of light spilled under Chuck's closed bedroom door. At the top of the stairs I closed my eyes and took several deep breaths, trying to calm my heartbeat.

"Anyone home?" I called.

No answer.

"Chuck? Are you home?"

Nothing.

I went to his door, hesitated, feeling a strange, almost sexual excitement deep in my stomach. I shoved the door open and quickly switched on the light.

The bed was empty. It was still very carefully made up, as though he hadn't been home at all since I'd left.

I leaned against the door frame, feeling like a balloon being deflated. All of my planning and sneaking had been for nothing. I could have stayed another full day in San Francisco—and completely avoided that depressing encounter with John Adams.

I stood for a long time staring vacantly into Chuck's room; then I wandered inside and sat on the edge of his bed, despondently glancing around at the walls—at the high school pennants, the blue-bordered Awards for Scholarship, a poster of the Caterpillar from *Alice in Wonderland*, and another of a gloomy-looking man with a black hat and a long beard, with a stained-glass window behind him. By the head of his bed was a tiny cartoon, pinned where the light from the bedlamp would shine on it, of Charlie Brown, leaning his head forlornly against a tree. There was no caption, but it didn't need one; the simple cartoon spoke eloquently of resigned frustration.

The room didn't seem like a teen-ager's bedroom;

there were no model airplanes, no pictures of sports heroes, no football or basketball or track awards. If my son were a reliable example, teen-agers had changed a great deal since I'd gone through that stage.

As I stood up to go out, I noticed two photographs on his dresser. One was of Chuck and me: a snapshot I'd completely forgotten, taken many years ago on one of our vacations before the girls had been born. Chuck had been about eight years old then. We were standing in front of Old Faithful in Yellowstone Park, hand-in-hand, both of us grinning happily at the camera. The other picture was an enlarged color Polaroid of Kate and the girls. I'd seen it a hundred times before, but looking at it now, Kate's smile appeared pathetically forced and there seemed to be a haunting sadness around her green eyes. Even so, she was a beautiful woman; no matter how I felt about her, I had to admit that. And the girls would look just like her eventually; they were both carbon copies of Kate as a child; both had her fair skin and freckles, her red hair which would deepen into auburn as they grew older. Like Kate, they would both be "plain" children and teen-agers, and then blossom in their twenties.

The pictures made me feel extremely uncomfortable, and I quickly moved out of Chuck's room, switching off the lights, closing the door quietly after me.

The house felt suddenly chilled.

I turned up the thermostat, then went into my room and wearily took off my coat and tie. I sat for a long time on my own bed, listening to the silence in the house. I felt I'd reached a dead-end, with no place to turn, no other road to follow. There was no way of knowing when Chuck might be home, or even if he'd be home at all. I cursed myself for ever having planned the stinking deceptive trip in the first place; it had caused nothing but problems, from beginning to end.

Finally I decided there was no point in just sitting. I

might as well go get the car and bring it around; if Chuck came home now, he'd see the lights and know I was home anyway.

I pulled the car into the driveway, then brought my luggage upstairs, intending to unpack and then shower, and maybe go out to a late movie. I was opening my suitcase when a blinding pain suddenly slashed through my head!

It was over and gone before I knew what had hit me, but I must have blacked out for a moment because I found myself sitting on the bed, clutching my head, with the suitcase and my clothes in a heap on the floor.

"What the hell...?"

I sat up slowly, blinking, gently shaking my head. I could still feel a dull throbbing, but no real pain. I hoped I wasn't going to start getting migraines! Monday, I'd have to go see Dr. Carter and tell him about this; maybe I ought to have a full physical. I hadn't been taking very good care of myself these last couple of weeks.

Maybe *that* was the cause of those other strange things that had been happening—those feelings of being watched, the spells of depression, that trembling, the headaches. Maybe I just needed some kind of tonic, or vitamins, or something in my diet. Yes, I'd go to see Sam first thing Monday morning.

I gathered the clothes from the floor, put most of them in the dirty-clothes hamper, hung up the rest, undressed, and was just starting out for the shower when I saw the envelope, propped up against the mirror of my dresser.

I grabbed it, then sat on the edge of the bed, my hands trembling, cold sweat tickling down from my armpits.

The first letter had come in a plain white business envelope, with my name and address printed in ink; this envelope was a 5x7 manilla, and there was just one word on the front of it: *ROBBER.*

When I saw what was inside, my stomach lurched and threatened to spew out the meal I had had on the plane!

"Oh...my God...!"

There were six photographs. Six unbelievably disgusting, evil photographs!

I lowered my head, closing my eyes, clutching the bed, desperately trying to quiet the nausea. Even with my eyes closed I could see the disgusting things! As though each one had been indelibly burned into my brain! I'd heard on the news, and read stories in the *Tribune*, that such filth was being printed and sold, mailed to unsuspecting children, peddled in "smut shops" to those so-called "adults" who were sick enough to enjoy looking at such things—but I had never expected to see such things myself!

I remembered one street in San Francisco—the only part of the city I'd seen that had made me glad I didn't live there—with "adult book shops" and "adult movie houses" block after block after block!

What kind of a sick mind...?

I wanted to crumple the evil things, burn them, destroy them. I half-expected the ceiling to collapse on me just for having them in the house.

But in spite of my revulsion and terror, my eyes kept returning to the pictures. Slowly I spread them out on the bed.

They were all of the same two men (neither was Chuck, thank God!) both muscular and—even then I couldn't stop myself from thinking it—both rather handsome. "Manly-looking". One wore a black leather jacket, a motorcycle cap, and high shiny black boots; otherwise he was completely exposed. The other wore nothing but boots, and his hands were tied behind his back. The first picture showed him kneeling in front of the other—you could see the rope around his wrists looped tightly down to his boots—watching as the standing one played with himself. The second one showed him...*licking* the other one's testicles, his chin up between widespread legs, and a large, slick penis lying on his forehead. In the third and fourth shots the standing one had moved around behind the other—had him bent backward, his body arched so that his own erect penis stood straight out—and was holding his head tilted back at a painful angle, trying to force his hard organ into the man's mouth. The fifth was a closeup, showing lips pressing hard against pubic hair, the entire penis completely engulfed by that mouth!

And the sixth photograph, the most disgusting, and yet somehow the most spellbinding of all, showed the kneeling one's face, his mouth open wide, tongue sticking up—and above it, a slick-shiny hand tight around the thick head of that amazing penis, milking a thick bright gob of semen down onto that upreaching tongue. There were other gobs and shining trails all over the kneeling man's face—on his forehead, down his cheeks, in his hair!

I couldn't stop looking at the filthy thing!

My stomach was churning, my mind roiling with disgust and fear—but I could not take my eyes from that frozen moment of depravity! I kept wondering how anyone could be so desperate for money—or so mentally deranged—or so doped-up—as to pose for such photographs. At first I was sure that the shots had been faked, the two models photographed at different times, but the last shot disproved that idea. It was too clear, too sharp, too obviously real to be faked. That semen was real and that penis was real, and...

I jerked my head up, turning away. I stood quickly, fighting to steady my breathing, to keep my stomach under control.

I heard something—a laugh? Someone moved, just over my left shoulder.

I spun around—and looked at myself in the mirror over the dresser. I stood there stark naked, looking back at myself. I had an erection!

A deep tingling was boiling in the pit of my stomach. Now the nausea came full force! With my hand tightly clamped on my mouth I ran stumbling into the bathroom and fell over the toilet and heaved! Raw alcohol and bile gushed out of me!

I slammed the seat down and flushed the toilet, then knelt there, my head resting on the cool white enamel, asking myself who it was that hated me so much as to send that letter and those photographs. What kind of desperately sick mind could be that disgustingly evil?

Weakly I sat up, becoming aware of the icy-cold tile under my legs.

This latest turn of events forced me to reconsider my earlier evaluation. The first letter could have been mailed by anyone, but the pictures had not come through the mail. That meant they'd been deliberately planted in my room by someone who had access to the house, and that limited the field of suspects considerably. What I needed to do now was to find out which of Chuck's friends he'd had over in my absence. Jerry Ashby was still number one on my list. But now a new name had added itself: Chuck himself.

Did he hate me so much he could go to such lengths to hurt and embarrass me?

He might.

I remembered the time, just a few months ago, when Kate had been turning the mattress on his bed and had found a small plastic bag filled with marijuana taped to it. I could still see Chuck sitting on his bed looking bored, refusing to meet my eyes as I threatened him, then pleaded with him, then threatened again. I remembered him looking up when I'd finally, in total frustration, run out of words.

"You gonna kick me out?"

I'd slammed my fist down on his dresser, then struggled to control myself, clenching my teeth to keep from hitting him. "Is that...what you think I should do?"

He had shrugged then—so utterly casual and contemptuous: "That's up to you, man."

"Goddammit, Chuck! Stop calling me *man!* I'm your father!"

"You're a man, aren't you?"

"That has nothing to do with it!"

"Oh?" He had studied me, then shrugged again. "Whatever you say...*Pop.*"

In the bathroom I struggled to my feet, rinsed my mouth out, washed my face in the basin. I studied my red-eyed reflection in the mirror. "Why does he hate me so much?" I asked aloud.

No one answered.

It wasn't likely that anyone would answer tonight. I could feel the silence and emptiness of the house pressing in on me. There was no sense looking for Chuck tonight. My plan had failed. If he came home now with one of his friends, he'd see the car in the driveway and leave without even bothering to come inside.

And I was too sick of the cloak-and-dagger routine to want to hide the car again, turn off the lights and sit in the darkness waiting on the offchance that he might bring someone home later.

Perhaps, after all, the best approach would be a direct confrontation tomorrow—or whenever he finally decided to come home. Kate and the girls would be gone for a full week, and Chuck and I would have the house all to ourselves. Maybe, just maybe, I could approach him in a way that would inspire at least honesty, if not respect.

When we'd caught him with that bag of marijuana, I'd started off on the tack that I didn't know what the stuff was (even though it was painfully obvious, with the cigarette papers in the sack with the powdery green stuff). By playing it wide-eyed innocent I'd engendered only contempt in him: "Oh, come off it, Dad! You know damn well what it is. Why don't you come right out and say it? It's *grass!* Pot! Dope!"

Just come right out and say it: "Chuck, I got this letter in the mail...do you know anything about it?"

Yes or no. If I didn't hedge, maybe he wouldn't either.

"Are you, Chuck?"

"Am I what, Dad?"

"What it says in the letter?"

"And what's that, Dad?"

"You know perfectly well! You've just read it!"

"Can't you say it out loud, man? Saying it out loud won't make it more real than it already is. Like that bag of grass. It was grass whether you could say it out loud or not."

"All right, then, Chuck–are you...queer?"

"Do I suck cocks, is that what you mean, Dad?"

I shuddered, shocked by my own imagination! I detested that phrase!

I tried to turn the scene off, but it continued in spite of me. Chuck was entirely capable of being just that blunt about it. I'd seen copies of the underground paper he worked on, and that phrase, along with others, was rather common. If it came to that, I'd have to say: "Yes, Chuck, that's exactly what I mean. Do you... suck...cocks?"

"No, Dad, I don't."

Imaginary or not, a surge of relief poured over me.

"You see, Dad? If you'd just come and asked when you got that note..."

I'd been judging Chuck guilty without benefit of a trial–with no more evidence than an evil, illiterate note. In effect, I'd been as disgusting as the note itself, assuming that it told the truth.

There were dozens of other possibilities beyond the obvious ones: Chuck was a good-looking boy, very popular at school, except with the administration. It was entirely possible that one of his classmates—maybe someone who worked with him on that underground paper, or simply anyone who resented his wide popularity—had sent the note, not to hurt me, but to get back at Chuck for something I knew nothing about. And if that were the case, I'd allowed myself to be taken in by the lie; I'd compounded that lie by believing it—or, just as bad, by being afraid it was true. And by doing that, I'd made the rest of the note true: by believing the accusation, I'd been, truly, "a wicked and terrible man".

I forced a smile at myself in the mirror. For the rest of the night, at least, I promised myself I'd stop being a damned fool!

Relishing the sense of relief my decision brought, I turned on the shower. I stood under the nozzle, letting the water spray on the top of my head, run down over my body. Slowly but surely the helpless frustration seemed to wash away. I closed my eyes and allowed myself to enjoy the tingle of the water pelting my skin. I could feel the relaxation spreading out through my body.

The thing that would feel really good right now, I thought, was one of Antonio's rubdowns.

I turned my back on the spray and applied soap to my front parts, again closing my eyes to relish the feeling of my hands slickly kneading my tense muscles. How great it would feel to relax in a steamroom, take a quick dip in the cold plunge, and then let Antonio pound and stretch me back into feeling like a decent human being again. The only trouble was, the Sugarhouse Businessman's Health Club was closed weekend nights. So, unfortunately, a steam and massage were out of the question. Still, dammit, it seemed like a good idea—there were other steam baths in the city.

And I had to do something!

I knew if I went to bed now, I'd lie awake all

night—if for no other reason, just worrying about Chuck, waiting for him to come home.

At least I could check the yellow pages.

I got out of the shower with a new sense of purpose, feeling better than I had for a week, maybe longer. I towelled dry, then went back into the bedroom. I cringed, seeing the photographs still lying there! What if Chuck had come home when I'd been in the shower and seen the things? I scooped them up, intending to take them downstairs and burn them in the fireplace.

Then suddenly it occurred to me that I might still use these pictures to catch whoever was playing this stinking game. Fingerprints! If I did have to go to the police after all, I could hand over these pictures as Exhibit B. Let them check for fingerprints. There would also be fingerprints on the letter. Find a matched set—besides my own, of course—and we'd have the troublemaker!

I got the letter out of my coat pocket, handling it carefully by the edges, and slipped it into the manilla envelope along with the photographs. I glanced for a last time at the final picture. The sheer depravity of it was overwhelming. I simply could not imagine anyone actually...catching semen in his mouth!

What would it taste like?

I stopped myself from even trying to imagine it, remembering that I'd just heaved my guts up into the toilet.

I tried to think of a good place to hide the envelope. I didn't want Chuck getting hold of it—or Kate, for that matter, although I chuckled at the idea of Kate finding such pictures under my shorts; it was almost worth doing just to see her reaction. I looked around the room. The dresser, of course! But not in a drawer—under the bottom drawers, where the skirt of the thing went all the way down to the floor. You couldn't see under it—and how often did anyone take the drawers all the way out?

I pulled out the bottom drawer and carefully pushed the envelope back into the farthest corner, then stood up, nodding to myself in the mirror. I couldn't help comparing my own image to those of the men in the photographs. They were younger, of course, but not that much younger. I was only thirty-five, and that was a long way from being "old". And I still had a rather good build. There was maybe a little excess fat around the midsection, but not if I stood straight. There weren't many others in the Health Club who had bodies half as good.

It was just a shame that I didn't have someone besides myself to appreciate it. Kate had once taken great delight in my naked body, as I had in hers. It had been a long time ago, but I remembered how it had been then, the lights out, under the covers, her hands exploring my body as though each time were new. Gentle fingers trailing over my chest, down my stomach. That little noise that she made in her throat when she touched my excited penis. I remembered how beautiful it had felt, then, to ease into the warmth of her body, how the feeling had come into me, spreading out....

In the mirror I watched my penis begin to rise. This time the reaction was coming from thoughts of a woman, which was normal and sane and acceptable, and I stared at it with fascination.

I stroked it lightly, watched the tingling gooseflesh spread down over my legs. How long had it been? Five years, at least. I hadn't touched Kate since that terrible day when she'd told me about Cindy and Dorene, when I'd moved forever out of "our" room into "mine"—the guest room. It seemed impossible, thinking about it. Five years!

In all that time I'd had no sexual outlet beyond what my imagination could devise for me, lying in the dark with the covers pushed back, masturbating to fantasies of how it had once been. (Even in my fantasies I'd been "true" to Kate.)

It felt so good, squeezing it.

Five years!

How had I ever got myself into such an impossible mess? I glanced up, eye to eye with myself. How much longer could I endure the situation? Sex was a natural function of the body. That was why the Mormons had rejected the idea of celibate priests: part of man's function was to marry and, through sex, have children.

I leaned back, beginning a slow kneading motion. I had a *good* body! Just tighten it, like this, and it looked every bit as good as either of those guys. Tight, you could see all the little ridges of muscles, that flat shield at the base of my belly, the thick auburn hair trailing up from my crotch, curling over my stomach, spreading out on my chest—and my chest was a good chest! Firm and full. No fat there. My pecs didn't look like sagging breasts, the way Ed's did. But then, Ed was a slob. He hadn't been, in the beginning, when we'd first met in college, but he'd turned into one. I couldn't understand what Kate saw in him. Certainly he was nowhere near as "well-hung" as I was—at least, he didn't seem to be, those times I had seen him in the showers at the Club. (But then, Kinsey has proved that women are not particularly interested in the size of a man's organ, but more in the techniques used to deploy it.) Well, she was welcome to him and to it, and to whatever pleasures either could give her. Over the years I had stopped resenting the fact that she had him to please her while I had no one but myself—*almost* stopped resenting it. There were times, such as now, when the resentment came back, when I wished I could be as careless a whore as she was, times when the need became so overpowering that I couldn't help resenting her.

What would it feel like to have it sucked by another man?

My hand stopped massaging and jerked away. I felt a

coldness grip my body. I turned away from the mirror, thoroughly ashamed of the thought.

I had to stop thinking about sex! There was simply no sense frustrating myself, torturing myself.

And I had to get out of this house. Empty and silent, it seemed to be forcing my mind into areas I did not want it to explore. If possible I wanted to find something to do tonight which would stop me thinking entirely.

I decided another drink wouldn't hurt anything; I'd heaved up all that I'd consumed on the plane and in the car. I dressed quickly, then hurried downstairs to the kitchen, where I mixed a good stiff Screwdriver. Then I went into the hallway to check the Yellow Pages. There were three or four listings for "Baths", but one ad attracted my attention instantly:

Now Under New Management
Uintah Plunge
Natural Hot Springs
Men Only–Expert Masseur
Open til 2 A.M. every nite
Come! Relax! Enjoy life!

That sounded just fine.

I turned off the lights and started out, then paused at the door; if Chuck did come home tonight (with or without a friend) there was no reason for him to worry about where I had gone (it seemed silly to leave him a note saying "Gone for a steam-bath"). I hurried back through the house, making sure everything was put away as though no one had been there. Once again at the front door, I paused to look back–and the house didn't seem nearly as depressing or threatening now. Just another empty house.

I relaxed more and more as I followed the old highway out to the north section of town. I decided that one reason I felt good again—besides the booze—was that I'd passed a certain crisis successfully; I'd made the decision not to spy on Chuck, not to trick him into anything, but to confront him directly and honestly. Now at least I had a goal I wasn't ashamed of. Not a very long-range goal, but a goal nonetheless, and that was something I hadn't had for a very long time.

It was as though there had been a voice in my mind, sitting back in a dark corner whining and complaining and criticizing, and generally forcing my life in a direction I hadn't wanted it to go; and it seemed that by making the decision, I had pushed the voice back into a dark little room and closed and locked the door.

Even the memory of those photographs had lost a lot of its power to disturb me. After all, they were only photographs, not "reality"—and certainly not any part of my reality—and those men were two out of millions of men; why should the images to two unimportant perverted men bother me in the slightest? Quite simply, they shouldn't!

I even turned the radio on, and hummed along with the music as I drove. I was fairly sure I remembered the place I was headed for; as a child, whenever we'd come to Salt Lake, I had wanted to go swimming in those mysterious "Natural Hot Springs" in a place that reminded me of a sultan's palace I had seen in a history book. Then the place had seemed huge, the lawns and the shrubbery like those of an "estate". I seemed to remember the name *Paradise Spa.* But neither of my parents had enjoyed swimming, and they never would trust Bill and me to go out by ourselves. If my guess were correct, tonight I would finally get to see the inside of that once-fascinating place.

At night, and in the few dim lights burning in the parking lot and along the sidewalk in front of the building, my "sultan's palace" didn't seem to have changed much at all, except that it looked a great deal smaller. As I walked up the front steps, I saw broken glass and pieces of plaster and strips of peeled paint lying everywhere in the rank lawn and under the untended shrubbery. No wonder it looked the same as it had fifteen years ago; from all I could see, it seemed fairly likely they hadn't painted or repaired anything in all of those fifteen years! An aura of gloom and decay seemed to hang in the huge foyer; it was like walking into a set for a Tennessee Williams play. There were ugly white plaster holes in the peeling, pea-green painted walls. Tiles were missing from the"mosaic" on the floor. Beyond the entry to the pool there had once been an elegant coffee shop; now the doors had been boarded up, and a crude sign that looked ten years old read *TEMPORARILY CLOSED.*

Behind a once-handsome, now chipped and ragged, long marble-topped counter a young man sat in an ancient swivel chair, his eyes intent on a book. I was surprised to see someone so young; I was used to seeing middle-aged men behind desks at health clubs. This boy couldn't have been much over twenty-one, if he was that. His age probably wouldn't have bothered me if it hadn't been for his condescending, contemptuous attitude, which seemed to have become a trade-mark for the young people recently. The chair squeaked as he reluctantly stood up, but only once did his eyes flick away from his paperback novel, and then they very blatantly started at the top of my head and swept slowly down to my feet, without so much as a flicker of friendliness. He shoved a battered tin box at me and muttered, "Two bucks. Put yer stuff you don't want stolen in there."

I forced a laugh, nervously wanting to get some kind of human response from him. "Two? Is that all?"

"It ain't the Ritz, honey," he growled.

I laughed foolishly. "No, I...guess it isn't."

He put my money in the cash register, put the box

into a cabinet, tossed a towel and the key attached to an innertube ring—on the counter before me, then sat down again in his swivel chair, without once taking his eyes off the book (which was called *Queens Of The Range*—with a grotesquely amateurish drawing of half-naked cowboys that looked, in my opinion, more like cow*girls* except for the blatantly detailed *bulges* in their crotches).

I turned away from the desk almost in a trance; I couldn't believe it. It was more like a dream than reality. Some distant, sober part of my mind whispered *Get out of here!* and although I realized the sense of the warning, I couldn't shake myself loose from that hypnotized feeling. It was like finding an abandoned mine-shaft in an area where no mine-shaft is supposed to be, and in spite of the crumbling walls and the loose timber you feel compelled to go inside, if for no other reason than a morbid curiosity to see if the thing will collapse once you get in.

I walked down a long hallway where most of the lights in the ceiling were out, through swinging doors, and into a large, cracked, peeling, boiled-egg smelling room. There were perhaps fifty toilet-sized stalls in two back-to-back rows, with narrow corridors between them. The floor of the room was concrete, and once upon a time it had been painted maroon, but the corridors and the floors of the rooms had been worn to the original grey of the cement. Many of the rooms had no doors on them at all, and many more had no locks. My stall, number 17, was in the middle aisle, and it was only a verification of a certainty I'd felt since entering the front door, that this wasn't the place I'd been looking for. The walls of my cubicle were literally covered with grossly crude drawings and childish propositions:

Show hard on for blow job.

Don't bother. Jack off. These queens should take cocksucking lessons.

You didn't find the right queen, honey.

Honey! I suddenly realized the attendant had called me *honey!* It hadn't even registered at the time! I wanted to be outraged, but all I could do was giggle drunkenly. The giggling made me dizzy, and I sat down on a narrow bench to avoid falling. It felt as though a depth charge had suddenly exploded in my stomach, shooting raw alcohol out into my bloodstream. My head was swimming! I couldn't even think.

I put my head down between my knees and took deep breaths, and the dizziness passed. I'd never had such a strange reaction to alcohol before. But I felt much better as I stood up—almost cavalier. I'd seen no one, heard no one moving around or talking; it was quite likely that I was the only one here. In which case, why should I worry about what kind of place it was? If they had a steam room, I'd use it. If they had a masseur (which I very much doubted) I'd use him. I wanted a steam and a massage and I'd paid two good dollars to get in the place, so I'd get my money's worth and then get out. Why not?

I undressed, wrapped the towel around my waist, and ventured in search of the steam room. I found it next to a crumbling shower area where the three old-fashioned nozzles all were dripping with fascinating counter-rhythms: *Splash-splash, drip-splash, plop-drip-plop, splash....* When I saw the door into the steam room itself, I stopped short and laughed out loud: the hinges of the wooden-slab door had been wired together with bailing wire! I pushed the door open and steam billowed out, licking me with warm fingers. It felt great!

The light in the ceiling was so dim I couldn't see two feet in front of me. I moved slowly into the room, my hands sweeping the air in front of me until my knees struck a tiled bench and I almost fell on my face! I sat down, reached around, found a wall, and slid back to lean against it. I sat for a minute, hugging my knees, then tentatively spread myself out until I was lying full-length on the warm bench. The towel around my waist was uncomfortable. I loosened it slightly, then, reminding myself I was alone, removed it entirely and rolled it into a pillow for my head.

It was like lying naked in a huge, warm, wet, dark womb. The steam swirled between my legs, feeling like somebody breathing. I allowed my hands to move down over my slickening body, down to my genitals. The sensations were delicious! The steam and the warmth of my hands and my own perspiration—the darkness, the wetness—safe in a womb, shut away from the world, where no one could see or know what I did. All of my problems seemed so far away! No past, no future, just the present now. The letter, the pictures, Chuck, Jerry Ashby, Kate, the girls, Ed Bogen—all these seemed like insubstantial ghosts left behind in another world, exorcised by the soft-swirling steam.

Masseur or no, the steam had been an excellent idea.

Someone coughed.

I sat up, grabbing my towel to spread it quickly over my crotch. My throat suddenly felt like a hand had grabbed it. The cough came again. I tried to sound casual: "Hello. I thought I was alone."

"Not quite," said a voice. "I'm here."

"Sorry."

"What for?"

I laughed. "I don't know."

The voice was silent for several long minutes, and I peered through the steam trying to see its owner; I could see nothing but a dim void.

"Would you like to trade rubdowns?" the voice suddenly asked.

"Do what?"

"Trade rubdowns?"

"Oh." I laughed again. I knew I ought to be nervous, perhaps even frightened, but in the darkness of the room nothing seemed quite real. For all I knew the stranger was sitting back in some corner holding a knife, ready to slice me into small pieces—but I couldn't get worried about it. His voice was soft, rather gentle. He didn't sound dangerous. Just another guy like myself enjoying the steam. "I'm afraid I don't give very good rubdowns," I told him. "I was hoping they'd have a masseur."

"That's just in the daytime."

"Oh."

He was silent again, and I finally decided the conversation had ended and lay back, adjusting the towel more comfortably over my midsection. Not that I was particularly worried about his seeing me. If I couldn't see him, he shouldn't be able to see me.

"Would you like one?" His voice seemed to be nearer. I sat up again, squinting, trying to see through the steam. I thought I could make out a dark form vaguely in the shape of a man, standing by the bench, down by my feet.

For some crazy reason I remembered the scrawl on the cubicle wall: *Show hard for blow job.* I remembered my imaginary conversation with Chuck: *"Just come right out and say it."* Feeling giddy and daring, I said, "One what?"

"You know—a rubdown."

"Oh. Sure, I'd love one. Are you a masseur?"

"Me? Goodness, no. But I'm pretty good—or at least some people think so. We do it all the time out here. Trade rubdowns, I mean. It's much less expensive than Joseph. He's the real masseur. And, anyway, he's not very good. He doesn't go all the way—if you know what I mean."

I decided to let that one pass. I had a pretty good idea of what he meant, but I wasn't about to let him know that. Also, I didn't want to get myself into an embarrassing situation by misinterpreting his remark. It was possible I didn't know what he meant.

"I'll get some soap." The dark form moved to the door. Light suddenly billowed into the room. For a moment I saw him almost clearly as he passed through the doorway. He was young-looking, tall, very thin, and completely nude. I couldn't be certain, but it looked as though he had half an erection—his penis arching out and down from his crotch like the trunk of a baby elephant.

As I waited for him to return with the soap, that locked-up, sober part of my mind told me to get up and leave, but my body seemed to have a will of its own, and it didn't want to move. And besides, it was a little like gambling—a vice I had never allowed myself—was he or wasn't he? Would he or wouldn't he?

I remembered those photographs. One by one they presented themselves to me, superimposed on the steam. I thought about John Adams in the Men's Room, reaching out, wanting to fondle my penis, muttering, "Very nice, Robert." Such things did go on in the world; I couldn't stop them by pretending they didn't exist. But surely I had the moral strength of character not to feel threatened by other men's perversity!

The door swung open again and I twisted to look up, but the door had closed before I could get a really good look at him. I felt a hand on my stomach. A wild shudder wrenched through me. "Want to turn over?"

"Sure." I rolled over, trying to keep the towel over my middle, covering my buttocks—but he pulled it away.

"You don't need that in here."

I put the towel under my face.

He started at my shoulders, soaping my back, down to my buttocks. His touch was gentle, but surprisingly professional. Almost as good as Antonio. In a way, he was better; Antonio started pounding the minute you were spread out on the table, but this guy took his time working up to the pounding. He massaged my shoulders, fingers probing into the tense muscles, relaxing them, down my spine.... When he kneaded my buttocks the sensation was fantastic! Then, almost too quickly, he worked down my legs, down to my feet. I felt like a limp bundle of delicious sensations. When he kneaded my feet, my entire body quivered. Slowly he worked his way back up to my shoulders. I felt something brush against my upturned palm on the bench. An uneasy chill spread out through my body as I realized that it was the head of his penis I could feel.

My own penis had grown progressively harder—nothing I had tried to do could keep it down. Lying on my stomach, it hadn't particularly worried me, but I was beginning to wonder what I would do when he asked me to roll onto my back. If he were queer and he found out I did have a hard-on, he'd assume I was responding to him—and if he weren't queer, he'd think that I was.

"Okay, roll over."

"I...uh..."

"Hmm?"

"Nothing. I just..." I sat up, stalling for time, desperately thinking, *Go down! Go down!*

"Is anything wrong?"

"No!" I said quickly. "No...nothing."

"Then lie down. Gee, you're so tense."

"Sorry."

"Come on..." He put a widespread hand on my chest and pushed me back. "Relax...." Reluctantly I lay down. His hand stayed on my chest as his other went searching along the bench for the soap. When he found it, he worked over my chest, down across my stomach. "You certainly have a nice body. Are you an athlete or something?"

"No," I said softly, painfully aware of his fingers on my stomach, just inches away from my penis. I held my breath, waiting for him to touch it.

But he didn't. Instead he went around it, down to

my legs. He soaped the insides of my thighs, absently brushing his fingers against my testicles. "Gee, come on, relax. You're so tense! Why are you so tense?"

"It's been a bad day."

"Gee, that's too bad." He clicked his tongue. "You have nice legs. Strong."

"I walk a lot."

"Um-hmmm. Walking's very good for you. I wish I had thick legs like yours. Mine are so spindly and ugly."

Down to my toes again, then slowly back up. "Relax.....relax...."

It was so strange having another man comment on my body. No other man had ever done that—at least not on the positive side. Usually it was something like: "Hey, Robert, you're getting a pot there," or something equally negative. I wanted very much to relax. I wanted to accept this guy's compliments and feel good about them. Obviously he was being very open and honest in praising my body. Obviously my body pleased him.

But that was perverted, and try as I might, I couldn't accept it. The steam seemed to have sobered me, allowing that locked-up part of my mind to come forward and take over again. I lay there waiting for him to touch me in that forbidden area, just once, just a definite touch. Up to now he'd been giving me an excellent rubdown, better than Antonio's, and I could enjoy that. But just let him step out of line and I'd have to do something about it. I didn't enjoy the idea of embarrassing him, but if he asked for it, that's what I would have to do.

And of course, just as I'd feared, just as I'd known he would, he touched it. Offhandedly, as though completely by accident—but we both knew better. I felt my penis quiver; a sweet tingling shot up through my stomach.

"My goodness," he whispered, "you *are* tense."

"Don't worry about it."

He chuckled. "Who's worried?" His fingers closed lightly around it. "You've got a beautiful cock. You should be proud...."

"I am," I said coldly.

I knew that the moment had come. I knew I had to push him away, get up, dress and leave—but I couldn't! It felt as though a huge hand were pressing down hard on my body, pinning me there on that bench.

His soapy-slick fingers began a slow motion, up and down—and the sensations were almost overwhelming! It had been five years since another human being had touched me there, and the feelings seemed a thousand times more intense than when I masturbated myself.

But it's wrong! It's dirty! It's perverted and evil!

But it feels good!

I don't care what it feels like, it's wrong!

I tried to sit up. "I think that's enough."

"Oh, come on, relax." He tried to push me back down, but I shoved his hand away. He giggled nervously, stepped back. My body felt suddenly cold. "All right," he said sullenly, "have it your way."

"I will."

"Oh, I'm sure you will. I've met your type before."

"Have you? And what's that—my *type?*"

"You know perfectly well. You come in here, knowing exactly what goes on, and when someone tries to do something nice for you..."

"Is that what you call it? Something nice? You know what *I* call it?"

"Oh, I'm sure you have all sort of horrible words. You're the kind who just *loves* to have someone make a fuss over *you*, but when it comes to pleasing *them*, then you start..."

The truth of his words jarred me, but that only made me more angry. "And what could I do for someone like you—to *please* you?"

"Absolutely nothing!"

"Oh, no! No, you wanted something, didn't you?"

"Don't be preposterous! I was only being friendly."

"Like hell you were! Come on, tell me what you wanted."

"I didn't want..."

"Say it!" I stood up, facing him, my heart pounding with cold fury. "Say it! Tell me what you want."

"Oh, *really!"* He started toward the door but I stepped quickly in front of him.

In the light filtering in from outside I could see him more clearly. His eyes blinked rapidly. He was frightened. His fear started an excitement churning in my body. He knew we were alone in the place. It wasn't very likely the attendant would hear if he yelled for help as long as I kept him in the steam room. I planted my hand on his chest, pushing him back; his body was slick and hot. "Not so fast," I said softly. "I want to hear you say it."

"No!" He bolted away from me, lurching toward the door. I grabbed his arm, spun around, twisting it. "Don't hurt me!" he cried. "Please! I didn't..."

"Just shut up! Don't start yelling, or I *will* hurt you!"

"Please..."

I twisted harder, forcing him down on his knees, facing away from me. *"Say it!"*

"You're hurting me!"

I leaned over him. "Say it, God damn you! Say it out loud."

"Please...don't...hurt me."

"You wanted it, didn't you? You wanted to suck on it, didn't you? You wanted to suck my cock!"

"Yes!" he sobbed. "Yes-yes-*yes!* Please let me go!"

"Oh, no! You wanted me to *please* you? Well, by God, that's exactly what I'm going to do."

"No! I don't want..."

I grabbed his hair, jerking his head back. I stepped

over him. "Just hold still. Hold perfectly still. I'm going to please you!"

I could tell he was crying. I couldn't see the tears but I heard his sobs clearly. The sounds made me feel powerful! I felt I could do anything I wanted to him.

Like the man in those pictures!

I took his head tightly between both hands, stepped over him, bending so my testicles brushed down the back of his head and my penis lay hard on his forehead. "Open your mouth, you cocksucker! Open it! That's what you wanted, isn't it? You..."

"You're hurting me!" he wailed.

"You miserable sonofabitch!" I pushed my cock painfully down, trying to force it between his clenched lips. He twisted his face sideways but I grabbed his hair with both hands and twisted it upright again.

Suddenly it seemed as though this had all happened before, like a dream I'd had hundreds of times and was doomed to go on reenacting again and again and again. He did it each time, turned his head away, refusing to do what I wanted him to.

"Suck me, Billy, please!"

"I can't, Bob! Don't make me! I just can't!"

I pushed him hard, down onto the floor; he sprawled on his back under me and I fell over him, thrusting my crotch heavily in his face. His legs started thrashing; his arms flailed at me, trying to push me off. I had to get *in* him! That was the only way I could finish the dream! I had to get my cock inside those clenched lips and shoot my jizz into him! I had to! The dream would keep coming back, over and over and over until I did!

I saw his cock—dark, long and hard—only inches away from my face. At that moment all vestiges of sanity left me. I desperately needed to finish that horrible dream! I lunged forward and thrust my mouth over his long cock.

I heard a sharp cry bubble up from between my legs.

Thick heat pelted into my mouth! Tacky spurts of his semen shot into my throat, coursed back over my tongue like a flood.

His body went limp under me.

I suddenly realized I had a man's cock in my mouth! I had a man's semen in my mouth! I could taste it!

My stomach convulsed and I threw up into his crotch.

I stood up, shaking, completely enveloped in sick disgust. I grabbed for my towel and spat into it, then heaved again, but my stomach was empty and only a raw sewer taste filled my mouth. My legs wanted to buckle but I forced myself, staggering, toward the door. I limped weakly to my dressing stall, drying myself as well as I could with my wet, soiled towel. Even though I was still damp, I dressed as fast as I could, praying he wouldn't come out of the steam room, desperately hoping he was frightened enough just to stay where he was. If I had to face him again, knowing what I'd just done, I'd be tempted to kill him.

I heard laughter—the sound shot through me like knives.

As I came out of the stall, I saw two young men standing down at the end of the corridor, both naked, their towels hanging over their shoulders. Their laughter stopped as they saw me, and one said, "Well, my dear, we're not the only ones here." They both looked me up and down. "Don't hurry away on our account."

I shoved past them without answering, pushed through the swinging doors, then almost ran down the dark hallway to the front desk. Behind me I heard laughter again.

It wasn't until I was many blocks away from the place that I allowed myself to relax at all. Then I pulled to the side of the street, under the shadow of a large tree, got my vodka from under the seat, and then sat hunched down, gulping the burning stuff until I had emptied the bottle. Then I sat up and looked around, wondering what to do next. I didn't want to go home, but I couldn't think of any place else to go. It was one o'clock, Sunday morning—Easter Sunday—and there was no place else to go. I started the car and pulled back onto the street, heading home.

Home, I thought bitterly. No, I wasn't going *home*—only to the house that I lived in. I had no home.

I had nothing. Nothing at all. No home, no family, and now no self-respect, no honor, nothing! In one night, a few brief drunken minutes, I'd managed to ruin everything I believed in, to invalidate everything I had worked for my entire life. So now it didn't matter where I went or what I did—and the house on 13th South was the only place I could think of to go.

I remembered the feeling I'd had that morning, in the hotel room (had it actually been such a short time ago? It seemed more like a year!) that something disastrous was going to happen. I tried to work up a sense of relief now that the disaster was over—but, as I drove slowly along the deserted streets, a new uneasiness began to creep into my mind: Suppose my premonition had not yet been completely fulfilled?

Suppose the insane events of the past day and evening were only the *beginnings* of that fulfillment?

Chapter 3

It wasn't until I'd parked the car in the driveway that I realized Chuck must be home: the light in the kitchen was out. For a moment I sat in the car, wondering whether or not I should try to sneak into the house, catch him at whatever he was up to—but at that point, after what I had done, I could hardly work up any anger at Chuck for maybe doing the same thing.

I could hear music as I walked up the front steps; through the narrow glass panels around the door, I could see firelight flickering. As I opened the front door, rock music rushed out to engulf me. Two figures lay on the living room floor in the bright glow from the fireplace. Chuck and Jerry. Both were sprawled comfortably, spread-eagled, arms outstretched, hands *almost* touching. Neither seemed to have heard the car or the door; apparently both were completely engrossed in the music—which, strangely enough, I found rather melodic and soothing. I closed the door and stood there watching them, waiting for one to look up and see me. For a long time neither moved; I wondered how they could both be so happy and contented while I was so miserable.

Then Chuck sat up—slowly, dreamily; he leaned on his elbows as his eyes wandered slowly around the room. He looked so peaceful! When he finally spotted me, for a moment he made no move, nothing in his comfortable expression changed. Then, as though suddenly realizing who I was, he stood up. "Hey, Dad!" he said loudly—and Jerry quickly looked up. "Hey, you're...uh...home early. I...uh..." He hurried to the phonograph and the music died. In the heavy silence both boys regarded me.

"Hello, Mr. Thorne."

"Jerry..."

"You okay, Dad?" Chuck asked—there was something strangely fuzzy about his voice, as though he needed to clear his throat. "We...uh...were just...uh...listening...Hey, are you okay?"

I moved away from the front door, feeling extremely uncomfortable. By all indications both boys seemed drunk—and yet I knew that Chuck avidly deplored alcohol. I had no choice but to conclude that my son and his friend were both "stoned". I knew I ought to be furious; I knew I should chastise them; but I couldn't. I simply could not work up any anger. "Yes," I said quietly. "I'm fine. Turn your music back on. I'm just going up to bed."

"We don't need to listen, Dad. I mean, if you're..."

"It's all right, Chuck," I said firmly, and started for the stairs.

"We didn't expect you."

"I know. I decided to come back early. Go ahead, turn the music back on."

"If you're sure."

I nodded wearily. "Chuck, I'm too tired to let anything bother me." I started up the stairs, then paused to look back. "Let's talk tomorrow, Chuck, can we? Will you be home?"

Chuck glanced at Jerry, then up at me. "Yeah, sure, I guess. We, uh, were sort of planning like a camping trip. You know, in the mountains for a couple of days..."

"I don't want to change your plans," I said. "If you're here, fine."

"Maybe in the morning, okay?"

"In the morning will be fine. Well...goodnight, son. Jerry."

They both told me goodnight, watching me with puzzled expressions. The music came back on as I started up the stairs—a lovely female voice softly singing what sounded like a lullaby: "Everything's all right... everything's fine..." I wondered what it was they were listening to; I'd never heard "rock" music quite so relaxing and beautiful.

I went to the bathroom, then into my room, where I closed the door and undressed in the dark. I got into bed and lay there quietly, hearing the distant music, thinking about Chuck and Jerry and how peaceful they'd seemed. I really should have said something, I thought; as it was, I'd given a tacit approval to their conditions. But then, what right had I to chastise them—or anyone? "He who is without sin, let him cast the first stone." It was curious, I thought—drifting slowly into sleep—that the quotation I'd thought of had contained the word *stone*. And there was another Biblical statement sneaking around in the back of my mind. Isaiah or somebody. "If men lie together, let them be stoned." Strange how words took on totally incompatible meanings.

There was a soft knock at my door, then a dim light filtered in as the door opened. "Dad?" Chuck said softly. "Are you sure nothing's wrong?"

I started to say, "Everything's fine," but changed my mind. I wanted to be finished with the lying and deception. "I don't know," I said frankly.

"Look, I'm, uh, sorry...I mean, I guess you could tell we're kind of, you know, high."

I felt myself smiling. "Well, you're high and I'm drunk, and it's no time to discuss it, is it?"

I heard him chuckle softly. "No, I guess not. Look, I'll put off the camping trip if you want."

"Let's talk about it tomorrow."

"Sure. I'll be here, Dad. Goodnight."

"Goodnight, son."

He started to close the door, then leaned back in: "Dad...thanks. I mean for not...well, you know what I mean. Goodnight."

The door closed and I lay in the darkness, remembering the tone of Chuck's voice. I'd never heard him sound so truly concerned. And it had been years since he'd thanked me for anything. I didn't understand how it could be, but maybe, somehow, everything *was* "all right".

I almost felt good as I drifted...deeper...deeper.... I dreamed I was back home, back in Glen Falls, Idaho, where my brother and I had grown up. I was younger–not a child, but not an adult either: I seemed to be myself, at my present age, but there was a "young" feeling about me. I was back on the farm where I'd spent most of my childhood, before we had moved into town, before my father had bought into a business and got himself involved in Church work. At first I wandered through the house looking at things I'd long-since forgotten: the patchwork quilts on the beds, crocheted doilies on the tables, afghans on the sofa and chairs, oval-framed sepia portraits on the walls, the old stove that my father would crank every morning at daybreak, shifting down the dead coals from the night before to start a new fire for a new day.

But the house was empty, and I began to feel uncomfortable and out of place, so I went outside, looking for someone. It seemed to be midsummer; the neatly trimmed lawns were a velvety green; the huge cottonwood trees around the house were in full leaf, with deep delicious shadows under them. I could smell growing things. I wandered through the garden: tomato vines thick on the fences, row upon row of lettuce and cabbage, radishes, turnips, carrots, Swiss Chard, pole-beans, yellow-ripening cantelopes, green-striped half-grown watermelons peeping up from the tangle of vines at the bright sun. I stood at the fence which surrounded the garden, looking out at the fields–alfalfa and wheat and a tall stand of field corn. The sky and the sun and a gentle breeze waving the corn and the wheat. The sound of birds singing, bees humming, leaves and trees and growing things moving softly.

Then I heard someone calling my name–not *Robert*,

but the name I'd been called as a child, *Bobby*. It came drifting through the cornfield on the breeze like a birdsong: "Bobby...oh, Bobby...Bobby-o."

I'd completely forgotten that my father used to call me that. *Bobby-o.*

And then I was running through the corn, the sharp papery leaves gently slapping my face, pollen-dust falling like rain, clinging to my face and hair, and the smell of loose earth and tassle-silk filling my nostrils. "Bobby-o! Bobby-o!"

The corn ended. I stepped out at the edge of the wheatfield and stopped. He was standing in the middle of the field, watching me, the golden wheat rippling around his knees. He was naked.

I'd never seen my father naked, and it shocked me at first—but then it seemed so totally natural, standing in the wheatfield, with the fields green and golden beyond him.

"Bobby-o! Hello!" It had to be my father; no one else had ever called me *Bobby-o.* And yet it wasn't the bulldog-jowled, scowling, fat, Marine-corps-cropped whitehaired man I knew. He was young, deeply sunburned, firm-jawed, muscular, beautiful as a god. Like the old, faded sepia pictures of grandfathers and great-grandfathers back in the house, my father now wore a beard and his dark hair was long. "Bobby! Come to me! I've got a secret! Come to me!"

I ran through the wheat, felt the sharp spears of the heads prickling my legs. Then I knew I was naked too. I knew that was how it should be. I felt no shame in my own nakedness or in his. He put his arms out as I ran to him. "Hurry, Bobby! Hurry! Run! Run!"

I leaped over the furrows, the golden field seemed to blur with my speed. Then I was before him and he was reaching out to me, smiling—as I never remembered him smiling before—and just as our hands touched, he said, "I love you, Bobby-o."

And then I awakened, feeling tears running over my

cheeks. The memory of his voice seemed to echo around the dark room, calling me back to the beautiful dream. For that moment, awake, I felt I could do anything in the world! Anything man had ever dreamed about doing. I could fly like the birds and swim like the fishes. I could, just by wanting to, take myself from this bed and put myself anywhere I chose, just by willing it. But I didn't want to go anyplace except back into the dream. Those fields no longer existed in reality; now they were tract houses. Now my father was a grumpy old man, too engrossed in loving his church to give love to the people around him. I wanted to know instead that beautiful bearded naked man, arms outstretched, saying: "Bobby, I love you."

I closed my eyes, felt reality slipping away again—but the beautiful dream did not return. Instead I found myself standing deep in the dark heart of some city, with ugly grey-sooty buildings reaching up to a grey sky where the sun was a sickly white day-star and the air all around me was heavy and thick. The man was still there, still reaching out, but he was no longer naked. He wore a heavy black overcoat and a black broadbrimmed hat that shadowed his face. "Follow me!" he commanded, and his voice was like thunder. He turned and hurried away.

I was frightened. I wanted to wake up, to stop this dream and get back to the other, but my feet took me after him. Faster and faster he walked, our footsteps beating out staccato echoes on the walls of the buildings. Then he ran, I followed him, running, my heart pounding as fast as my footsteps. The air grew darker and thicker.

Suddenly he stopped and turned. I stopped short. "Hello, Bobby-o!" his voice boomed.

"Who are you?"

"Who do you think I am?"

"Who are you?"

"You know who I am!"

"Who are you?"

He started to laugh. He threw back his head and the laughter poured out like a river, engulfing me.

"Who are you?" I screamed.

The laughter stopped abruptly. He stood tall, looking down at me. "Look." He threw off the hat, ripped the buttons from the overcoat. Once again he stood naked before me. The city disappeared. The white sun became golden. The birds sang and the breeze fingered my body. "I am *you*, you fool!"

He leaped up and for a moment hung suspended above me. Then he raised his arms straight above him and rose into the clear air.

"Wait!" I cried, and jumped after him—and I felt myself rising up, flying! The earth slowly moved away under me, the fields growing smaller and smaller. My body was filled with the most exhilarating excitement I'd ever known. I was free of the earth and of all the miseries and sorrows it represented. I was free! Flying! Following my naked father, diving upward into the sun!

But then I looked down, and I felt the fear gathering. What would happen if I fell?

And the instant I thought it, I felt myself falling—but not to the earth! The earth was no longer there. There were screaming sounds, blackness, emptiness—and then a light, a blinding exploding light, churning, expanding, blossoming all the colors of the spectrum. And I fell into it helplessly.

I heard a voice, soft, but filling everything: "Where is thy brother?"

I heard my own voice, seeming tiny and impertinent: "Am I my brother's keeper?"

"Yes!" the voice cried, and the sound of it crashed through me. *"Yes!"* I screamed at the fury of it. *"YES!"* The sound was like worlds crashing together.

Suddenly the light exploded. I exploded. I screamed...

...and awakened...

...ejaculating!

Someone was pounding on my door. "Dad!"

I was not in my bed! I was standing naked in the middle of the room, both windows wide open and the light from the streetlamp outside reflecting my dim image in the mirror. Bright splotches of semen lay on the floor and the top of the dresser—trailed like thick rain down the mirror.

Chuck was pounding on the door, yelling. My mind was spinning helplessly. I stared at the closed door, waiting for it to open, wondering stupidly what he would do when he saw his father naked with an erection.

"Dad! Answer me! Why's the door locked?"

Relief surged over me, and with it a sense of reality returned. I fumbled along the bed for my robe, stuffed my arms into the sleeves as I called: "It's okay, Chuck. It's okay." My penis was still stiffly erect; I pressed it tight to my stomach and covered it with the robe, strapping it tightly to my body with the belt. I opened the door.

Chuck stared at me, blinking and frowning. A light came from behind him, from his own room, down the hall. He was wearing only his shorts. For a moment I stared back at him. My son was a beautiful young man, broadshouldered, firmly muscled. In that moment I realized that he was truly a part of me; he had come from my body. "You were yelling," he said, and I heard genuine fear in his voice.

"Sorry." I leaned in the doorway; my body wanted to collapse under me. "I guess I had a nightmare."

"Why was your door locked?"

I looked up, into his eyes, then shook my head. "I don't know," I said. "I don't remember."

"You okay, though?"

"Yes, I'm fine."

"You sure?"

I found myself chuckling, reaching out, taking his

forearm in my hand and squeezing it. "Yes, Chuck, I'm sure. Thank you."

He shrugged, then glanced down at my hand as though he couldn't understand why I was touching him. I released the grasp and stuffed my hands into the pockets of my robe, feeling foolish and uncomfortable.

"Dad...?"

We regarded each other, eye to eye. Then he shook his head and turned away.

"What?"

He shrugged, glanced at me, turned away again. "I don't know. You're, uh, okay, though?"

"Yes."

"Well...okay." He started slowly down the hall. At the door to his room he turned briefly and grinned. "You scared me."

"I'm sorry."

"It's cool. See you, okay?"

"Right," I said. "In the morning."

"Right. G'night."

As the door to his room closed, I felt an emptiness creeping up through me. I looked back at my own bed and remembered the dream and the terror. I hurried to the bathroom and took two sleeping pills, went back to my room and cleaned up the mess on the dresser and floor, then collapsed in the bed. Total exhaustion sucked me down into sleep, but in the last fading moments of consciousness I heard an echo of that booming voice: "Where is thy brother? Where is thy brother? Where..."

Chapter 4

The sound of churchbells brought me up from a heavy sleep, and I lay for a long time, listening, staring at the ceiling. "Happy Easter," I told myself softly.

I felt absolutely rotten! My head ached, my body ached, and my stomach felt as though it had been twisted and tied into knots. My legs and back were so painfully stiff I could hardly lift myself out of the bed.

It was just ten o'clock.

I sat on the edge of the bed, remembering other Easter mornings a long time ago, when Chuck was just a small child, before Cindy and Dorene were born. I remembered warm bright sunny days, jonquils and daffodils, my small son clutching my hand, wearing his newest little suit and white shirt and necktie. Singing in Church, speaking of the glorious resurrection of Christ. And afterwards, Chuck and his young innocent friends had scrambled for Easter Eggs hidden in the yard, laughing, yelling, while Kate stood beside me, watching proudly and smiling.

Something incredibly ugly had come into our lives since that happy time. No, not only into our lives, I thought, but into the entire world. Had I still been a religious man, I'd have thought the prophecies of John were indeed coming true. Wars and rumors of wars, pestilence and famine, fathers against sons and sons against fathers, women against men, sickness and degeneracy spreading like a plague across continents. Murders, assassinations, bombings, hijackings, rapes, robberies. What possible happiness could they be celebrating in Church this morning?

I did not want to believe—could not force myself to believe—as so many claimed, that God was dead. Life would make no sense at all if that were true. But something was wrong, obviously. Perhaps God had got thoroughly disgusted with the human race and had gone away to try it all over again, someplace else in the Universe, leaving man to destroy himself, as he seemed so determined to do.

And if that were true—as it certainly seemed to be—what difference could it possibly make that I'd sucked a man's cock last night?

I shuddered, and pain jolted out through my body and head like fire through my nerves. No, I thought. Nothing could justify what I had done. And yet, I *had* done it, and nothing could blot out the memory.

For a long while I sat on the bed, staring at the floor, thinking of nothing except how wretched I felt. When I finally realized I was only wallowing in self-pity, I forced myself up, put on my robe, and headed for the shower. The door to Chuck's room was partially open and I paused to glance in at him. He was sprawled peacefully, half-uncovered, on the bed, one arm under his pillow and his face cradled in the crook of his elbow. *My son*, I thought, *my beautiful son. What kind of heritage have I given you—has the world given you?*

Sixteen years ago it had seemed such a beautiful idea to have a child, especially a son. I'd been so proud, so happy; I'd promised myself I would give him a good life, a better life than I'd had, growing up. But so many things had gone wrong in those sixteen years. Too many things.

But then as I stood there, watching him sleeping, I remembered how concerned he'd been for me last night. I remembered how he'd thanked me for not blowing up when I found out he was "high". And I remembered a phrase of that song they'd been playing: "Everything's all right...everything's fine...."

Perhaps things were not quite as bad as they seemed.

In the bathroom I took a couple of aspirins, then showered and shaved. My body still ached and my head felt as though a steel band had been permanently tightened around it, but I'd relaxed enough to feel halfway human again. I dressed, then went downstairs, intending to fix breakfast.

I stared into the refrigerator. No eggs; no bacon; two stale butt-ends of a loaf of bread. Well, hell, the idea of food hadn't really appealed to me, except that I knew I should get something in my stomach to straighten out those knots. I made toast and a pot of instant coffee, then wandered out, cup in hand, into the back yard. It was a beautiful day. The sky was brilliantly clear, the sun warm. The grass was beginning to lose its winter-dead brownness, bright yellow-green spears reaching up to the sunlight. Kate's tulips were beginning to open, and the deep green shoots of gladiolas and peonies were nudging the dark earth aside. Any other Sunday morning I'd have been happy to sit out and sip my coffee and enjoy the spring sunshine, but this particular day, it all seemed so worthless. I looked around at the greening bushes, the new grass, the budding flowers, at the house and the trees, and I thought: *This is it! This is my life. This is what I've worked ten years to achieve. A few flowers and bushes, an old house, a couple of cars, and what else?*

A son *maybe*—but that was a new maybe and I wasn't yet sure enough of the possibilities to count on it. I was too used to thinking that Chuck hated me; I couldn't overcome the idea just with the encouragement he'd given me last night. Otherwise, nothing. No one to love or be loved by. No one to help or be helped by. No close friends. A wife who hated me; two "daughters" who liked "Uncle Ed" better than their "father". And even if Chuck did like me, was concerned about me, there was little common ground between us. He was part of me, part of my body, but he'd rejected all of my values. He accepted my money but without appreciation, as though it was simply his due, as though I *owed* it to him for having sired him.

And the job? If someone had walked into the yard right then and said, "I want to get into advertising," I'd have said, "Here! Take my half of the business and welcome!" Because the truth was, I hated my job. Once I had loved it, but that, too, had been a long time ago, before I'd found out about my wife and my partner. Now every day was like hell at the office. I still arrived every morning on time, still spent the day working dutifully, but there was absolutely no enjoyment left in it for me. Going to work was simply the better of two evils, *slightly* preferable to staying home.

What does a man do when his life becomes worthless?

One answer quickly presented itself, but I rejected it instantly. I might not be religious any longer, but I could not contemplate an end to my life, especially an end self-inflicted.

Perhaps I could go away somewhere. Thirty-five wasn't old, not really. And I'd have enough money from selling my share of the company to start something. Perhaps I should give Kate the divorce she so desperately wanted. Give her the house and a car, let her marry Ed and give the girls a real father. Ed could buy me out. I assumed he'd be willing to marry Kate.

But what could I do? Where could I go? How could I ever forget what a mess I had made of my life? Could I ever overcome it?

Although the sun was bright, I felt chilled. I went back inside and poured some fresh coffee, then sat at the kitchen table, despondently tracing the green ivy patterns in the table cloth. The house was so silent!

I tried to remember good things about the house, about sitting at the kitchen table, about tracing patterns in tablecloths. If there had been such times they were too far back in the past to remember.

Perhaps I could go back to Idaho, buy a farm, settle down in some remote corner of some remote valley and get a good dog, raise my own food, depend upon no one. And have no one depending on me.

Thinking of Idaho reminded me of the dream. The old house...the garden...the green fields...and my father? No, that was impossible. That beautiful naked man could not possibly have been my own father. Thinking about it now, I doubted that the man had ever been naked in his whole life, at least not since Grandmother's midwife had first diapered him. My father's abhorrence of nudity had been the genesis of my own. At one point in my life I had practically worshiped my father, incorporating all of his ideas about life literally as "gospel". And even though I'd found myself at odds with the man these past six or seven years, I still found so many of his attitudes cropping up in my own thoughts.

Then how, why, had I dreamed about a naked man?

The realization jolted me! I'd *never* dreamed about naked men! At least, not that I remembered.

At first, in the dream, I'd been sure that the man was my father, but later, as I'd followed him through those dark ugly streets, I'd started to realize that it couldn't be. And then when he'd turned, when he'd thrown off the overcoat, saying "Look!" I'd been certain.

I could still hear his taunting laughter as I'd asked, over and over, "Who are you?" And then: "I am you, you fool!"

But that too was impossible. I didn't have a beard or long hair—and I certainly wasn't planning to grow them. The dream didn't make sense. And the longer I thought about it, the less sense it made. I was forced to decide it was only my mind's unfathomable way of working up to a sexual climax—although I'd never had a wet dream quite like it before.

But that flying sensation had been delicious. I hadn't dreamed about flying since....

"Where is thy brother?"

I sat upright in the chair, staring hard straight ahead, but not seeing the kitchen—seeing, rather, a young boy, about the same age as Chuck. A boy dressed in pajamas and an old plaid bathrobe, standing in the doorway....

The image faded, but the idea remained. *Bill!*

Of course! What an idiot I'd been not to think of it sooner!

"Where is thy brother?"

That man had been Bill! Not me, not my father, but my brother, Bill!

I'd completely shut Bill out of my mind—erased him. We'd been so close as children, two years apart in our actual ages, but more like twins than just brothers. And then we'd had some kind of fight.... I remembered the anger, but I couldn't recall what we had fought about. Or had it been Kate that we'd argued about? I remembered he'd hated her. And that would have made it about the right time. I'd been seventeen when I'd started dating her, and that would have made Bill about fifteen.

The last time I'd seen him had been at my wedding. A year or so later, Mom had written that he'd run off and joined the Marines. It had been...Good Lord! Seventeen years since I'd seen my own brother!

But why should I dream about Bill? I still hadn't answered the riddle of the dream: "Where is thy brother?" That was what God had asked Cain, who had killed his brother. I hadn't killed mine.

I stood up to get another cup of coffee, but I never got as far as the stove. The cup slipped from my fingers and shattered on the floor as I glanced into the front room and saw the envelope tucked under the front door!

My hands were shaking as I ripped off one end and extracted the single folded page. I leaned against the door, holding my arms tight to my sides to stop my hands from shaking the paper. This note was printed, but now the printing was not quite so childish, and the contents were not quite so illiterate:

DERE ROBBER. YOU CANT GET AWAY FROM ME NOW. I NO ALL ABOUT YOU. I HOPE YOU HAVE THE DESENSY TO KILL YOUSELF. YOU DESERV TO DIE. YOU ARE TRYING TO RUNE CHUCKS LIFE THE SAME WAY YOU RUNED MINE. IM GOING TO GET YOU ROBBER! LOOK OUT! XXX YOU KNOW WHO

I took a deep breath and leaned back against the door, closing my eyes. Suddenly I saw John Adams as clearly as though he had been there physically—standing up to the urinal, milking his thick half-hard penis as he looked down at mine. I seemed to feel his hand squeezing my shoulder. "Just remember, Robert, it's your word against mine. And you don't know who I am, do you? They might just believe me and think *you* were the *pervert.*"

"Oh, no," I whispered. "No, it couldn't be....."

You don't know who I am, do you?

YOU KNOW WHO

Where is thy brother?

And, last night, in the steambath, I'd heard myself say: "*Suck me, Billy, please!*"

The pieces were suddenly falling into place!

I remembered, on the plane, thinking that John Adams was not what he seemed to be. I'd been right! And his name wasn't John Adams. The pieces fit together too neatly to be a coincidence. Our meeting had not been accidental. Nor had it been a coincidence that I'd been worrying about Chuck and that note. Jerry Ashby hadn't written the note, nor had Ed. Now I knew who had written it, plus the one I'd just read: the man who had called himself John Adams; the man I had dreamed about, only slightly disguised, last night: Bill Thorne! My brother!

Because now a new piece of the puzzle presented itself. Suddenly, clearly, the memory came back—and it hit me with such a shattering impact that I had to sit down on the couch.

I was sixteen and my brother was fourteen. As children we'd been so close, going everywhere together. But then I'd reached puberty first, and Bill had begun to seem like a silly kid, always carping at me: "Don't do this, Bob, you'll get us in trouble. Don't do that, Bob, it isn't right. What will Dad say? What will Mom say? What will people say?" The thing that had galled me was that most of the time he was right. He was always the "sensible" one, I'd been the "crazy" one, just out for a good time. Driving Dad's car, filled with half of the basketball squad, down to Boise to a whorehouse, leaving poor Bill in the car to keep watch for us. What a bastard I'd been then. Cocky, smug, self-satisfied. I'd stopped going to church, started drinking, swearing....

We had moved into town by then....

It was some time late in July.... I'd been out on a date that night. Bill had wanted to come along but I'd told him to get lost. I was planning to get myself laid and I didn't want him messing it up for me. (He'd come into his own, as far as growing up was concerned—he'd shot up two or three inches taller than me, and his body was better: bigger, fuller, broader shoulders, thicker chest—and his whang was the talk of the shower rooms—and yet it seemed he couldn't get out of that "goody-good" stage. As far as I knew he'd never even jacked off. So I didn't want him watching over my shoulder as I tried to get some action out of Jenny Lou Fisher.)

The night had been pure frustration. Jenny Lou had insisted on taking Karen Simpson along, and Karen's boy friend, "Whimpy", was the biggest, fattest, dumbest cluck in the Junior Class. All through the movie, and afterwards parked up on Cemetery Hill, I'd tried to make out, but with Karen and Whimpy along, Jenny Lou wouldn't even touch me. Oh, she'd let me put my arm around her and sneak my fingers inside her blouse, but then suddenly she'd push me away and turn around in the seat to gossip and giggle with Karen. To top it all off, Jenny decided to spend the night with Karen, so I couldn't even take Whimpy and Karen home first.

By the time I got home, three o'clock in the morning, my nuts ached so bad I could hardly walk. And of course I was furious. I slammed into the house and turned on the lights, not giving a damn if I woke someone or not. I rummaged around in the kitchen, massaging my aching groin, getting a hard-on, almost wishing my father would come charging down to see me playing with myself. But he didn't. And I managed to get myself so worked up I knew I'd have to do something to get rid of the pressure. I couldn't go up to my room. Bill was sure to wake up and whine, "What are you doing, Bob? You shouldn't do that. It's not good for you." And I didn't need that on top of everything else.

So I went outside, out into the back yard. There had been a moon earlier, but it had gone down and now everything was dark. Our big elm was only a darker shadow against another shadow of the Wilberson's house next door. I'd left the light on in the kitchen, but it had to filter through the screen door and then the screens all around the back porch, so even if someone did see me, they wouldn't be able to see what I was doing.

I unbuttoned my fly and eased my cock out and started slowly working it. I thought about Jenny Lou and let myself imagine what I *should* have done. I should have just raped the dumb bitch. Everybody in town knew she fucked like a mink. One night I'd been one of five guys she'd taken on, out behind the bleachers on the football field, lying on one of the benches the team used, letting one fuck her while she sucked on another one, getting him ready to screw her next. And Karen knew what a whore Jenny was; Karen wasn't any churchgoing virgin herself. They were probably home right now sticking things up each other's cunt. I should have raped both of them! And let Whimpy watch! Let him stand there and play with his teeny dink while I screwed his girl friend.

I wandered around the yard, completely caught up in my fantasy, seeing myself shoving Jenny up against the trunk of the car, ripping her skirt off, jerking her pants down, shoving it in! Like a damn bull! Fuck her like a stallion! Harder and harder until she screamed–but not stopping. If she did scream I could grab her and force her down and shove my cock into her screaming mouth and shoot my jizz into it!

"Bob, is that you?"

The voice came from the back porch behind me! My heart did a wild somersault in my chest as I tried to shove my cock back in my pants, but it wouldn't go! I turned around, hooking my thumbs into my pockets, spreading my hands over my crotch, fully expecting my father to come striding down the back steps, ready to knock me flat on my ass on the lawn.

Bill stood there, outlined by the light from the kitchen, wearing my old plaid bathrobe. I said, "Oh, shit, it's you! Jeez, Bill, you scared me!"

He came down the steps. "I'm sorry. What are you doing out here? I heard something and..."

Watching him step down like a kid scared to death to dive in a swimming pool, hearing his whining voice, all the anger and frustration of the night welled up and went straight out toward him. I wanted to hurt someone, shock someone, get back at someone–and Bill had politely presented himself. I pulled my hands away from my crotch and stepped into the dim spread of light where I knew he could see my hard-on. "Oh, that cunt

Jenny Lou," I said, knowing the word *cunt* would chill him clear through. "One of these days somebody's going to strangle her! Goddamn pricktease!"

"Wouldn't she...*do* anything?"

The goody-good wouldn't say *shit* if he had a mouthful! I'd told him earlier, just to torment him, that I was going to get Jenny Lou to *blow* me, and he'd gone red as a beet!

"Naw, shit," I said. "She just wanted to tease me. Besides, Whimpy and Karen went with us. That dumb Whimpy—he still thinks his pecker is just something to pee through." I turned slightly in the light and started to play with my cock again.

"You shouldn't do that out here, Bob!" Bill whined. "Somebody will see you!"

"Aw, for Christ's sake, Bill! When the hell are you going to stop being a chickenshit? Who's going to see me? Everybody's asleep in this burg!"

"Dad might. You slammed the door. Maybe he heard you. Maybe he'll come down...."

I laughed and bent backward, working my fist even harder on my cock. "Yeah...I wish the old bastard would come down. I'd show him a thing or two. I'd say, 'Hey, Pop, watch me beat my meat! Watch me shoot my hot jizz all over your fuckin' lawn!' "

Even in the dark I could see his face turn bright scarlet. Every swearword I used hit like a fist in his nuts. "Bob!" he whispered. "Be quiet!"

"Aw, shit!" I turned away from him, still pumping away, and stepped out of the light, into the shadow of the elm tree. I stood there, staring into the darkness, praying he wouldn't go back into the house. An idea had started to form in my mind—a sick, but very exciting idea. I kept moving slowly until I reached the thick trunk of the tree, then I turned and leaned back against it, spreading my legs apart. He was right behind me. "Is this better?" I asked him.

He hunched his shoulders. "I guess so."

"C'mere, Bill." He stepped closer. "You know what Conrad Bigelow told me? He said him and his brother do things for each other. You know what I mean?" (I was making it up, but I knew Bill wouldn't have the guts to ask Conrad about it.)

"No," he said softly, shaking his head.

"Conrad says any time they go out with some girls that won't come across, him and Ed *do things* later."

I heard him swallow hard. "What kind of things?"

"Conrad says Ed takes it up his...you-know-what. And then sometimes they both do what crazy Noel Becker does."

He swallowed again, and his voice was tight when he said, "Noel Becker's a queer! Dad says they should shoot him, just like they would a freak animal."

I laughed. I was really enjoying this. Each time I made him cringe, something inside me tingled wilder and wilder. "That's because Dad's never had Noel Becker *blow* him!"

"Bob!" he gasped. He looked back at the house, then at me. "Have *you...?*"

"Oh, boy, you really are dumb, aren't you? Shit, every guy in school has had old Noel suck 'em off!"

That wasn't quite true, but it sounded good. Maybe not all of the guys had let him, but a lot of them had. Noel Becker was a legend in Glen Falls; if you saw him out walking someplace late at night—and you did almost every night—you just stopped and said, "Hey, Noel, I got something for you." I'd done it twice now.

"That's terrible!"

"Like hell it is. Boy you should try it sometime. He loves it. He sucks and sucks and then swallows your jizz. Jenny Lou spits it out." I was watching his face; I was used to the dark now and I could see that his eyes were looking straight down at my cock! I even imagined I could see his, hard, under his robe, and that really excited me. I knew Bill had a big one, but I'd never seen it hard. I decided right then that I would look at it, one way or another. "Jenny Lou thinks she'll get pregnant if she swallows it. But she's lousy anyway. She's not even a good piece of tail." I took my hand away again so he could see my cock clearly. "Billy..." I said softly. "Do you really like me?"

"Well, sure I do."

"If I asked, would you do something?"

He took a step backward. "Not that, Bob!"

"Then you don't like me!" I turned my back on him. "Go back in the house, chickenshit!"

"What are you going to do?"

"I'm gonna *jack off!* What the fuck do you think?"

"Don't be mad, Bob," he whined. "I just couldn't."

I turned to him. He looked so damn pitiful it disgusted me! This big strapping kid scared to death of the least hint of sex. I wanted to kick him right square in the nuts! And then rip off those fucking pajamas and shove my cock right up his ass!

I reached out and grabbed his robe, jerking him toward me. By then I couldn't have stopped myself if I'd wanted to. I wanted to hurt him. I wanted to do something so bad that he'd never forget it. I ripped his robe open. Sure enough, his cock was as hard as a rock, sticking straight out from his gaping pajamas, so damn big it looked like my forearm! Just the sight of it sent chills all the way through my body. Nobody I'd ever seen had one like that! I reached down and grabbed it and knelt down. "Well, *I'm* not a chickenshit!" I opened my mouth and shoved my face forward and took his cock inside my mouth.

Suddenly his hot cum was spurting! I gagged, but I kept my mouth tight around it, pumping my own cock furiously. I jumped up and forced him down to his knees and shoved my cock into his face.

"Please, Bob! Don't!"

I grabbed his hair tight in one fist, pumping my cock with the other one. I was trying to get the damn thing in his mouth before I came, but his lips were clamped tight.

Then everything exploded! I watched my cum splatter all over his face. It gushed into his hair, his eyes, all over his cheeks. The full load I'd been building up all night!

Then I twisted his hair, forcing his head back, his face up toward me—and leaned over—and spat his cum into his face. "That's *yours!*" I stood back and stripped the last gobs from my cock, flipped the stuff from my fingers. "There now!" I said. "Now you're just as rotten as I am!"

He didn't move. He just knelt there in the grass with my cum and his own mixed together, running over his face, dripping down from his chin onto his pajamas, trailing onto his hairy chest. He didn't say anything. He just looked up at me. I couldn't tell if he were crying or it that was our cum streaking down from his eyes.

The last of my anger drained out of me. I wanted to cry, to kneel down beside him and take him into my arms and tell him how sorry I was I had done such a terrible thing. But I couldn't move either. We just looked at each other. Then finally he stood up, his face shining in the dim light. He wiped the stuff off with the sleeve of his robe. He went into the house without saying a word.

I knew as I watched him go back up the steps that he'd never forgive me. And I knew I would never forgive myself. I felt like Cain in the Bible—except I had done something even worse than killing my brother.

At that point the memory became very hazy. I'd had a terrible fever the next day—screaming, cringing in the bed, as hideous Hell-Monsters slobbered in the shadows of my room, waiting for me to die, waiting to eat my soul, suck it out of my body.

I seemed to remember my mother and father having an argument about calling the doctor—and then some men, standing around my bed, leaning over me, putting their cold hands on my head and praying to have this "affliction" taken from me. And then later, my father sitting on my bed, telling me that I'd been following the paths of Satan, and that the sickness was a warning from God to repent of my evil ways. I remembered him praying: "If it be Thy will, Oh Lord, let this cup be taken from him."

Had I told my father the terrible thing I had done to my brother? Had I, in the delirium of fever, terrified of the consequences of my sin, twisted the truth to make Bill the guilty one, implying that my brother had "tempted" me in a moment of extreme weakness? For reasons I'd never clearly understood, my father had always preferred me to Bill, and I'd learned very early in life the fine art of implication—not really *lying*, simply leaving certain things to my father's imagination, letting him make the decision that Bill was the guilty one.

I must have said something, because I remembered Bill, standing by my bed, his eyes red from crying, just looking at me, pure hatred written all over his face.

And that had been the end of our friendship.

Bill had stopped going to church—the same Sunday that I started again—and, even before school had started that fall, he'd taken up with the Caldwell brothers, going out night after night, getting in trouble with the police. I could remember how disgusted I'd been when I heard the guys talking about what a big prick he had, and how he was making out with all the Junior and Senior girls, and how they loved it, and how he'd get drunk and show off, making bets that his cock was the biggest in town and that he could shoot further than any other guy.

It was during the winter that followed that I got to know Kate Jensen. She was one of the school's "wallflowers", the complete opposite of Jenny Lou—shy, plain, serious, and a virgin. We didn't even *talk* about sex until just before the wedding, when the Bishop gave us his "little chat" about marriage and the "proper" use of sex as a means of multiplying and replenishing the earth, as God had commanded in the very beginning, and not simply for pleasure, which was Satan's tool for leading us astray.

I studied the note again: *You are trying to ruin Chuck's life the way you ruined mine.* That *had* to be Bill! If that one horrible night had changed my own life so drastically, I was sure it had changed his just as much. His helling around in Glen Falls had seemed normal—in the sense that he messed with girls rather than boys—but I hadn't seen or heard from Bill for seventeen years; it was possible he'd turned queer in the service, or afterwards, and blamed it all on that night, and on me.

And now that I could remember how it had really happened, maybe he was fully justified in blaming me. I could understand why he would want to punish me by sending those notes, those pictures.

As ye give, so shall ye receive.

Obviously, though, he had no idea how much I'd already been punished—by Kate and by Ed and by Chuck, and, perhaps, even by myself. *Well,* I thought, *the time has come to let him know.* My sin had caught up with me and now I had to make reparations. I had to find Bill and apologize. I was sure now that nothing was wrong with Chuck; Bill had simply used him as a means of getting back at me.

It was amazing, now that I thought about it, how simple the true explanation really was. It would have been easy for Bill to have found me: I was listed in the telephone directory. Knowing my address, he'd have known which school Chuck would go to, and a few "casual" inquiries would have given him the name of Chuck's best friend. He'd simply used the same deceit with me that I'd used with our father—*implying* that Jerry and Chuck were homosexual lovers. Or maybe he'd approached Chuck himself, gained his confidence. Maybe...

I cringed at the thought that Bill might have hated me enough to seduce Chuck—but I pushed the idea out of my mind. I'd made the mistake of believing the note once; I didn't want to make the same error again.

At any rate, somehow Bill had found out I was going to San Francisco, and he'd followed me. He'd been the one in my hotel room. He'd been the one following me on Van Ness, watching me in the coffee shop, dogging my every move, waiting for his chance to approach me, get me drunk, then seduce me. He'd tried to get me drunk on the plane; afterwards he'd suggested a beer. It was ironic that my reason for not succumbing to his charms, for not having that beer, was the very note he had sent me. Had it not been for that, I might have gone to a bar with him, might have let myself be duped into going home with him...."Let's go to my place for a nightcap, Robert. Nobody's expecting you. If you want, you can spend the night there. I've got an extra bed."

I could imagine what he would have done then, with me too drunk to fight him off—holding me down, opening my pants.... And then, afterwards, spitting the stuff in my face, saying: "There! That's yours! Now you're just as rotten as I am!"

Obviously the next order of business was to find Bill and talk to him, and to do it before I got into any discussion with Chuck. I could see that my brother had planned all this very very carefully; if I hadn't guessed who "John Adams" really was, I'd have gone through with my plan of confronting Chuck—and that would have been the real disaster I'd felt coming; Chuck might never have forgiven me for accusing him of being homosexual. Yes, one way or the other, Bill would have had his revenge. I could appreciate how diabolically clever my brother had been.

I still wanted to talk to Chuck about his being "high" last night, but now that could wait—until after his camping trip if necessary.

I put the note back into the envelope and went upstairs intending to get the other note and the pictures, then find the slip of paper "John Adams" had given me—and then take them all to confront the man.

But the note and the pictures were not where I'd left them! In a panic I felt all around under the dresser, removing both bottom drawers. Nothing! I searched through each separate drawer, moved the dresser away from the wall and peered behind it. I found a dime and a pen I had lost several months ago, but no envelopes.

I pushed the dresser back and reached under it again. And this time I found something. Not the envelope: it felt like a small plastic bottle. I'd probably dislodged it from its hiding place by moving the dresser. I pulled it out. It was an old prescription bottle of mine with the label still on it: Nembutal. At first there seemed nothing but cotton inside it, but when I extracted the top layer, there were six small white capsules.

They were not sleeping pills!

I had a sickening feeling that I knew what they were—and an even sicker feeling that I knew *whose* they were.

Dope! Pure poison!

I felt miserable.

Wearily I replaced the drawers. Just a few minutes ago everything had seemed so clear and so simple. Now things were all mixed up again. Who had taken the note and those pictures? Chuck? Jerry Ashby? Or had Bill somehow managed to get in the house last night, between the time I'd gone out and the time Chuck got home? It was possible. We kept a spare key hidden under the front steps. Bill could have kept watch until he'd seen somebody use the key. In fact, Bill might have put those pills under the dresser! Not Chuck at all!

At least that slip of paper he'd given me was where I

had left it, in my coat pocket; but all it had was his name and a phone number, no address.

I went into the hall and checked the directory. Just as I'd suspected, there were several John Adams, but none with the number he'd given me. I called the operator and asked her to verify the number. Yes, it was a new one. His address? Thirteen-twenty-five Richards Street.

Chuck was still sleeping peacefully so I left him a note: *Had to go out for an important meeting. Should be back early afternoon. If possible, put off your camping trip until later today.* I signed it *Dad*, read it over, then inserted *love* before *Dad*, and left it on the floor, just inside his door. I took the little bottle of pills downstairs and locked them in one of the drawers of my desk; no one had a key to that lock except me. I decided to have a quick drink, just a small shot to bolster my confidence; then I got in the car and headed for Richards Street.

As I drove, I tried to decide the best way to approach Bill. My original impulse had been to tell him straight out that I knew who he was and what he'd been doing, to apologize honestly for what I had done to him, and ask him to stop writing those notes. But the more I considered it, the more I began to doubt that the direct approach was the best one. I did not want to risk making him even more bitter toward me than he already was; if possible, I wanted to settle the problem and still remain friends with him—after all, he *was* my brother, even if he was queer. And now that I understood why he was queer, I felt that I had an obligation to help him, if he'd let me. Maybe some of his actions last night on the plane hadn't been completely insincere; maybe he really had wanted to get to know me. There was no way of knowing what had truly been going on in his mind; maybe he'd wanted to tell his troubles to me. I had to be very careful about putting him off again.

If I went to him as though I hadn't figured out anything, as though I really believed he was John Adams—as though the fact that he was queer didn't bother me at all—that might take some of the wind out of his sails. If I could make him believe that the idea of sex between men didn't upset me, then the idea of using it as a kind of emotional blackmail would suddenly become pointless. But beyond that, it would imply an acceptance of him, regardless of his...unusual desires, and that might make him feel better about himself. He might even admit to writing the notes without my having to tell him I'd figured it out.

Strangely enough, now that I'd remembered that evening, back in Glen Falls, I didn't feel nearly as self-righteous as I had last night. Some of the wind had been taken out of my sails, too. I even began to wonder whether, given the chance, he'd try to seduce me again. What possible harm could it do now, anyway, after what I had done in the steam bath?

I found his address easily, a fairly large two-story frame house, sitting back from the street behind a low stone wall and a neatly trimmed yard. It looked as though it had been painted just recently. I felt an excitement starting deep in my body, not entirely unpleasant, as I went up the walk to his front door and rang the bell. For a moment the excitement began to fade when it seemed that no one was home; but then I heard: "Just a minute!"

Suddenly my heart began racing. Suppose I'd been wrong about all of those pieces fitting so neatly into the puzzle? Suppose they fit together *too* neatly? I felt dizzy and reached quickly to steady myself on the doorframe. *I shouldn't be here! I shouldn't be doing this!* I didn't want to become friends with a queer, no matter whose brother he was!

The door opened. He frowned angrily, and I thought: *Please! Just say "Go away!" and close the door!*

But he didn't. He stood there regarding me with a kind of half-triumphant smile slowly erasing the frown, wearing paint-splattered levis, so old and tattered they looked as though they might disintegrate any moment, and an equally old faded brown army shirt. There were small flecks of white on his forehead and hands, and I guessed he'd been painting. "Well," he said. "I didn't expect to see you today."

The sound of his voice, so calm and self-confident, made me feel easier in one way, but much more nervous in another. For a moment I couldn't even remember the reason I'd come here—or the reason I'd given myself for coming. Looking at him now, I remembered vividly that feeling I'd had on the plane, of wanting to touch him. With a shock I realized that I still wanted to. It made not one bit of difference whether he was my brother Bill, or John Adams, or someone whose true name I might never know. He radiated an aura of self-assurance and strength that I wanted to share, to feel for myself. How had I ever got it into my mind that he was miserable? *I* was the one who was miserable! By all of the values I prized so highly, he should have been cringing at the sight of me, terrified that I might have the police waiting out on the street to arrest him, and *I* should have been the one looking triumphant.

"Hello...John," I swallowed hard. "I guess I should have called...but...I was afraid you'd hang up on me."

"I probably would have. What's happening?"

"I want to....apologize."

"I see."

"May I come in?"

He studied me carefully, his eyes moving slowly from my face down to my crotch and back up again. He shrugged and stepped back. "Sure. Why not."

I went inside, intensely relieved. It was dim in the front of his house, with all of the drapes drawn over his windows, but I could see he'd been doing some extensive construction: there were saw horses in one corner; a large part of one wall had been cut away to join a parlor and living room. Paint-splattered drop-cloths lay over most of the furniture. He closed the door, then leaned back against it, folding his arms. "Okay, Robert. Now what?"

I looked up at his face. He was regarding me steadily, unblinking, waiting for me to explain myself. His gaze was so intense that I had to look down—and I couldn't help asking myself if a man guilty of "emotional blackmail" could look his victim in the eye so unwaveringly. Now I remembered the way he had appeared to me *before* that moment at the urinals, before I knew that he was a homosexual; somehow I'd forgotten his original appearance, or had distorted it totally beyond recognition in my imagination. This was not a man who would seduce a sixteen-year-old boy, even if he did hate the boy's father. And there was no hatred in his eyes. There was anger, perhaps.

I wanted to tell him: "I've made a mistake, sorry," and leave. Obviously I was wrong about many things concerning this man, whoever he was, my brother or John Adams—just as I'd been wrong about so many *many* things recently. If I stayed longer I was certain to make even more of a fool of myself than I already had, one way or another. And yet I knew I couldn't leave. I couldn't let the man remain a mystery to me. I shrugged helplessly. "I'm sorry," I said. "I knew what I wanted to say, driving here, but...I don't even know where to begin now."

"May I make a suggestion?" I looked up, meeting his intense eyes again. "How about starting with: 'I'm sorry I called you a filthy pervert'."

I cringed and looked down. "Yes," I said softly. "I am sorry about that."

"You know, Robert, that's really a rotten thing to call a guy. I don't give a damn how upset you were. I mean, as far as I was concerned, you cruised me just as much as I did you. Sure, I'd seen you at the airport, but I hadn't been staring. But, man, you zeroed in on my crotch like you had every intention of doing exactly what I wanted you to. You know? So I tried to be friendly, and you gave me the old fuck-off routine...."

"It wasn't that at all, John," I protested. "I really was upset about something. I did want to talk to you."

"I know. That's what you kept saying. So I thought, 'Okay, the guy's got his mind on a problem, fine, I can appreciate that, but he wants me to come back later.' Well, hell..." He shrugged and moved away from the door. "I should have said something. Instead of being cute and telling you I wasn't married, I should have told you: 'Robert, I'm a cocksucker.' I shouldn't have groped you, especially there in that head. But, man, *filthy pervert*—that's a very bad trip to lay on somebody."

I stared at the floor, feeling like a very small child being sternly reprimanded—but not unjustly. He was right: it was a rotten thing to call a man—especially him. I couldn't help thinking how ridiculous I'd been, imagining that I could "help" him, make him feel "reassured" about himself. He didn't need reassurance from anyone.

"I'm sorry," I said again. "I didn't mean it."

"Are you sure?"

I nodded. "Yes. I wasn't even thinking. I just wasn't expecting..." My voice faltered as he stepped up to me, reached down and brought his hand up under my crotch. Wild tinglings exploded in my stomach, up my spine, on the top of my head. I flinched—then shut my eyes tight, forcing myself to stand absolutely still, to make no move at all that he might misinterpret. His fingers found my penis, now beginning to harden, and closed around it. For a moment it felt as though my body might melt on the spot.

"I still think that's very nice, Robert," he whispered.

I shuddered and swallowed hard. I muttered, "Thank

you," then instantly felt like an utter fool. He squeezed gently, then patted my arm. "Would you like a beer?"

"Uh...yes...I, uh, yes, I would, please."

"Let's go into the kitchen. It's the only room finished down here. I just bought the place a few months ago, and it's still pretty much of a mess."

Weakly, still tingling, and with my hand deep in my pocket, holding my erection firmly so it wouldn't show, I followed him into a large, old-fashioned kitchen. Any other time I might have appreciated all the careful work that had obviously gone into giving it that warm, relaxed feeling–it was very much like our kitchen had been in the farm house, back home–but my mind seemed to have gone almost totally blank. He gestured toward a beautifully-restored old wooden table. "Sit. Make yourself comfortable." He took two cans of beer from the refrigerator, then hesitated. "Would you prefer something harder? Than beer, I mean?"

I shook my head numbly. "No. Beer's fine." He opened the cans and put one on the table before me. I took several deep, cool swallows, then muttered, idiotically, "Mmmm, good."

He chuckled, then leaned against the table, drinking his beer, watching me drink mine. I flinched again as his fingers touched the back of my hand, then traced slowly along the thick vein; the touch was like an electrical current flashing up through my arm and down into my body. "Okay, Robert," he said. "Now tell me the real reason you came here today."

I looked up at his face, feeling like a child again. ("Tell Daddy where it hurts, Bobby.") I shuddered and looked down again. "To apologize...."

"Yes, but you've done that," he said. "If that was all that you'd come for, you'd have said your piece and gone, right?"

I nodded. "I guess so."

"Well?"

My heart was starting to pound again, and my mind

was a helpless jumble of confusion. Did he know why I'd come here, thinking he was my brother? Or did he mean something else by the question? I realized that now was the time to ask him about the notes, about his true identity, but my mind refused to form the questions. Dimly I realized that I didn't want to know the answers—not yet; I wanted something to happen first. "I'm not sure, John," I said.

He went to the refrigerator. "You want another?" I nodded, lifting the can to my lips to finish it. He put the new can on the table, then wandered back to look out of the window above the sink. He stood there silently for several long moments and I found myself looking at him in a way I had never looked at a man before, at the way his levis clung tightly to his muscular legs and his buttocks; his body had become an exciting thing to consider.

"Robert...Clear up something for me, will you? Are you gay?"

I couldn't help laughing; the question seemed ridiculous. "Not particularly."

He looked over his shoulder, frowning; then he grinned. "I wasn't asking if you were happy. But you answered the question anyway, didn't you? Gay means queer, Robert. I was asking if you were a cocksucker."

"Oh." The word jarred me, and my first impulse was to react angrily, to say "No!" emphatically—but I knew if I said it, he might simply shrug and say, "Too bad. Why don't you go home now?" I took a long drink of the beer, feeling my penis starting to rise again. "I've... done it...a couple of times."

"Oh?" He turned to face me, leaning back with one elbow on the top of the sink, standing as he had when I'd first seen him in the airport, leaning on that counter of the bookstand. "Well, that's interesting. I wouldn't have guessed it." He regarded me with a look of challenge in his eyes. "Did you enjoy it?"

Again I wanted to say "No!" but now I could see the firm outline of his genitals under the thin faded denim—and his penis was growing, slowly lengthening, thickening. My mind was churning, but I understood that something completely new was happening to me: one of the most exciting men I had ever seen was getting excited himself—over *me!* Twice I had wanted almost desperately to touch him; it occurred to me suddenly that I *could* touch him! He was a homosexual; he *wanted* me to touch him! It wouldn't be dirty and perverted to him—and if it wasn't to him, how could it be for me? It couldn't be both dirty *and* beautiful; it had to be one or the other. I wanted it to be beautiful.

"I was...drunk," I said. "I don't remember."

"Are you drunk now?" he asked.

"...A little."

He pushed himself away from the sink and walked slowly across the room until he was standing before me. I could not take my eyes from his crotch; the closer he came, the more clearly the outline of his penis stood out; I could even see the ridge around the head of it.

He unbuckled his belt. "This is what you came here for, isn't it, Robert? This is how you wanted to apologize, isn't it. You decided it might not be bad like the others. I'm not like the others, am I, Robert?"

"No...."

"You think maybe with me it would be good..." He tugged his shirt up from his levis. "...Because I'm a man..." He opened the buttons, slowly. "...Because I've got a man's body...and I *act* like a man."

A fantastic vacuum was opening, deep in my body—a need so desperate, I knew I could never control it. I *needed* to touch him! Yes, that's how I wanted to apologize—in the most meaningful, the most personal way possible!

He opened his shirt, pulled it over his arms, and tossed it onto a chair. I reached out and touched his stomach. It was covered with thick black hair—but the hair felt so soft—and the skin of his belly was tight over firm muscles. And warm! The excitement within me became a storm! My penis strained painfully, frantically hard against my pants. He opened the top snaps of his levis, inched the zipper down. I could see just the base of his cock, nestled in a thick tangle of black pubic hair. He reached into the spreading V...closed his fingers around his cock...inched it upward...then pulled it out!

A brilliant thrill lashed through my body!

Slowly I moved my hand down from his belly, down over the white hollow of his leg.... I slipped my hand slowly under his cock, cradled it in my palm, watched it jerk and grow harder, rising upward. It was beautiful! I'd never thought of a man's cock as beautiful, but his was—like a living piece of sculpture—almost like a holy thing.

I leaned forward, closing my eyes; felt the warm tight head of his cock touch my lips. I shuddered—but not with revulsion—now I trembled with hunger. I needed to take him inside me, take his cock into my mouth, to engulf it, *his cock!* The most beautiful, personal part of his body. I opened my mouth and took it in. He moaned softly. His hands touched my shoulders—and the touch felt so good!

"Suck it, Robert," he whispered. "Suck my cock, Robert." In my mind I could both feel and see his warm blood surging into his cock, swelling it thickly inside my mouth. "That feels so good, Robert...."

His hips started a slow easy rhythm, and with each gentle thrust his cock hardened and reached deeper and deeper into my mouth. His hands tightened on my shoulders. I cupped my hand under his balls, felt them tightening upward. Inside me fantastic sensations were swirling and building. "Oh, God!" His body tensed, his fingers dug hard into my shoulders—and then sweetness exploded! I felt his cock surging, felt thickness and heat shooting into my mouth! His semen came gushing out, out from his beautiful body, through his beautiful cock, to flood over my tongue—and I swallowed each starchy torrent like a man dying of thirst!

He moaned and leaned over me, breathing heavily; the warmth of his breath tingled my cheek. "Oh, yes...." He laughed weakly. "Oh, man, I needed that." He squeezed my shoulders. "And I needed *you* to do it, damn you. I was so fucking frustrated last night."

"I'm sorry."

He stood up and took a deep breath, then grinned down at me. "That's okay. You made up for it." He leaned over me again and gripped my shoulder—then his hand moved down my arm, to my leg. He knelt down before me, pushing me gently to lean back in the chair. He unfastened my belt, unzipped my pants, pulled them down. I stared at his face as he concentrated on tugging my shorts down, saw him grin as my cock flipped up. He tugged my hips forward—his touch was like fire on my buttocks. He leaned his head down. I gasped and closed my eyes as a warm flush spread slowly through me: the sweetest, most delicious feeling I could possibly imagine. He took my cock into his mouth slowly, deliberately, as my body flinched and trembled in the chair, inch by inch, until it was in him completely. A hand squeezed my balls and the other gripped one cheek of my ass, and his throat started constricting, milking my cock. I raised up in the chair and his mouth went down even further; my body convulsed, and I came! The sweet storm inside me went cascading out of my cock into him, one incredible explosion after another, until I collapsed in the chair, my arms like limp cloths dangling at my sides, my body feeling like a shapeless lump of flesh.

"You needed that too, didn't you?" The sound of his voice brought reality crashing back into my mind. I sat up in the chair, running my tongue over the slick residue of his semen still clinging to my teeth and the roof of my mouth. I clenched my teeth hard to keep from being sick. A voice whispered in my mind: *"Now you're just as rotten as I am."*

I opened my eyes and saw him, sprawled in a chair, his cock still hanging out of his gaping fly. I looked down at myself, saw my shorts and pants down around my ankles, my cock limp, shining wet, white semen still seeping out from it onto the chair. I stood quickly and turned my back to him, pulling my shorts and pants up.

"Something wrong?"

I shook my head, fighting to keep my voice steady. "No. Everything's just fine."

"Well, good," he drawled. "Cause that's how it should be." He sat up, grinning broadly. "How about another beer?"

All I wanted at that moment was to get out as quickly as possible; but I knew that I had to stay long enough to ask a couple of questions. I sat down again. "Sure."

He stood up and casually tucked his cock back into his levis, then sauntered over to the refrigerator. I watched him, thinking, *He's still beautiful!* But the voice in my head lashed at me: *"He's a pervert! And so are you!"*

He brought back the beer, then sank heavily into the chair. "Jesus, I'm exhausted."

I took a long drink, then set the can down with a thunk on the table. "Who are you?"

He looked up. "What?"

"Who are you?"

"What do you mean, *who am I?* I'm me. I don't..."

"What's your name?"

"Are we playing some kind of game? You know what my name is."

"Please! Just tell me your name."

"John Adams."

"Are you telling me the truth?"

"What is this, Robert? Of course I'm telling..."

"You're not Bill?"

"Bill?" He shook his head. "No, I'm not Bill. Who's Bill?"

"What did you mean...at the airport?"

"What, when I groped you?"

"No. You said I didn't know who you were. You said, 'You really don't know who I am, do you?' Tell me why you said that."

"Oh." He started to laugh, then apparently saw my expression. "Sorry," he said quickly. "This is something serious, isn't it?"

I nodded.

"Well...It can't hurt anything now. I wanted to scare you—that's all. I realized what a dumb thing I'd done and I thought maybe you might actually call the cops. And if you had...quite honestly, they *would* have believed me. You see, Robert, I'm an attorney."

I blinked at him stupidly, feeling cold all over. "An attorney?"

He nodded. "And there I was, doing the very thing I tell all my clients not to do—cruising the head—groping a guy in a public can. You don't believe me, do you?"

I shook my head miserably. "I don't know. Yes, I guess I do."

"Just a minute." He stood up and went into the hallway; when he came back he put a small white card into my hand: *John Christopher Adams: Attorney at Law.* The address was one of the professional buildings downtown. "Did you really think I was someone named Bill?"

I stood up, putting the card on the table. "Yes," I said. "That's why I asked if I knew you."

"And all this time, you thought... I don't know whether to be pleased or insulted."

"Neither," I said quickly. "Well...John. I think I'd better go."

"Do you have to?"

"Yes. My son's waiting."

"Okay." He followed me out to the front door. "Are we still on for dinner this week?"

I turned to look at him—naked to the waist, his body still bright with sweat. I wanted to say yes, but I knew that I couldn't. "I don't think so. But thanks."

He put his hand out and took mine to shake it firmly. "If it makes you feel better," he said, "I really enjoyed that. I'm sorry if you didn't."

"But I did, John. And that's the whole trouble." I hesitated, waiting to say more, but it seemed there was nothing more to be said. I stepped outside, glanced back at him. "Goodbye, John."

"Robert."

I hurried out to my car without looking back.

Chapter 5

Driving home I heard the churchbells again. Easter services letting out. I glanced into the rearview mirror at my own eyes. *Cocksucker!*

What a way to spend Easter!

It had all become too utterly ludicrous to be believed.

And I still had not found out who was sending those notes—who had stolen those pictures. But that no longer mattered. Nothing mattered. I was a robot driving the car, making all the appropriate motions, but not giving a damn what they accomplished. My life as I'd known it was finished. It might start again—or it might not—but it made not one bit of difference to me at that point whether it did or it didn't.

Chuck was gone when I got home. The note I had left him was on my bed, with a new message scrawled under mine: *Jerry came by to pick me up. Back around three. Chuck.*

I was glad he was gone. In the mood I was in there was nothing I could have said to him. I lay down on the bed, listening to the silence in the house, remembering John Adams and what I had done to him; but now there was no emotion whatever attached to the memory. I felt the exhaustion creeping up through my body and abandoned myself to it.

Some time later I heard the front door bell. I sat up, realizing I had been asleep. Drained and exhausted, I got up and went downstairs. This time when I saw the envelope under the door, I felt nothing. I was simply too weary to care any more. I picked it up, ripped it open, and unfolded the single sheet. Something small and white dropped onto the floor, but I ignored it and read the note:

DEAR ROBBER: IV DECIDED TO PUT YOU OUT OF YOR MISEREY. YOU CAN FOOL SOME PEEPLE BUT YOU CANT FOOL ME. BUT THAT DOSNT MATTER. YOUR DYING ANYWAY. YOUR BRAIN IS ROTTING. HA HA. SO HERE IS A LITTLE PRESENT FOR YOU, ROBBER. HA HA.

YOU KNOW WHO

I bent down to pick up the thing that had fallen—a small white capsule. I stared at it for a moment, then put it back into the note, which I carefully folded and reinserted into the envelope. I went back upstairs, put the envelope onto the dresser, then lay down again. As I drifted back into sleep, I thought about John Adams again; in my mind I saw him vividly, standing by the kitchen table. I laughed to myself. *I should have known* I thought. I should have known the minute he unzipped his fly. Bill's cock was much bigger than John Adams'. Much *much* bigger.

So the joke was on me. Ha-ha!

I sat up, wide-eyed, my heart pounding madly. My body was freezing cold, drenched with sweat.

I remembered a voice—laughter—ugly, evil laughter.

"Who's there?" I wanted to shout but my voice came out a strangled whisper. "Is anyone there?"

I told myself I was still in my bedroom—which made sense, because I was lying on top of a bed, and it seemed to be *my* bed—but the room was all hazy; I couldn't see the walls. The room was filled with shadows, evil, menacing shadows. I could hear someone breathing!

"Who is it?" My voice sounded tiny and lost, swallowed up by the shadows. "Answer me, please!"

No one answered.

I blinked hard, trying to focus my eyes. I could make out the edges of the windows—a brilliant light was shining around the edges of the blinds, so bright that I couldn't look into it—but it didn't penetrate the shadows.

And I knew someone was hiding in those shadows.

"Please!" I begged. "Please answer me! Who are you?"

No answer. Only that slow rasping breathing.

I struggled to move, to get up from the bed. If only I could get to the light switch, turn it on—then I could see who it was in the shadows. But I couldn't make my body respond. It felt disconnected, like beads on a string. I couldn't make it move! I'd forgotten how to move!

Was I still dreaming? Why couldn't I move?

Something was wrong with me—desperately wrong!

Why was my heart pounding? Why was I drenched with sweat?

Then I became aware of something in my hand, something crumpled. I managed to look down. One hand was clenched tightly around something. An envelope lay on the bed. I opened my hand. Slowly I brought my other hand over and extracted a wadded paper and shakily unfolded it; it was the latest note: *I've decided to let you kill yourself!*

"Oh my God!" I said aloud. Frantically I grabbed for the envelope, ripped it open. The pill wasn't inside it. I looked all around on the bed, shook the paper. That little white capsule was gone!

Someone laughed.

I looked up. The shadows were thicker—and closer! They were gathering around the bed, moving in on me. They were whispering, *"Robber...Robber...you're going to die!"*

"No!"

"Die, Robber, die!"

"NO!" I screamed. *"Get away from me!"*

"Die! Die!"

"GET AWAY! GET AWAY!"

Madly I scrambled over the bed, tumbled onto the floor. *I'm still asleep! This isn't really happening! Dear God, please! Don't let it be happening!*

But I knew it was too late to pray. I knew I had poisoned myself. I was going to die.

"Our Father....who...who art..."

"*Die, Robber, die!*"

"Our Father....in Heaven...hallowed..."

I couldn't remember the words!

Something was slipping away. I didn't know what it was, but I could feel it slipping—draining out of me!

Now I could barely make my voice work!

"Somebody....help...me!...*Please!!!*"

Suddenly it seemed I was floating above myself, up near the ceiling, looking down. I could see myself clearly, spotlighted, cringing like a terrified animal, curled up on the floor. I understood, in a very detached way, that my body was dying. For all practical purposes it was already dead. Poisoned. I hovered there, floating peacefully, waiting for my body to finally die. I heard my voice whimpering, "Father...forgive me...."

Silly, pathetic man, I thought. *Doesn't he know that he's already dead?*

Then I heard a strange sound, a wild clattering; the echoes of it crashed through the room, piercing my head like raw bolts of lightning. Through the clattering I heard a voice: "Dad! Dad! Dad! Daddad-daddaddaddad!!!"

I was back in my body again. The voice was getting closer. I knew the voice, remembered it from somewhere. It was a friendly voice, not evil, not threatening. The name *Chuck* came into my mind, but I couldn't remember who Chuck was.

I found I could uncurl myself—my body felt solid again, only slightly disarranged. I could move my arms, uncover my eyes so I could look at the door. In the process I had to look over my own body—and I saw I was naked!

Abruptly the room changed. The walls became black, moved away. There were dim orange aureoles hanging in black space. A policeman was coming up the stairs to arrest me. Any moment now the door would crash open and he'd rush in with his gun in his hand. Someone had told them about me and now they were coming to get me! They would put me away in a room in a dungeon, chain me up to the wall. They would torture me, cut parts away from my body, make me confess to my sins.

The door banged open. Light exploded above me, blinding me. I screamed and covered my eyes as the pain swept like fire into my brain. "Dad!"

I curled myself tightly again, holding my breath, praying that he wouldn't see me, that he'd look around, decide there was no one here, and go away. I didn't want to be tortured! I knew I had sinned, knew I had to be punished, but not that way!

I felt hands on my shoulders—warm and sticky. I went limp. Let him think I was already dead; let him think he was too late to torture me!

"Dad, answer me!" That didn't sound like any policeman's voice! I sneaked my eyes open to look at him, but all I could see were feet and legs. He shook me hard, forced my body to uncurl, but I stayed limp, allowing him to straighten my body on the floor, lay me out on my back. "What's wrong with you? Dad! Goddammit! Answer me!"

Chuck!

It was Chuck! My son!

I was naked and my son was touching me, looking at me! *God forgive me!*

I tried to curl back into a ball, but his hands held me flat. "Please," I begged. "Go...away."

"Dad, what the hell is the matter? *Tell me!*"

His voice was so forceful, so determined, I couldn't help answering. "I...took something."

"What did you take?"

"I don't know. It was...p—p—p—" I tried desperately to say *poison*, but all I could manage was "p—pill... pillllll."

"What kind of pill? Dad, tell me!"

"W-white."

"Oh, Jesus!"

He jumped up and rushed to the dresser. I leaned up and watched him, thoroughly confused. He pulled out a bottom drawer and reached inside. I remembered doing the same thing myself, but I couldn't recall what I had found.

At first he looked frightened, and that frightened me, but when he stood up and turned to look down at me, he was *smiling!* He was shaking his head slowly, back and forth, smiling! "You found my stash, didn't you?"

"What?"

"My stash. My caps. You found them."

"In...a bottle?" I asked—it was so hard to make my voice work. Years seemed to pass between the time that I thought the words and the time that I actually said them.

"About so big. With six caps, right?"

"I...don't remember," I lied—I remembered it clearly. I remembered counting the little white capsules. I remembered the one in the envelope. The conclusion was obvious: Chuck had poisoned me! Chuck had written those notes, left those pictures, and then he had stolen them back from their hiding place and put poison there instead, knowing I would find it.

And as I looked up at my son, he changed. He grew larger and his face lengthened. Deep hollows appeared under his cheeks and around his eyes. His skin became transparent and I could see his naked skull leering down at me. He was Satan!

They had taken my son and put Satan himself in his place! Satan would torture me, cut me apart—not the police!

I screamed and tried to crawl under the bed, but he caught my legs, dragging me out, yelling, "Stop it! *Dad!*"

"Leave me alone! Let me die!"

Suddenly he slapped me, hard! Lights and colors and screaming sounds exploded in the room! "You're not dying!" he yelled. "Don't even *think* it!" I tried to crawl in another direction, but he caught me again. "Do you hear me? Dad—*do you hear me?*"

"*Yes!*" I yelled. "Yes! Yes! *Yesssssssss!*"

"Now stop it or I'll clobber you! So help me!"

I went limp, collapsed. He knelt close beside me, his hands on my shoulders. Warm hands, not cold. Satan's hands would be cold—or burning hot—but these hands were just warm. Human hands. Maybe it really was Chuck after all.

"Listen to me. Are you listening? You're not dying, you're just stoned! Do you understand that?"

If men lie together, let them be stoned! Had Isaiah said that, or had it been Jeremiah?

But it didn't make sense. I'd been poisoned, not stoned.

"You're okay, Dad. Believe me, you're okay."

I couldn't help laughing. "I'm...not...*okay!* I've been...poisoned!"

He slapped me again. "That was *mescaline!* That's all!"

"What?"

"Mescaline! Dope! Now settle down, please! Do you trust me, Dad?"

"Trust you?"

"Yes. Do you trust me?"

"I don't...know."

"You've got to! Please. I know how to handle it, Dad. I know how to help you. But you've got to trust me!"

"I don't... Yes! Oh, God! I...don't...know! I *want* to."

"All right, then, do it! Trust me. I know what I'm doing."

"How?"

"Oh, shit! Because I've *taken* it."

"You've...?"

"Yes, man it's just mescaline."

"*Just???*"

"I know you don't understand it, Dad, but it's true. It won't hurt you."

"It's...terrible!"

"Only if you make it terrible! You're forcing yourself on a bummer. Just relax and you'll be okay. Dad, I promise you, you'll be okay. Believe me."

I nodded. I wanted to believe him. I wanted to trust him.

"Can you sit up?"

I remembered I was naked. "No!"

"Sure you can. Come on."

"No...Chuck, I...I don't want to."

"Why not?"

"I... You'll *see* me!"

"Oh, for... What does that mean? I see you right now! You're not invisible, man."

"I'm naked!"

"Oh, wow! So what else is new?"

"Don't laugh at me!"

"I'm not laughing, but Dad, you're not making sense. I've *seen* you."

"But I'm *naked!*"

His hands gripped my arms. "Dammit! I don't give a

fuck! Now sit *up!*" He jerked me up and leaned me back against the bed. I covered myself with my hands.

But somehow I felt calmer. Partly because I had a new problem to deal with: My son had said "*fuck*". He'd said, "*I don't give a fuck!*"

"You...s-said a bad word." Even as I said it, the old-maidish prudishness of it appalled me!

"*What?*"

"Bad word."

"Dad, come on! Don't get hung up on that."

"But...you... You...said..." Now I couldn't even remember the bad word he had said.

He knelt down again, this time with his face close to mine. I looked into his brown eyes. They were so deep! It seemed that if I wanted, I could dive right into one of them. I'd never seen eyes so rich...or so deep...or so *beautiful!* "Hey," he said quietly. "Will you listen to me, man? I mean, just listen, and don't get hung up with *things*, okay? Just listen a minute."

I nodded unsurely. His voice was so patient and calm that I couldn't maintain any anger with him. His calmness reached out to me, spread over me and seeped into my body and mind.

"Okay, now just listen. All you have done is dropped dope, okay? Now I know how you feel about dope because you've swallowed all the shit they—sorry—all the *stuff* they put out on it. But that's all crap, Dad! I mean, sure, some people O.D., and that's it, but you just took a cap, and it's just pure stuff. No speed or strychnine or anything like that. It's not acid and it's not snow or coke or anything. It's just mescaline. Okay?"

"Chuck..."

"You promised you'd listen."

"I'm listening, but..."

"Please, Dad, just hang in, please. I'm trying to explain it."

I couldn't help laughing again. He looked puzzled, then angry. I reached out and took his arm. "Chuck, I'm sorry."

"Jesus Christ, I'm just trying to *help* you!"

"I...*know that*...son! *I know.* But...I...can't... understand...a w-word you're...saying!"

He grinned. Then he laughed—and I laughed with him. We sat on the floor of my bedroom, me stark naked, with my sixteen-year-old son's arm clutched in my hand, laughing like fools! Every time we would start to compose ourselves, we'd look at each other and laugh again.

And as we laughed, all the darkness passed. The fear withered away and went scuttling out the door and down the stairs and out of the house. I felt a beautiful calmness beginning to settle. My body felt solid again, part of me. And I realized how silly, how utterly foolish I'd been acting. All these years I'd been trying to "protect" Chuck by never letting him see my naked body! Always closing the doors, wearing those ridiculous uncomfortable pajamas, or my bathrobe, or something. Something covering up my terrible, shameful body!

Why?

Why had I ever felt that my body was shameful or terrible? God made man in his own image! *His Own Image!* The idea seemed totally new to me, although I knew I had known it all of my life. I could quote chapter and verse. And yet it had never even occurred to me the true implication of the words: IN THE IMAGE OF GOD CREATED HE HIM!"

I felt that I'd discovered one of the most momentous truths in the history of mankind.

Or if not for all mankind, at least for myself, because it meant that *I, me,* Robert Randolph Thorne, had been created in the image of God.

My own Church had taught me that!

As man is, God once was; as God is, man may become.

Why hadn't I believed it? What possible *right* did I have to be ashamed of my body? That would mean that I was ashamed of God!

And that seemed to me to be a sin far worse than anything else I could think of—short of murder. How utterly petty it suddenly seemed to feel guilty for drinking vodka...or coffee...or for that matter, having sex with John Adams! How cosmically inconsequential such things must seem to a God who created man. A God with such vast understanding that he knew how to *create* a living man could not possibly be ignorant of all the problems a man of flesh was heir to. If my own church's doctrine were true, then God had gone through it Himself!

But how terrible, how loathsome, to be *ashamed* of God! And I had been. Ashamed of myself. And by logical extension, that meant I'd been ashamed of my Creator. Clearly that was the sin that I had to repent of.

Suddenly a memory presented itself, brilliantly clear: One day in the fifth grade—it had been springtime; I remembered a flock of robins were where I could see them, out on the greening lawn—our teacher, Miss Bartlet, had brought a very special book to school. We'd been studying *ART*, and this, she said, was the most beautiful art of all, and she'd brought it from her own special collection of books at home. She'd split us up into groups and had one group come up to the big table to look at the book while the others were working on problems.

I could *see* the classroom and Miss Bartlet so clearly! I hadn't thought about Miss Bartlet for...twenty years! And I could see the book. A beautiful, expensive book, with a red cover, wine-red, with gold leaves and stems twining all around one name: *Michelangelo.*

I could understand now that Miss Bartlet had made a basic error of judgment. A teacher in a small country-town school doesn't show pubescent children "naked pictures". At least, not back in those days she didn't.

There were hundreds of pictures—some in beautiful soft colors—of *naked* people! Oh, of course they were statues, and paintings, and drawings, but to us they were *people*, and they were naked, and we giggled and sniggered, and afterward, out in the play-yard, we'd poked one another in the crotches and giggled all over again. We giggled because the pictures had frightened us and we didn't know what else to do. One in particular had frightened me, shocked me more than I'd ever been shocked about anything: a drawing which said under it: *The Risen Christ.* And it showed a muscular man, stark naked, rising up out of a tomb, with a cloth falling away from him. In Church, all the pictures of Jesus had him clothed. Usually he had on long robes where all you could see were his face and his hands and feet. Even on the cross he was wearing a thick cloth wrapped around him to hide the *offending* parts of his body.

My God! How blasphemous to be ashamed of Christ's body!

Of course, I'd told Bill about the book, and, just goading him because he took it so seriously, I'd told him about *The Risen Christ.* And he had told Dad—good old Dad. Good old holier-than-anyone, wife-hating, children-hating, God-loving Dad. And the next day we'd had a new teacher, the one we called Miss Grump—Miss Gray, wrinkled like a prune, with her high screechy voice saying, "What are you giggling about back there? I will not have giggling in this classroom!" Miss Grump who slapped our hands with our rulers and gave us demerits if we had to go to the bathroom and we couldn't get a good mark on our report cards if we had too many demerits. Miss Grump, who said, "Art is for artists," and refused to be tricked into a question about Michelangelo, *or* what had happened to Miss Bartlet. We never saw Miss Bartlet again.

I remembered my father looking smug for weeks after that. Years later, he'd told me he'd had the woman fired—still smugly, still proud of the fact that he'd rid Glen Falls of an Evil Menace. What kind of man could be proud of his own shame? And what kind of fool had I been to allow that man to teach me that shame, to wrap it up in a bright package and say "Here, son, with my blessings"? He had cursed me with his sin!

And I had been trying to curse Chuck with mine!

I wanted to tell Chuck something of the astounding ideas that had been flying through my mind, but I realized that I'd have to explain the ideas, and amplify them, tell him when and how—and I couldn't.

"You okay?"

"Yes, I'm fine."

A sweet voice sang in my mind: *Everything's all right. Everything's fine.*

"Help me up...will you, son?"

"Sure thing. Feeling better?"

"Much."

"Groovy."

"Yes," I chuckled. "Groovy."

And I did, I felt *groovy.* I felt *good.* I couldn't remember feeling this good—this *aware* of myself, of my body and its senses—for a long, long time. I felt strong, and tall, and supremely healthy!

Chuck helped me to stand, and I saw us in the mirror, with me facing it, Chuck turned away. I studied myself; I *looked* good!

"Okay?" Chuck asked.

I turned to look into his eyes. He was smiling, but his eyes showed concern—and something else, something I'd never really seen before, not in Chuck's eyes, not in anyone's—I saw *love!* I saw it and felt it. My son loved me; his eyes said it beyond doubt. My son was concerned for me. My son wanted to help me! And my son didn't give a *fuck* if I was naked or not!

Tears welled up in my eyes and I started to turn away. All the garbage out of my past bubbled up in me, making me ashamed again, this time of my tears, my emotion. Man must not cry, must not show his emotions, must keep everything hidden, his body, his genitals, his emotions, everything! Everything that makes him the least bit worthwhile to his fellow man.

I had dreamed of a man in a black hat and a black overcoat. He had thrown off the overcoat, thrown off his shame, and had risen, like Michelangelo's *Risen Christ,* up into the sky, naked and free. And the man had said to me: "I am you, you fool!"

And there I stood, naked—and feeling more *free* than I'd ever felt! With tears trailing down over my cheeks I squeezed my son's arm and said, "Thank you, Chuck."

He blinked unsurely and shrugged. "What the hell, right?"

I laughed and wept at the same time. "Right.... What the hell?"

Chuck glanced away, blinking, and I realized I was embarrassing him. And with that I also realized what a shock it must have been to him, to hear me yelling at shadows, to come racing up the stairs thinking someone was killing me, only to find me cringing like an animal on the floor. What an overwhelming responsibility he had automatically assumed, to talk me out of my irrational terrors. What grown man would have done it? Could have done it? Surely none that I knew—and that included most of the good Mormons I knew. They'd have gone screaming for the ambulance. Or, worse, if they'd realized what had actually happened, that I'd swallowed "dope", they'd have gone for the police. And now to see his father weeping, on top of everything else, of course it embarrassed him.

"Well..." I said, concentrating hard on putting the words together, "I think...maybe...I can manage...to get dressed." He glanced up at me, grinning. "I still...feel... foolish...even if you...don't care."

"Hey, man," he said quickly, "you shouldn't. No. I mean, you know...I mean, you look just fine."

The tears started again and I moved quickly to the closet. My body still felt slightly awkward, but I found if I didn't try to concentrate on what I was doing, my arms and my legs would do it themselves, automatically. It seemed to take an hour for me to decide what to wear; then I finally decided to copy Chuck's costume; it seemed somehow appropriate: old levis and faded blue shirt—my gardening outfit.

And to hell with shorts!

I'd suddenly become extremely aware of my body, of the pressures and textures of clothes on it. It felt so fantastically good just slipping my old levis on over my legs. And I decided to just let my penis—my *cock* and my *balls*—hang free. From now on, the less I "bundled up" the better I'd like it! It felt marvelous just to move, just to breathe! I'd never imagined the human body could feel so deliciously sensual.

Now that I'd pulled myself more-or-less together, now that Chuck had talked me out of my "bummer", I was beginning to notice all sorts of wonderful, fascinating things: the way things around me took on whole new dimensions. *Light* became a phenomenal thing; *colors* were breathtaking, spellbinding! Things I had seen every day, such as clothes in the closet, the bedspread, the rugs, suddenly seemed totally new to me. The colors and patterns and shapes presented themselves to me like precious gifts—gifts I had blindly ignored until now. Everything I looked at seemed to assume a brand-new *reality*, a "higher" reality than the one I'd been living in.

I had the feeling that I'd done something particularly special and as a reward, mysteries were being revealed to me; hidden truths about the nature and meaning of sizes and shapes, of patterns and colors and textures, became brilliantly clear to me—not in words that I could have expressed, but in understanding, in true appreciation.

It wasn't as though these truths were "new" in any sense of the word; obviously they had existed within each particular thing for as long as that thing itself had existed—and perhaps much, much longer, since the very beginning of anything. I was only now able to perceive and appreciate what had been here all along. At the same time, it seemed that I'd always known those truths, deep in some subconscious, unconscious well of knowledge. There was even a feeling that I'd seen all these things, thought all these thoughts, some time long ago.

Chuck's voice brought me suddenly back from my flight into colors and lights and new/old memories: "I mean...I've always wondered, you know?"

It seemed to me that thousands of years had passed since I'd last heard Chuck talking, and I hadn't the slightest idea what he was talking about. "Wondered... what?"

"About you."

"What about me?"

"Well, you know—what you, you know, looked like."

"Oh."

"I mean, you know, this house has been so fuck—I'm sorry! I didn't.. "

"Chuck," I said, turning to face him, "if...you use... the word with...your...your friends...use it with me... because I want to be your...friend. Okay?"

"Oh, wow! Hey, don't blow my mind all the way, man!"

"Sorry."

He chuckled. "It's okay. It's kind of wild, having your old man blow your mind. Wow!"

He was silent for a while, as I went to the dresser for socks.

"Oh, yeah," he said softly. "What I started to say was important. Because, like, this house, you know, has been so uptight that I've wanted to just stand up and yell at you, you know? And Mom. Both of you. I mean, what's the big deal? What's the point? You know?"

I leaned on the dresser and waited for him to explain himself; when he didn't I said, "No...I don't...know. What are you...talking about?"

"About you! You know...bare-ass, you know? I mean naked. I mean, what's the mystery? Jeez, I've seen naked people before. But here it's like, well, like some, I don't know, big terrific...*secret* or something. Like you didn't see me when I was born or something, or never had to take me to the toilet. You know?"

"Yes. I know."

"Hey, wow!" He laughed and hugged himself delightedly. "I'm actually *talking* to you! I'm sitting here *talking* to my old man! Oh, Jesus, that's beautiful! That really is beautiful." He lay back on the bed, chuckling and turning from side to side. I laughed, just watching him.

When he sat up he shook his head and said, "Yeah, well, I just wanted to say you looked okay. Like Jerry's old man, I mean he's got a pot out to here and he runs around their house in his shorts, even when kids are there. But you look...groovy. I just wanted to say it, that's all."

"Thank you, Chuck."

He shrugged and looked down again and nodded. "It's cool." He stood up quickly. "Hey, was I right?"

"About what?"

"Feelin' good. You feel good, don't you?"

I nodded. "I feel...*wonderful!*"

"Oh, wow! Yeah, you can tell. Man your eyes are like...like fuckin' stars! Hey, I know! Look, can you move?"

I laughed. "Haven't I...been moving?"

"I mean walk, you know, like outside?"

"Outside?" The idea should have terrified me, but it didn't. I knew I was drugged, but I felt a fantastic sense of self-confidence. If Chuck had asked me, "Do you think you could fly?" I would have seriously considered it. "All right," I said. "I...think I can." I hesitated. "Do *you* think...I can? You know...more about this...than I do."

"It strictly depends. I can do it. But like Jerry just gets bombed. It's wherever your head is. If you think you can, then you can. Don't worry, I'll watch out for, you know...things. Anyways, we won't go far. Just up the block, there's this place where I go when I'm tripping." Suddenly a strange expression came onto his face and he seemed about to step back away from me. "Oh, wow!"

"What?"

He shook his head, started toward the door, hesitated, turned: "You know what I just flashed on? When I said that—about when I go tripping? I expected you to clobber me. And you didn't. And that blew my mind." He sniffed and cleared his throat, keeping his face turned away from me. "I'll, uh, be right back, okay?" He spun around and hurried out. I followed him to the door, watched him duck into the bathroom and close the door. Moments later I heard him blow his nose, and I guessed he'd been on the verge of tears himself.

It hadn't even occurred to me to hit him! And yet, thinking about it, I knew that I would have, if I hadn't been "stoned". I had taught my son to be afraid of telling the truth! I had taught him to lie and to cheat and to hide and to sneak out behind my back. I had taught him that when he did tell the truth to expect to be "clobbered" for his efforts.

We were strangers to each other, Chuck and I. Total strangers. It was deeply disturbing to suddenly realize that Chuck knew no more about me and my life and my private thoughts—those that really mattered—than I knew about his. I had shut him almost totally out of my life, and by doing that, had forced him to shut me out of his—as surely as though I'd deliberately planned it!

What an absolute idiot I had been!

I could not understand, could not truly comprehend, how I had lived for thirty-five years without once having realized what a damned fool I had been! It was so patently, painfully *obvious* now! I saw clearly that all of my life I'd been digging a cave for myself—a private, dark, unhappy, miserable little cave where I could hide from myself and from people, from everything! And I'd *forced* myself to stay locked inside it.

With other people's *garbage* piled up over that cave's door! My father's garbage. My mother's garbage. Kate's. Ed's. And my own. Yes, I couldn't blame others for all of the garbage; a good part of it was my own.

I wasn't sure how to get out of my cave—to crawl out from under the garbage—but I knew that I had to. No wonder I constantly told myself I felt "rotten"! I had every reason to feel that way. Anything else, stuck away, buried like that, would have rotted thirty years ago! Perhaps, I thought, it said something about the human spirit to realize how well mine had survived suffocation and premature burial.

Chuck came out of the bathroom, giggling about something, and my mood instantly shifted up into a brighter level. Seeing Chuck happy was something new and delightful to me. But then, I supposed, seeing me happy was an equally "mind-blowing" experience for him.

"We gotta hurry," he said, "or we'll miss it." He started down the stairs. "I saw it out the window. Wait'll you see."

"What is this...this wonderful thing...we're going to look at?"

He looked up with a frown and said, "The sunset!"—as though I'd been the dunce of the world to ask such a dumb question.

The sunset! Of course!

My son Chuck, looking at sunsets?

Why not? What was so outrageous about that? Yes, of course! My beautiful son looking at beautiful sunsets! How long would it take to get it through my thick head that Chuck could not possibly be the monster I'd made him in my miserable imagination? Perhaps the children had indeed discovered a secret their parents had forgotten, or lost. I hated to think that it might be a drug, but that had to remain a possibility. At least it was better than alcohol.

That thought started another one bounding around in my mind as I carefully went down the stairs: Chuck was sixteen. I had started to drink when I was eleven! Eleven years old. I clearly remembered taking my first shot of *Four Roses* out behind old man Witherspoon's barn. I and five other kids my same age. We'd got falling-down, throwing-up drunk and gone stealing watermelons—after first tipping over Mr. Witherspoon's outhouse. And I'd had my first cigarette that night, too. A Fatima. I, myself, had stolen the pack from the drug store.

And Chuck took a pill that made him feel happy. In the total scheme of things, that no longer seemed so enormously alarming. I'd never got drunk and gone out to look at a sunset! I'd got drunk and gone out to look for trouble.

It was far more alarming to realize that it had taken that drug to make me understand myself—or begin to understand myself.

I followed Chuck out of the house—and into one of the most exquisite experiences of my life! *Trees! Flowers! Green leaves*—every possible shade of green. And coolness. The textures of a sidewalk! A lawn-sprinkler, in fading sunlight, became the most dazzlingly beautiful fountain I'd ever seen; millions of droplets of liquid gold on the deep-deep green grass—spiralling into the air—falling! Chuck had to call to me twice to keep me moving.

Halfway through the block, the street climbed steeply up a sharp rise in the hill, and on top of the rise was a vacant lot, with a huge, ugly *For Sale* sign, with a *Sold* sign tacked over it, and rank weeds overgrowing the burned-out remains of the house that had once stood there. (I remembered the house and the night it had burned down.) Chuck led me into the lot, waist-deep in last summer's weeds. I'd long since forgotten what we'd come out to look for, and I thought it might be something in the ruins. They were fascinating. Water-pipes sticking up, rusted and twisted. Smoke-blackened bricks of the basement where someone had scratched *Fuck You* in the soot. Children, probably. I'd known the word at the age of seven,—long before I'd had the slightest idea of what it meant—and I knew that long before I reached puberty. At Chuck's age I was laying Jenny Lou—or Mildred Robbins—or Grace Schulz—or that waitress, what the hell was her name? Carla Something—at least every other week. And I'd already had at least two blowjobs, courtesy of Noel Becker.

Somehow I'd forgotten all that. Somehow I'd managed to pretend that Chuck was still some kind of infant, blissfully ignorant of all the things I'd known long before I was his age. I'd gone skulking around, taking a totally unnecessary trip to San Francisco, sneaking back a full day ahead of my schedule, in order to trick my son into committing an act that I had performed on his uncle when Bill was fourteen. And if I remembered correctly, at least half of the boys in my scout troop "cornholed" each other on our numerous outings. And at least half of those had been with Noel Becker at least once. But that had been *then*, in the past, in a memory, not real any more, and I'd insanely expected my son to be miraculously different.

If I'd respected myself in the least, I'd have realized that Chuck couldn't possibly turn out any worse than I had for undergoing the same kinds of experience. But perhaps that was part of the problem—perhaps more than just part; perhaps almost all of the problem—the fact that I didn't respect myself. I hadn't even liked myself. How had I expected Chuck—or anyone else—even Kate—to like me if I didn't like myself?

"Hey, Dad, turn around."

I turned to face him. "What?"

"Look." He pointed toward the west.

I turned—and the panorama exploded into my mind! Colors! Lights! I was wrenched out of my private world and scattered all over the city, all over the countryside!

A small rounded paring of the sun was still visible over the black jagged rim of the world, out beyond the Great Salt Lake, blinding, pulsing red; and that color was reflected in a long brilliant trail through the dark lake. Above the horizon were thin clouds, floating like bright golden cobwebs around the sun, shifting and changing their patterns as I watched. The sky all across the horizon was dull white, turning grey, silhouetting the black mountains as though they were pieces of a stage setting, lit from behind. Their long-long shadows stretched out almost to the city, where thousands of houses stood out in stark relief, glowing all around their etched edges with the light on their west sides that I couldn't see. All the way down 13th there were red and green traffic lights, brilliant as bright stars on a summer night, changing colors in strangely meaningful patterns, with bright little explosions of orange as they changed. And the cars on the streets were turning their lights on, and the lights were like fireflies floating toward me.

I looked up, straight above me—and fell helplessly into the color of foggy violet! Helplessly into an incredible vastness of sky! As I watched, darkness deepened, creeping up from the east; the color lost its fogginess and became a fantastically soft purple, and then ultramarine; and then a star, just the tiniest pinpoint, started to sparkle, and then more. I felt the light fade from my face. The stars brightened. The sky deepened. The universe opened above me. I understood why poets had called stars "candles". I could understand why the ancients had believed that God hung out the stars—I could almost see an unseeable hand tossing them out into the heavens as a farmer would toss wheat into his field. And it seemed as though that Cosmic Farmer was sowing His stars just to please me, to delight me—and to remind me of His reality, unseeable though He might be.

The stars became intensely personal and enormously meaningful. They seemed, literally, *my stars,* because I felt I was part of the same thing they were part of—everything! And it seemed we had always been part of that totality. Perhaps we had shifted positions, been born and grown old and died and been born again, but the whole was unchanging, eternal—or if it did change, it did so in a way, at a rate which my limited mind could not grasp—any more than it could grasp the meaning of *eternity.* I felt tiny and huge at the same time. Infinitesimal in one sense, boundless in another. A tiny speck on a tiny speck in a cluster of tiny specks floating in an unimaginably vast universe—and yet each speck was like a particle of an atom, and the atom was part of a molecule, and a molecule was a part of...whatever. *Something.* That I couldn't comprehend what that *something* might be was no more alarming than the idea that an atom in my own body could not comprehend me. I laughed at the idea of atoms feeling so self-important that they had the audacity to "know" the thing they were part of.

Chuck's voice drifted into my thoughts, returning me to earth, to the vacant lot, and the dark, cooling ruins of the burned-out house. "What?" I asked.

"You were laughing."

"Oh." I tried to remember what I'd been laughing about. Parts of it came back, but not the whole thing. I looked up into the sky again and said, "I wonder if God even knows when a speck of Him does something."

I realized what I had said and looked at Chuck, fully expecting him to say, "Oh, shit, religion!" Instead, he looked up and nodded his head. "One trip I had," he said softly, "I felt like I really knew. You know? Like I understood the whole thing, but just couldn't tell anyone. And it was like, well, maybe He didn't know, not the way we do, but He knew just the same. Like He *felt* it."

"Do you honestly believe in God, Chuck?"

He said, "Oh, sure," as though he were saying, "Thank you for passing the salt," as though it had never occurred to him not to believe. "I just don't understand Him, that's all. But man, what does that mean? Like you take the world—or those stars. Now, man, I don't know what a star is! Fuck what they teach you in school, man, *I don't know.* Sure, they're suns—but what the hell is a *sun?* I just know they're stars, and, like I say, 'hey, groovy,' you know? But that doesn't change them, or make them real or not real, just because I say, 'hey, stars, man! Wow!' Like these guys going around telling everybody they know what's coming down. Man, they don't know one damn thing more than I do—and that's *nothing!* Some cat told me the other day I was going to Hell, and I just looked at him, you know? I mean, what can you say to a dumb thing like that?"

I stared at my son for a long time, and then turned away, looking out over the city; it was starting to sparkle.

"Like today," Chuck said, "Jerry's folks made him go to Church, you know, *mass,* because it was Easter, and he's Catholic, and they have some kind of big deal thing, you know, about the resurrection and all that. He laughed. "But you know what that dumb nut did? He sneaked out and blew a joint in the bathroom. He told me it wasn't a bad trip at all if you got stoned—all those robes and candles and that organ. That's when he came by for me, after church." He stood up. "I'm sorry I wasn't here when you got home."

"Well," I said, shrugging my shoulders, "that's how it goes, right?"

"Yeah, right."

"Besides..." I hesitated, not sure that I wanted to say the thing I was thinking—but it needed to be said: "If you'd been there, none of this would have happened, would it? Right now we'd probably be stomping around the house hating each other."

"Dad...I couldn't *hate* you. Get pissed off at you, maybe, but..."

"Well, you know what I mean."

"Yeah, right. Well...things work out right, you know? I mean they really do."

We started back down the hill, walking slowly, side by side. I had an impulse to put my arm around Chuck's shoulder, and for a moment I resisted it—but then, when I couldn't think of a single good reason why I shouldn't, I did. He turned to me and grinned. He was almost as tall as I was, and, God, he was a handsome young man! I felt so proud for having sired such a fantastically beautiful manchild!

Back in the house Chuck suggested that we listen to music. Just "light stuff"—as opposed to the "heavier trip" which he had decreed I was not yet ready for. At first I was very reluctant. I'd heard his music before and didn't even consider it music—just a lot of loud banging and twanging and screeching and wailing. But I'd made up my mind to go along with whatever he decided, to trust him as honestly as he'd honestly asked me to. As it turned out, my reluctance quickly faltered and flew away under the onslaught of the music, and I totally lost myself to a world I had never suspected existed. And this time it was a brand new, virginal experience! I'd seen sunsets before (though never so beautiful) but

I'd never really *listened* to rock music. And after the first album, I found it impossible to reconcile what I was listening to with what I had heard before. The Beatles made sense! And that truly amazed me. Some young men named Crosby, Stills, Nash and Young sang fantastically beautiful songs, some so true and piercing that I wept—and I wept without shame. Because those songs became the most intensely *personal* experiences I'd ever had. The singers sang to *me!* They told me about things I had known all my life, about love and beauty and caring, precious things I had thought gone forever from the world—as they truly had in the world I'd been living in; but in Chuck's world they were alive and well. More than that, they were happy! No—*happy* is an empty word compared to the pure joy that those singers gave to me. "We love you," they said, "we really do." And the sounds I had once thought were banging and twanging soared through my head like rivers of rainbows, augmenting and proving the love that the singers proclaimed. *Love one another. Love us. Love yourself. Love the world.* And, to my utter amazement, they even sang about loving God! I understood what Chuck had meant with his expression "mind-blowing" when a man George Harrison said, "You don't need a church-house..."

As Simon and Garfunkle, unlike their names, built a jeweled silver bridge far out in vast space, Chuck started a fire, turned out all the lights, and then sat cross-legged on the floor, watching me. When the last cut of the last album had played, he got up and turned off the set. For several long minutes a tense silence built up in the room. I could *feel* a reluctance—almost a fear—coming from my son.

Finally he sat down on the floor again, facing me. "Dad...when are you going to get to hell out of here?"

I sat up slowly and leaned back against the couch. "What do you mean, Chuck?"

"Dad...you know what I mean."

I did; I knew precisely what he meant; but I found I was still very reluctant to admit it.

"Look, I don't want to start you on a bummer, but, you know, I...I've just got to say it, Dad. I've been wanting to say it for so damn long...."

I took a deep breath and steadied myself. "Then say it, Chuck."

"Please don't get sore. I don't mean it bad any way. I mean, I...well, I just think...oh, shit!"

"Go ahead, Chuck. You think I should give your mother a divorce."

He nodded, looking very unhappy. "Yeah. I do. I mean, why make everybody miserable just because... well, you know, because the two of you can't get along? That's dumb. I mean..."

"Yes," I said softly. "I guess it is dumb."

He leaned forward. "Do you really?"

I nodded. "I guess I've known it was dumb for a long time, Chuck."

"Well...why didn't you do something about it?"

"I didn't know what to do."

"Dad, you do what you do when *anything* goes bad. You just let it go."

"What about you and the girls?"

"Oh, come on, Dad. I may be a dumb kid, but, man, I'm not stupid! I know where Mom goes in the afternoons."

"Where she goes?" That she went anywhere in particular was news to me.

"Don't you know?" he asked.

"I'm not sure. I don't know what you're going to tell me."

"Oh, wow, you mean...? Dad, she sees *him.*"

"Ed?"

"Right."

"On Thursday afternoons," I said quickly, as a new

piece fitted itself into the puzzle. "When he goes to play golf."

"I don't know what he tells you, but they both go to his place. Dad, they really dig each other—and you don't—so why don't you just let it happen?"

I leaned back and looked up at the ceiling, asking myself why it had never occurred to me that Kate and Ed might love one another? I'd been so tied up in my own misery as the cuckolded husband, the put-upon substitute father for two bastard daughters—*blaming them!* Blaming everyone but myself for my problems. Was it possible that Kate and Ed were actually in love with each other? Did Ed love Cindy and Dorene?

Mentally I slapped myself! What an assinine question! Of course he would love them! He was their father.

And me! Arrogant, garbage-inundated, self-hating *me*, had deliberately stood in the way of his claiming his own. If Kate had sinned in loving another man, I had outdone her a hundred times over by standing in their way. No wonder she hated me! No wonder she couldn't stop herself from teaching the girls to hate me too. She had every reason for hating me. How could I have been so completely blind and stupid?

In this new light of self-revelation, I was forced to reconsider Kate's "sin". All these years I'd been thinking of her as a "wanton" woman; it was far more likely that she'd been a "wanting" woman. Chuck had been born during my first year of college, and even though we'd both been delighted to have a child, still he'd been unplanned, and his birth had required Kate's quitting her secretarial position and my taking on two separate part-time jobs. I'd resented the extra work and had blamed it on her "carelessness". My interest in sex had become almost nil since that night with my brother, and I had easily convinced myself that our sexual indulgence was responsible for all of my hardships. We'd had no intercourse at all during the last few months of her pregnancy, and it had seemed not only easy but necessary to avoid it afterward. By the time of my graduation, having sex once a month, even less, had seemed perfectly natural. And Kate hadn't seemed to mind.

I could understand now that I'd practically driven Kate into an affair with Ed—my best friend, welcome at our house any time, night or day. Perhaps Ed had been the reason Kate hadn't minded my lack of attention. And now that I thought of it, Ed had never shown much interest in other women. Had they been having the affair all these years?

Kate had asked for a divorce just about a year before the twins had been born, but I'd still been a good churchgoing Mormon and, of course, had refused her flatly. It was possible that they had actually planned her second pregnancy in an attempt to force the issue!

Suddenly I could think of Kate in a new way—not the harping, sullen woman who grudgingly cooked my meals and kept my house, but a weary, unhappy prisoner kept here totally against her will. When I thought about her in that light, I was amazed that she hadn't long since tried to poison me. Instead, I'd been poisoning myself—and Chuck—and the girls—and Kate and Ed—with my hatred, my *revenge.* That's exactly what I'd been doing, taking out my revenge on them, making them suffer the way I'd imagined they had made me suffer. Worst of all, I realized I'd made two innocent children suffer for something over which neither had the slightest control. They had not asked to be born—neither of me nor of Ed. I understood clearly how unthinkably cruel I had been.

"Sometimes she goes on Mondays, too."

"What?"

"Mom."

"Oh." I took another deep breath. "Well, I guess...she has every right to go. I guess you're right, Chuck. Maybe I should...just let go."

"I don't mean it to sound like I knew more than you do, Dad, but..."

"That's all right, Chuck. Go ahead and sound like it. I'm beginning to think maybe you do."

"...but I think *you'd* be better off, too. Like, you never go anyplace now. I mean, what kick do you get out of anything? You're always so damn...well, you know."

"I know, Chuck. I know it now." I sighed heavily. "I know it now."

We were silent for a while, watching the firelight, feeling the warmth of it flickering across our faces. I knew Chuck was right, that I had to let go; I had to give Kate the divorce, sell the company to Ed, and go.

But where?

And how soon?

If I left, that would mean leaving Chuck, and I didn't want to do that–not now–not after finally beginning to get acquainted with him. "What would you do, son?"

"Me?" He sounded surprised that I'd even consider him important to my decision. "Dad, I can take care of myself."

I laughed, a little sadly. "Yes, I guess that's obvious."

"But look, I've been thinking, like, if you wanted to push it, legally I mean, you know, adultery and all that shit...you could force them to let you have me."

"I don't want to force anybody to do anything, Chuck. I want to be through with that."

"Well, then, what's the problem? Mom wouldn't mind if I lived with you part of the time, like the summers or something."

"Would you mind it?"

"Why should I mind it? I dig both of you. But, like,

I just can't take much more of you *together.* It's burning me out, Dad."

"Well, then...let's stop burning everyone out."

"Will you do it?"

I nodded. "Yes."

"Oh, man!" He leaned toward me and grasped my hand. "You're...you're just great!" He laughed, squeezed my hand, and leaned back, grinning from ear to ear. "You ought to stay high all the time."

I laughed with him. "I guess that's one possibility, but I'm not so sure I wouldn't get hooked."

"Yeah, well...don't get yourself hooked on *anything,* man. Anything. Like you were hooked on this whole thing. It's not just dope that gets you strung out. Like Jerry's old man—he's all strung out over this whole religion thing, and it's like he's got a monkey on him. I mean, it doesn't mean anything to him, he's just hooked on it. He goes through it like somebody shooting horse. And you talk about a bummer, man, I mean Jesus on the cross *all the time!* But, you know, that whole trip ended two thousand years ago—but they keep right on killing him...over and over and over. Man, if they'd just look around...."

"They wouldn't know what they were seeing, Chuck. I didn't."

He smiled. "I'm not really sure you do yet—but you will. It'll come through to you now."

"What will?"

He shrugged secretively. "You'll see. Just keep watching and listening. You'll see. And man, when you do see, it'll blow your head wide open!"

"All right. I'll take your word for it."

"Hey, you know something? I'm starved."

"Now that you mention it, so am I."

"How long you been up?"

"What?"

"How long ago did you drop?"

"I don't remember, Chuck, honestly. I must have been walking in my sleep."

"What a way to go! But, let's see, it was five, maybe five-thirty when I got home. And it's almost ten now...."

"Is it that late?" I suddenly realized I'd completely lost all consciousness of time. For some reason the idea delighted me.

"That's at least five hours, maybe more. You were pretty close to peaking when I got here. Sure, you should be able to drive. Think you could?"

"I don't know. I guess so."

"Things are back, pretty much, aren't they?"

"Yes," I said, "pretty much." Then it struck me that I was not only understanding Chuck, I was using some of his words. More and more through the evening his jargon had ceased being unintelligible and had taken on almost a private meaning between us. And of course, that's what it was—a jargon, a secret language, the private language of a subculture that only an initiate could understand. With the help of the mescaline I was beginning to understand it. I looked around the room, and it seemed relatively normal; the lights were still more vivid than usual, but otherwise things looked more or less as they'd always looked—with the difference that now I seemed to *understand* them. Rooms and furniture had taken on a new meaning to me, but the meaning itself wasn't new, except to me; it was just that I'd finally understood a meaning that had been there all along. "Yes," I said, "I think I can drive. Where should we go?"

"You want a mindfuck? I mean..."

"Why not?" I said calmly. "I don't know what a *mindfuck* is, but I'm willing to learn."

He grinned. "Nothing bad. It's sort of like the other, only in the head."

"Like the other..." I repeated.

"You know what I mean."

"Oh, yes, I know. And I wasn't...what do you call it?...putting you down. I was just thinking. *Fuck* isn't a bad word to you, is it?"

Chuck stood up, beaming. "Dad, you just took a giant step! Come on. I'll show you what a mindfuck is."

At first I felt very awkward, once again disconnected, as I backed the car onto the street and headed across 13th toward Sugarhouse—toward a new restaurant that Chuck called "The Yoko Ono Place" where the "head-crowd" went—but very quickly my mind adjusted itself to the necessities of driving. I was tempted to be distracted by the kaleidoscopic patterns of lights, coming toward me, but I found it increasingly easy to ignore them—realizing there was nothing at all new in what I was seeing and that I could look at lights any time. I was extremely curious about where we were going. I was briefly concerned that Chuck might feel awkward, taking such a "straight-looking" father in among all his friends, but then I understood that it would be nothing less than a kind of triumph for a boy to bring his father in among his peers. Chuck not only wanted to show me his world and to show me as much as he could in the time we had left on my trip, he wanted to show me off to his world as well. I understood that I'd been given a signal honor, being invited to share his world with him.

The restaurant was called *Mother Earth*—but Chuck explained why he called it "The Yoko Ono Place": on the back wall was a huge photograph, blown up to what looked like at least ten times life-size, of a moonfaced Oriental girl, who, he told me—as though announcing the name of a saint—was Yoko Ono. And as we ate, she smiled down on us at though she alone knew the answer to all riddles. The background music was also Oriental; I didn't know whether it was Japanese or Hindu or what, but I found it extremely relaxing, and it seemed to go perfectly with the strange but delicious macrobiotic food the place served. I found myself dreamily luxuriating in the textures and tastes of not just the food, but the music as well; one went with the other, augmented the other; each added new meaning to the other. But more than the food and the music, the thing which impressed me was the people: clean-scrubbed, long-haired girls, looking farm fresh, brighteyed and constantly smiling; shaggy-haired bearded men, looking like Biblical Prophets, smiling as brightly as the girls they were with. As soon as we'd stepped through the front door, a feeling of beautiful peacefulness had drawn me in. Complete strangers smiled at me for no reason at all—both sexes—and I found myself smiling back! It was indeed a new world I'd discovered. It was like finding Atlantis right under my nose. Or, better still, I decided—loooking around at the long hair and beards—almost like finding the New Jerusalem. Maybe John's prophesies were indeed coming true. Men—apparently normal men—*smiling* at one another!

I wished desperately that I could be Chuck's age once again, could be starting my life in this new world, rather than finding it halfway through. How different it was from the Brite-Spot Cafe where I and my own teen-age peers had gathered in Glen Falls: cheap-hamburger joint where we went nightly to "tip a few" in the cars parked out back, and get into a fight. I could hardly remember a night when there hadn't been trouble of one sort or another, usually one young buck beating the hell out of another to prove who was the most *manly*. It was a genuine relief to know that my son preferred places like Mother Earth to the Brite-Spots. Here the young men seemed perfectly content to be whatever they were, without having to prove anything. The thing that continued to amaze me was how peaceful they looked.

There didn't seem to be an ounce of hostility in anyone, and it didn't detract one bit from their masculinity!

Thinking about Glen Falls got me to thinking about Bill. I'd stopped worrying about the notes and the pictures. Something in my mind told me that I knew who the sender was, and that all I had to do was wait; the clues would come. And, anyway, those notes, along with so much of my former life, had become essentially meaningless; at least they no longer carried any kind of real threat. It was still a remote possibility that the sender was in fact Bill, but I didn't think so. Now that I'd disqualified John Adams—the only candidate—I was reasonably certain that Bill wasn't in Salt Lake after all. I'd been wrong about so many things it was almost a foregone conclusion that I'd been wrong about Bill. He probably wasn't a homosexual at all. He was probably married and settled down somewhere....

When we were kids, before that ridiculous scene in the back yard, if ever I had an insoluable problem, I knew I could take it to Bill, and he'd come up with a solution. Sometimes his solutions were not entirely practical, but he had the kind of mind that seemed to be able to see *into* a problem, to see its relationship with everything else. If I could talk to Bill, take a day, or a week, and relax with him, get to know him again, ask him what he thought I should do (not about Kate and the girls; I'd definitely decided to give her a divorce) about myself, and possibly about Chuck. Being younger, maybe Bill was more in touch with Chuck's generation than I was.

But above all, I just wanted to see him again. And this time, with the real one, I'd apologize honestly.

How to find him? The answer was so ridiculously simple, I wondered why I hadn't thought of it much sooner. Surely he kept in touch with the folks? I checked my watch; it was late, and I knew they'd have gone to bed hours ago, but I wanted to do it now while I still had the courage.

"Would it be okay if I made a phone call right now?" I asked Chuck.

"Sure. I'll rap with somebody."

In the back, near the doors to the rest rooms, was a pay-telephone. I dialed the operator and had her place the call, charging it to my special number at work. I counted seven rings, then mother's anxious voice said, "Yes? Hello?"

"Mom? It's Robert."

"What's wrong?"

"Nothing, Mom. Nothing. Everything's fine. Mom, I'm sorry for calling you this late, but...do you know where Bill is?"

"Couldn't it wait until morning?" she grumbled. "Well, since you're calling, just a minute." I could hear her muttering, and I pictured her leafing through all the clutter of Dad's roll-top pigeon-hole desk. He kept it looking neat, but nothing was ever where it should have been. "It was on his Christmas card," she said absently. "I wonder if Daddy threw it away."

"Don't you have it in your address book?" I asked.

"No, dear. We just heard from him a few *weeks* ago. Five whole years he just disappears, and then he sends us a Christmas card. Yes...here it is. Why are you suddenly interested in your brother? I thought..."

"It's a long story, Mom. Where does he live?"

"San Francisco," she said.

I cursed softly, away from the mouthpiece–*I'd just come from San Francisco!*

"I can't hardly read it, Robert, the post office smudged it. Two-something-something Fourteenth Avenue."

"Thanks, Mom, that's all I need. Sorry to wake you."

"How's Kate and the children?"

"They're fine, Mom. Everything's fine."

"We haven't heard from you since Christmas either."

"Well, now you have. Look, I promise I'll write soon and tell you all of the news, okay? Tell Dad hello, will you?"

"He's got a new gallstone."

"Tell him I'm sorry about his new gallstone."

"Why don't you come up for Decoration Day, Robert? It gets so lonesome around here. Sometimes I feel like I don't have any children at all."

"Mom, I'm going to try to call Bill tonight, so I have to hurry. I promise I'll come up sometime very soon. Okay?"

"Well... Give Kate and the children my love."

"I will. Goodnight, Mom."

"Well..."

"Say goodnight to Dad for me."

"All right, son..."

"Goodnight."

"Goodnight, Robert."

Finally I heard a click and the line went dead. I always felt terribly guilty, hanging up first when I talked to my mother.

Quickly, my hand shaking with excitement, I dialed the operator again and asked for Bill Thorne on Fourteenth Avenue, San Francisco. She muttered that I could find that information by dialing directly, then grudgingly got it for me. I listened to the empty buzz of each ring, praying that he wouldn't be out.

"Hello?"

"Bill?"

There was a long pause. "Yes...who's this?" He sounded very distant.

"It's Bob."

Another long pause. "Do...I know you?"

"You used to."

"Hey...come on...who the hell is this?"

"It's your brother."

"*Bob?*"

"Right!"

"Oh, my God! Wait...wait just a minute...I wasn't... *Bob?* I was just...thinking about you. Where are you?"

"In Salt Lake."

"Well... Hey, it's...it's great to hear from you. Just today I was...uh...I was thinking...about you. I...uh..." His voice drifted away. He was either drunk or being distracted by something. He was silent for several long moments.

"Bill?"

"Right! Yeah, I'm...I'm still here. What's happening?"

"Nothing much. I just wanted to talk to you."

"Oh. Well, uh...that's...just great, Bob. Really." It was quickly becoming obvious that Bill didn't want to talk to me. And suddenly I found that I couldn't think of anything else to say to him. I couldn't think of anything else to say to him. I couldn't even remember why I'd been so anxious to call in the first place. After a long, uncomfortable silence, he said, "Bob...listen...I'm sorry as hell, but...you called at a very wrong time. Give me your number and...and I'll, I'll call you tomorrow."

"That's all right, Bill, you don't need to. I just wanted to...say hello."

"No, honestly... Dammit, I do want to talk to you. But...it's really...the wrong time."

"I understand," I said flatly.

"*No, you don't, dammit!* I can tell you don't! Please, just...give me your number, and I'll call you."

"Bill, I can't give you a number. I've decided to move. I'm giving Kate a divorce."

"A divorce?"

I waited, expecting him to say, "I told you so," but he didn't.

"Bob...I really am sorry. You call me, then, tomorrow, okay? Before...uh...three, okay?"

"Okay."

"Promise me."

"All right, yes. I'll call you tomorrow."

"Okay. Listen...I'm sorry. Really. It's...great...hearing from you again. Tomorrow, okay?"

"Yes," I said, "tomorrow. Goodnight, Bill."

"Night, Bob."

I stared blankly at the telephone as I hung up the receiver. It was ugly. It was the first ugly thing I had seen all evening. The wall all around it was ugly too, covered with doodlings and phone numbers.

That beautiful euphoria had gone.

I'd been very foolish, expecting Bill to be as excited as I was about talking to each other again. Most likely, I thought, besides being drunk, he'd probably had a girl there with him—and that, to Bill, would be more important than talking to me. A whore off the streets would be more important than his brother!

Walking back to the table it seemed that the room had changed—and the people. Now it was just another ugly room, needing paint. Now the "Biblical Prophets" seemed like dirty hippies, needing haircuts and shaves.

For a few minutes Chuck's happy mood lifted my own, but it started to fade again as we left the restaurant. Luckily he was too happy to notice my dejection. To him, everything was still all right. I was determined not to spoil his illusions. "Well," I said, "it's time to take the old man home and put him to bed. He's not used to these late hours."

He studied me for a moment, then smiled. "Sounds to me like you're crashing. Don't worry. It happens to the best of us."

We got into the car and started home; the street was dark and depressing. Lights were nuisances, glaring into my eyes.

"Dad....?"

"Hmmmm?"

"Look, if you don't want me to, say so—but I kind

of promised Jer I'd come over tonight. I mean, we put the thing off today cause you wanted to talk. But we kind of wanted to start fairly early in the morning."

"Start on what?"

"You know, camping. His folks have this cabin up in the mountains, near Heber. They said we could use it if we call every day and stuff. Do you mind?"

"No, of course I don't mind. Do you want me to drive you to Jerry's?"

"If it's okay. If it isn't, I'll stay home."

The thought of spending the night alone in that empty house frightened me, but I said, "Of course it's all right, Chuck."

"We took my stuff over this afternoon."

"All right."

We were silent for several blocks, then Chuck turned to me: "You know...you never did say what you wanted to talk to me about."

"Well...I guess it didn't seem so important after all."

"You sure? Because, like, if I've done something that bugs you, I want to know. Really."

"It's all right, Chuck. It can wait."

"No, really, Dad. I mean, let's get it all out."

"Are you sure you want to?"

"Well, if it's still bugging you."

I told myself Chuck was telling me the truth; he wanted to know what had been bothering me. This was my chance to dispel any last remaining doubts I might harbor about him and his friend. We'd been so honest with each other all night....

But I didn't want to mention the notes or the pictures. There was no need for him to start worrying about who might be sending the things.

I took a deep breath, glanced at him, tightened my grip on the steering wheel. "I want you to promise me something first."

"If I can. What?"

"Please don't be angry with me for asking the question. It doesn't mean I...*suspect* you of anything...or even that I'll be angry with you if...well, one way or another."

"Okay," he said seriously.

I took another deep breath. "I've been...worried... well, not exactly *worried*, but...*concerned*...about you and Jerry."

There was a long moment of silence. Then Chuck said, "Oh," very flatly.

"It isn't that I don't think you're old enough to handle your own problems, Chuck. I've realized tonight that you're really a lot older than I was at your age. And when I was your age..."

"Dad..."

"Yes, Chuck?"

"I know what you're going to ask."

"Do you?"

"Sure. Funny thing. I expected it months ago."

I glanced toward him again; he was soberly staring down at his feet. The expression on his face made me feel like someone was getting set to open a trap door directly under me.

He cleared his throat. "Dad..." he said softly—and I was sure I could hear a tremor in his voice—"things... well, aren't the same, like when you were a kid. I mean, sex isn't...you know...such a big deal any more."

The trap door opened.

He did know what I was talking about!

"I mean," he continued, "if two people think they can groove with each other, well, they do. You know? Nobody gets uptight any more."

"I don't think that's completely true, Chuck. It might be true with you...and your friends, but..."

"Well, who else is important?"

"Myself. Your mother. Even your sisters. Chuck, something might seem completely innocent to you, but if someone found out...someone who didn't feel it was quite so innocent..."

"Okay, right. But, I mean, who's going to be hurt? I mean..." He made a helpless sound in his throat. "Dad...it just doesn't *mean* anything. Look, if, like you get upset, okay? About something I'm doing. Well, it's just what you're *thinking*, not what I'm doing! Don't you see that?"

"Chuck, let's get this straight. What are we talking about?"

"Me and Jerry. Aren't we?"

"I'm not certain we're talking about the same thing. What about you and Jerry?"

"Well, Jesus, Dad...I mean...isn't that what you wanted to know? Hey, I don't want to get in a mess. What are *you* talking about?"

"I'm...talking about a...a relationship...between you."

"You're talking about sex, right?"

"Yes."

"Okay. Right. You were right, Dad. I'm just surprised it took you this long to figure it out."

"Chuck, are you telling me that you *do* have a... homosexual relationship? With Jerry?" The words sounded like those of a judge, getting set to pronounce a dreadful punishment.

"Dad...we ball each other, okay?"

"I see."

"But it still doesn't *mean* anything. Not what you think it does."

"And just what do I think? I told you...promised you..."

"Dad, you think it's something terrible. You think it's some horrible *crime*, and I'll ruin my whole life or something."

"It could, Chuck."

"It's just *sex!* Dad, I dig Jer and he digs me. We like each other, the same kind of things. What's the big deal?

I mean, it doesn't mean we don't dig chicks too."

"Just sex." I remembered, earlier, discovering something; I'd said, "Fuck isn't a bad word to you, is it?" And my son had said, "Dad, you just took a giant step!" Apparently neither the word nor its implications were bad to Chuck; it was still "just sex".

"Have you been with a girl, Chuck?" I asked.

"Well, sure."

"Many?"

"Dad..."

"Let's be honest, Chuck. We've gone this far. Let's go on being honest. I promised I wouldn't judge you, and I won't. But I want to know."

"Okay. Sure, I've...been with girls."

"And Jerry?"

"Yes."

"Any other boys?"

"Yes."

"Many?"

"Jeez, Dad, I don't keep score!" He thought for a minute, then said, "Four. Four guys. They were all my friends. And there's another guy I know wants to."

We had reached Jerry's. Reluctantly I pulled into the driveway and sat staring at the bright splash of my headlights across the Ashby's garage. I had asked Chuck the question and he had given me an honest answer—and now I didn't know what else to do or to say. I felt no emotion whatever, neither anger nor relief. I felt empty.

"Dad..." Chuck gripped my arm. I looked down at his hand, his strong young fingers, then up into his eyes; I remembered how brown and deep and beautiful they'd been earlier. "Please don't get strung out about this. Please! Tonight's been so great. Don't spoil it, please."

I swallowed hard and nodded, trying to force a smile—but I couldn't. "All right, Chuck."

"Have you changed your mind?"

"About what?"

"About me going with Jerry. I mean, it's going to happen again, Dad. We'll be all alone in that cabin."

I nodded. I knew it would happen again, no matter what I said or did, if not with Jerry, then with somebody else. The note had been true; my son was homosexual. The bewildering thing to me was that he didn't seem the least bit concerned about it. He was concerned about my being worried, but not about the thing itself.

Maybe he was right and I just wasn't thinking clearly enough to see it; maybe it wasn't as much of a big deal as I wanted to make it.

"No," I said. "You go ahead."

"You're sure."

"Yes."

"Thanks, Dad. Look, don't worry, huh? I mean, really. I'll come out okay."

"Yes, I guess you will—with or without your old man asking you a lot of dumb questions."

"I'm glad you know, though. I wanted to tell you."

"Did you?"

"Well, sure. I mean, if something's a secret, then it always turns into a big deal—and this isn't, believe me. Times have changed, Dad. They're still changing."

"I hope you're right. Well...you'd better go inside."

He sat silently, then muttered, "Okay," and opened the door. "We'll talk more about it when I get home, okay?"

"Okay, Chuck."

But even as I said it, I knew that I wouldn't be there when he got home. I didn't know where I would be, but I wouldn't be there.

I wasn't even sure that I'd ever see Chuck again.

Desperately I reached out and clasped his hand. "I want to tell you just one thing, Chuck, so you'll know, so you won't worry about what I'm thinking." The words poured out before I could stop them: "I'm not angry. I can't be...because...I've...I've done it, too, Chuck. And...well, I just wanted you to know. Because you've been...honest with me."

There was no change in his voice or his attitude, no surprise or hostility; he asked, "Is that why you and Mom don't get along?"

"No. At least, I don't think so. I really don't know, to be honest, Chuck. But, anyway, I'm not angry with you."

He got back into the car, but now he was clutching my hand tightly. Suddenly he leaned forward and kissed me. He said, "I love you, Dad. I don't care what happens." He sniffed hard and extracted his hand from mine to quickly wipe under his eyes. "Look, I better go. See you, okay?"

I could barely make my voice work; my mind was nothing but a foggy daze. "Okay," I said. The door slammed. Chuck walked down the long driveway, paused, standing in the car's headlights, waved, and then disappeared between the garage and the house.

I backed the car onto the street, barely conscious of what I was doing. I could still feel the pressure of his lips on mine. I could not remember ever having kissed my son on the lips.

I couldn't make my mind settle down. Hazy, unintelligible thoughts seemed to be flying in a hundred directions all at once. I tried to remember all that had happened during the evening, to forget what Chuck had just told me, to bring back that delicious happiness, that clear, clean perception that allowed me to understand things–but it all seemed to have happened long ago, to someone else.

For no reason I could think of, I did remember one thing: I remembered, when I'd called Bill, saying, "This is Bob." I hadn't called myself that for at least fifteen years. But somehow I'd felt like *Bob*, talking to Bill. But now I was *Robert* again, right back where I'd started, and all of the problems I'd dismissed through the evening as inconsequential were back haunting me.

I pulled into our driveway and turned off the lights, then sat for a long time staring at the dark windows of the house. We hadn't left a light burning. I did not want to go inside. I kept telling myself that my fear was unreasonable, but I knew something deadly was waiting inside for me.

But I couldn't stay in the car all night. The night had become very cold. And I was so tired, I could hardly keep my eyes open. Finally I got out, and locked the car, and started toward the front steps....

I hesitated, seeing the shadows clustered around the front door.

I heard something behind me and spun around. I couldn't see anyone, but it seemed I could hear heavy breathing—*and I remembered that sound!*

Freezing fear started low in my spine and spread upward; my heart started pounding. I raced to the front steps, leaped up, frantically trying to get the key into the lock. Just as I managed to unlock the door and swing it open, a cold hand grasped my shoulder. And a voice, right behind me, said, "*Robber*—I'm going to kill you!"

I screamed and lunged into the house.

I saw shadows rushing at me, heard them hissing and growling. My foot struck the doorsill...and I felt myself falling....

PART 2

Chapter 1

I felt myself falling and tried to grab for the door, but I fell on my stupid face anyway. "Shit!"

I got up on my elbows and looked around. He was gone. He was always gone!

Damn him! Why was that?

He'd been so damn close this time, right there where I could reach out and grab him. But dumb me, I just had to yell at him and scare him. Why couldn't I stop doing stupid things like that?

This time would be different, though. He was still in the house. I was sure of it. He'd been just inside the door when I grabbed for him, and he hadn't run back out over me. He was too scared of me to do that.

But he might go out through the kitchen door.

I jumped up and turned on the light and then ran into the kitchen. Nope! The door was still bolted from inside. Detectives knew that meant somebody was still inside, because you couldn't lock a door like that from the outside.

So I knew he was still in the house.

But that didn't make it much easier. He knew lots of places to hide from me, places where he hid every time I got out of that room he kept me in. But this time I felt stronger than ever! This time I felt like I wouldn't get scared and pass out like I always did, and then have him really killing him. I just wanted to get out whenever I could and do things for fun. But not any more. No, sir! Once I stopped fucking around and figured things out, I knew that he had to die or I'd never get out of that spell of his. But this time I had to think it out and make plans about how to do it. I couldn't just do things or say things that came into my head, just for the hell of it.

*First of all I would find him, and then...*skoosh! *Right through the fucking heart. And then...then I would cut him up and throw him in the garbage can! Wouldn't that be just funny as hell, to find him out in the garbage can? With his eyes open, just staring at you....*

Well, that's where he belonged. In a damn garbage can.

"Hey, Robber!" *I yelled.* *"I'm gonna throw you in the gar—"*

Damn me! *I clamped my hand over my mouth. Why the hell did I do that? All that would do was just scare him and he'd find a place to hide where I never could find him.*

Dumb stupid shit!

Wouldn't it be great if I could get him tied down, like those pictures? Tie him down and make him watch when I cut his cock off! Whack!

My cock started getting hard, just thinking about it.

Whack!

Maybe I shouldn't really kill him, just cut his damn cock off! He didn't need the damn thing anyway. The dumb shit never used *it. That's why he hated me so much, because I liked to use mine, and he thought that was terrible! Oh, that was wicked and sinful and disgusting. The dumb shit!*

Get him gagged and tied up so he couldn't say anything but just sit there and go blink-blink *when I cut his cock off!* Blink-blink! *Cut his balls off too! Do it slow, real slow, so's he'd have to just sit there and watch. Maybe cut the skin off first and play with them hanging there. Maybe suck his old cock like I did Billy's and then just as he started to shoot—snip-snip! No jizz! Just air!*

And then *cut his cock off.*

But I had to go ahead and kill him afterward. He had to die. There was no other way I could ever get rid of him.

I could put his cock over the fireplace, like those things they did with deer's heads. Just his cock and his balls on this wooden shield. And the people from church would come in and be sitting there, talking about sins from the Bible, and they'd look up and see his cock sticking out! They'd just sit there and pee all over theirselves!

First I had to find him.

And then I would have my fun!

Whack! Whack!

Now where would he be?

He might be in the basement—but if I went down there and he wasn't there, he could be sneaking out while I wasn't looking.

For a minute I couldn't think what to do. I hated for things to get complicated so I had to decide *things. Then I got an idea! I grabbed one of the chairs from the table and propped it against the door, under the doorknob. Detectives did that. That way he couldn't get out if he was in the basement and I was upstairs.*

I went up the stairs two at a time. His door and Chuck's were both open, and I didn't think he would hide in the room with the door open—but he might! He was tricky that way. He just might be in one of those rooms, with the door left open, just to make me think *he wasn't there.*

I went to the door of his room and reached in and

turned on the light. From all I could see, he wasn't in there.

I left the light on and went to Chuck's room and reached in and turned on the light, but Chuck's room looked empty too. I listened to see if I could hear him breathing, but I couldn't.

I went to his wife's room—and then the girls' room—and then to the bathroom—and he wasn't in any of them! Of course I didn't go inside. I had to decide which one he was probably in before I went inside one myself.

I was confused and I hated to be confused! I liked things that were easy.

It was funny. The lights were all blazing away like we were having a party.

Well, I'd have me a party, by damn! When Robber was dead, I would have me a party! I'd take all my clothes off and run around and jack off on everything. All over his fucking house!

But I still had to find him. I kept getting distracted.

I could do all the things that I wanted to do when old Robber was dead!

Well, I had to pick a room. I couldn't just stand here all night. He might really be in the basement after all, and here I was wasting my time making dumb decisions.

Then an idea came to me. "Hey, Robber," I called. "I'm gonna stay right here until you come out. You hear? I'm gonna stay...right...here—in the hall!"

Then, holding the knife so I could stab him the minute I found him, I went tiptoe into his room. Quiet as a mouse I looked in his closet—felt way back to the back, even down on the floor, but he wasn't there. Then I went to the bed and looked under it. It was dark underneath, but I figured out lifting the covers so some light could get under—and he wasn't there either.

But on top of the bed was the last note I'd left for him. That showed what a fool he was, just leaving it lying there. I picked it up and smoothed out where he'd crumpled it, then I folded it and put it in my pocket. After I'd killed him I could hide it with the other things so they never would find any clue about who done it.

When I stood up and turned to go out, I saw him! He was standing behind the dresser.

Dumb, stupid shit! I had figured that all out the last time! When I poisoned him! He hid in the mirrors!

We stood there, just looking at each other. And then I began to feel funny. Damn him! He was working that spell on me again!

Damn him! Damn him!

Had to kill him!

Had to!

I raised my knife–but he had one too!

I felt dizzy!

What if he killed me too? I didn't want to die!

I had to do *something! I was getting scared again.*

I closed my eyes and yelled, "Die!!!" *and jumped at him, aiming my knife just as hard as I could at his heart!*

Glass splintered and I collapsed.

"Die!" The echo slowly faded: "Die...die.....die......"

My heart was pounding insanely! I was covered with cold sweat!

I sat up, clutching my chest, taking deep breaths to calm myself down.

Someone had just tried to kill me! A madman!

But he'd splintered...and vanished!

It wasn't until I stood up and saw the shattered mirror that I began to realize what had happened. I looked at my fragmented image and started to remember:

I'd felt hands on my shoulder, and I'd stumbled over the doorstep–and then I'd awakened, sitting on the floor of my room, in a cold sweat, terrified! The memory of coming through the front door, and then awakening in my room, were both vivid, normal memories. The rest of it seemed like a dream—but a dream I remembered.

I'd been a child again.

A child in a grown man's body.

I'd been looking for a man, intending to kill him.

The knife I had dreamed about lay on the top of the dresser. The man I now looked at in the mirror was the man I'd been trying to find in my dream—the one I'd intended to kill.

Myself.

"Oh, my God!"

I sent those notes to myself!

I could dimly remember—using "his" desk, "his own" paper and envelopes, thinking what a funny joke it would be on him. I remembered how hard it had been to write at first; I hadn't been sure how to spell the words or punctuate the sentences. But the second time had been easier, and the third even easier.

But those hadn't been dreams!

Nor had this been a dream! I remembered turning all the lights on, looking for "him"—and I'd thought about having a party and running naked....

I ran into the hallway. All the lights were on and the doors were all open. I ran downstairs and found the chair propped under the basement doorknob. I jerked the chair away from the door and replaced it by the table, then sat down, shaking all over.

A voice wailed, "*Robberrrrrr....*"

I leaped up, expecting to see him right behind me!

"Stay calm!" I told myself. "Think it through."

It felt as though something were *sucking* at my mind—something terrible!

"*Stay calm! Damn it!* Stay calm! Stay calm! Think it through! Don't panic, don't panic, don't panic!"

The sound of my own voice comforted me—but I knew that that sucking *madness* was still clawing to get into my mind.

"Coffee!" I raced around the room, repeating, "Coffee...coffee...coffee..." as I got a cup and a spoon and the instant coffee, my hands shaking almost uncontrollably. "Coffee...coffee...coffee..." I turned on the hot water faucet. "Coffee...coffee...coffee...coffee!" I couldn't wait for the water to get hot! It was only lukewarm but I stirred it viciously and gulped it down, then made another cup.

Slowly the trembling stopped. Slowly my mind seemed to cover itself with a barrier, forcing that madness away.

"Sit down," I said aloud. "Calm down and think it through." I sat down. "Okay, maybe if you keep talking...."

Why did this have to happen when I was alone!?

I didn't know what to do.

I was going insane and I didn't have the slightest idea of what to do!

"Please, God, help me!" I whispered. "I know I don't deserve it, but please! I don't want to go crazy! Please! Help me...."

I'd asked Chuck if he believed in God, and he'd said, "Oh, sure."

"I love him!" I said to the empty room. "I love him! He's my son and I love him! I don't care what he does! *I don't care!* I *love* him, God! Please...help me!"

I could feel my heartbeat slowly calming down....

That madness slunk back further...and further....

I deliberately forced my mind to think of unimportant things—like the tablecloth. I had sat there this morning, tracing the ivy. I thought about the table in my mother's kitchen, with the oilcloth covering it.

I couldn't just sit there, thinking of things! I had to *do* something—*take* something! But what? All I had were sleeping pills—and I was utterly terrified of going to sleep. That's when *he* got loose!

"What can I *do?*"

Kate's pills!

"Oh, God! Please let there be some!"

I raced up the stairs to the bathroom. For years Kate had been taking Dexamyl. She told everyone she was keeping her weight down, but I knew Sam had prescribed them as an *anti-depressant!* Just last week, I'd picked up a new bottle for her. If only she hadn't taken them to Ogden with her....

But she had!

I was almost ready to break down and start sobbing, curling myself up in a corner somewhere, when I saw her old bottle, still there. I grabbed it and opened it, holding my breath. There were four halves of those little triangular green ones, the old ones—she'd taken the spansules with her.

I took two halves, gulping the water from the palm of my hand. I put the other two in my pocket. These things were *supposed* to work for six hours or more, but I'd keep the other halves with me, just in case.

Back in the kitchen I had two more cups of coffee. And finally I felt settled enough to try to think through what had happened.

I'd stood here in the kitchen, playing with the knife, thinking hideous thoughts of mutilating "him"....

I couldn't keep thinking of myself as "him"—and yet there were obviously two...parts of me, two individuals, and each had to be "him" to the other.

I wondered if he had a name. The name *Bobby* came into my mind, but I rejected it angrily. That demented would-be murderer wasn't Bobby! Impulsively I decided to call him *Rob*—which was one of the nicknames for Robert that I particularly disliked. After all, he had called me *Robber.*

Idiotically I thought, *What's sauce for the goose is sauce for the gander.*

I chuckled at the incongruity of the thought. It was strangely comforting to know that I could giggle at something as frightening as this. Either it meant I had flipped out, or Kate's pill was beginning to take effect.

I did feel better! Wider awake...stronger.

Rob had thought about being strong. He'd been very sure that when I became tired, was when he became strong. But his strength had been growing recently, obviously! Other times I'd been asleep; but this time he'd come out before I'd got inside the house. Next time...

I hadn't taken that pill of Chuck's while "sleep-walking"! Rob had come out and taken it *for* me. That's when he discovered that I "hid" in the mirrors.

But how could he think about killing me? Didn't he realize he'd be killing himself? Apparently he wasn't bright enough to realize that.

"Idiot!" I said aloud. "You'd be committing suicide."

It seemed that a voice in my head answered, *Liar! Liar!*

"*Suicide!*" I repeated. "Do you hear me."

No!

Was I simply jibbering to myself, I wondered, or was I really in touch with him?

I thought, *This is insane!*

Then nodded my head in amused agreement; it was indeed!

But was *I* insane? I, Robert? Yes, that strange, childish...*thing* inside me was crazy, obviously....

But then I wondered: *Was he?* Remembering his thoughts, they seemed more like those of someone retarded–like Jeff Potter, my college roommate's brother. Jeff acted like a twelve-year-old, but he hadn't been "crazy"; he simply had never grown up; his reasoning powers had remained at the mental level of a child. And judging from those letters Rob had written, the way the spelling and punctuation had improved from one letter to the next, I wondered if that might not mean he was "growing up"–getting brighter each time he got out.

Now that I knew who he was, was it possible he had also guessed who I was? Maybe we could communicate with one another, work this thing out....

What the hell was I doing, thinking about *communicating* with an insanity?

It was crazy to sit here and think about being crazy!

I was tempted to call Chuck and beg him to come home. But what good would that do? This wasn't a mescaline trip; this was real; the person inside me wasn't just a phantom in the shadows, a "bummer". Calling Chuck would just frighten him, and he'd have to wake somebody up to bring him home—I was still far too shaky to drive over and get him.

If only Bill had been more responsive. God! I needed him more than ever now. I'd feel so safe, knowing Bill was around. I'd missed him so much all these years. I'd missed that safe feeling.

Maybe I'd misjudged Bill. Maybe he actually had had an honest reason for not talking tonight. At least I could give him the benefit of the doubt—even if I were clutching at straws. There was no one else I could think of. Mom and Dad surely couldn't help. And Kate wouldn't. Who else was there but Bill?

I ran to the telephone and called the airport. The next flight for San Francisco left at ten o'clock in the morning! I did not dare stay in this house alone all night! Even if I didn't go to sleep, I'd drive myself crazy by sitting and thinking. And if I did go to sleep, I might never wake up.

The clock over the refrigerator read 12:15. I'd have to wait ten hours for the flight. I could almost *drive* to San Francisco by that time!

I started back into the kitchen, then stopped short. *Why not drive?*

Driving would keep me awake, keep my mind occupied. It would take longer than ten hours, of course, but not much. If I drove straight through, I ought to be able to make it in no more than fifteen hours. That would get me there—with the time-difference—around three o'clock!

I didn't have much cash, but I had credit cards. Plenty of identification to cash checks on the way if I needed to.

I wouldn't be needed at the office. Tomorrow, I could call from someplace in Nevada—just tell them I'd changed my plans and wouldn't be home for a week or two. Let Ed run the business; he was going to get it anyway.

I ran upstairs and got out my suitcase and packed again, remembering unpacking it just last night. *Last night?* It seemed like months ago.

The clothes I had on were fine for traveling. I made sure I had my checkbook and credit cards, my driver's license, and as much cash as I could find—eleven dollars in paper and a few cents in change; well, it would have to do.

Downstairs I took several minutes, writing a note to Chuck, telling him where I was going and asking him to tell Kate I would call on the weekend. I signed the note *All my love, Dad,* and left it on the kitchen table.

I made sure all the doors and windows were locked. Outside, as I started toward the car, I found my attention being drawn to the garage. Something hovered on the verge of consciousness, a memory that the garage was *important.* I tried to resist the feeling, but it persisted. I turned on the VW's lights and opened the garage door. My black shadow scuttled quickly over garden supplies, trunks, boxes.... There was something inside the garage that I knew I could not leave behind.

Then, abruptly, I knew what it was I was looking for: Rob's "hiding place". The baby crib. I cringed as I stepped into the garage, sensing the deep shadows above me and back in the corners, but I reminded myself that Rob was *inside* me, and the shadows were just shadows, hiding nothing but the clutter of fifteen years' junk. I found the crib easily, folded, hanging on the back wall, with cardboard tied around it. I reached into an opening of the cardboard and withdrew the brown envelope.

The barrier between his memory and mine was growing thinner all the time. It was even possible that he had been trying to *tell* me not to leave his treasures behind.

In the car, I opened the envelope to make sure everything was there. I found both notes and the pictures, plus a small note-pad that had come up missing several months ago. The first dozen or so pages were covered with strange, grotesque doodlings, naked bodies of menchildren, parts and pieces of bodies—hands and heads, with blood dripping from them—and cocks: long fat cocks, wildly spurting, dripping....

I shuddered and put everything back into the envelope, and put that in the glove compartment. I wasn't at all sure that I wanted that barrier between his mind and mine to come down.

The lights of Salt Lake gathered together, tighter and tighter behind me; the black roadway zipped under me; dark unfathomable shapes on the sides of the freeway became grey blurs whizzing past, caught briefly in the fan of the headlights.

I could definitely feel Kate's pill taking effect. It was almost like being back on the mescaline trip; my mind seemed to be galloping at full speed. The only problem was, I was sweating profusely, and, in the cold air coming in through the wind-wings, my body was tingling, continually on the edge of a delicious shiver; it had a sexual quality to it, like being on the verge of an ejaculation. I'd forgotten how good that could feel!

The road angled south, now moving away from the lakeshore, and a black arm of the mountain began blocking the sparkle of lights in the Salt Lake Valley. If I looked slightly away from them, it seemed they were being snuffed out by a gigantic finger.

I wondered if I'd ever see those lights again. I had a growing sense of *completion*—and the vanishing lights seemed to substantiate that feeling. My life as I knew it—as I'd known it for thirty-five years—was ending. Or perhaps it had already ended. And ahead was my future, like the countryside, hidden in darkness.

Suddenly I understood something else: I'd awakened in my hotel room yesterday morning with a premonition of impending disaster. Now I could see that the notes and the premonition and the feeling of being watched and followed all were parts of the same thing: I'd been trying to tell myself that my life *had* to change, that, in effect, I had to "die". Well, the "disaster" had happened, but in a way no one could have foreseen. And Rob had accomplished his mission: "Robber" Thorne was indeed "dead"; we were leaving his remains scattered all over Salt Lake City—almost as Rob had intended—one part at each place where an aspect of him had died: in that sulphurous steam room, in John Adams' kitchen, in the Mother Earth. Bits and pieces of him lay in that vacant lot, among the weeds and the twisted pipes and the soot-covered bricks with *Fuck* written on them. More pieces were scattered along 13th East, where Chuck had insisted on one last exchange of honesty. What was left of him rested, like the fragments of the mirror, all over the dresser top and the floor of his bedroom.

"That ought to make you happy," I said aloud.

I imagined I felt something like a chuckle in response.

I laughed softly to myself. This was one Easter Sunday I wasn't likely to forget. In a way, the date and the circumstances seemed very appropriate.

Of course, if the old Robert were dead, who did that make me? I truly felt I had definitely changed, but I wasn't sure how, and in how many ways. I was neither Robber nor Rob, but who was I? What would I become?

It was fascinating to think about becoming someone

new. Earlier, on the mescaline, I'd imagined that the change had been instantaneous and complete; but I realized now that such wasn't the case. Now it seemed that the "trip" had been a kind of "visionary" experience—and, after all, that's what the Indians used it for. It had not brought about actual changes, but had given me a foretaste of what I *could* become. Unhappily I found I'd forgotten a good part of that fantastic clarity I'd had earlier. I could remember specific events, such as sitting in those ruins, looking up at the sky, being overwhelmed by the beauty and the idea of the heavens—and yet I couldn't bring back that pure intense pleasure I'd felt, nor even a small fraction of the ideas that had flowed through my mind. The Dexamyl had brought me "up"—out of the terror of lurking madness—but nowhere near as high as I'd been earlier.

Considering it, the events of the evening seemed almost unbelievable. Even more unbelievable was the way I was taking it. By all rights, I should have been jibbering in some corner—like a rat in one of those psychology experiments, where they deliberately drive the poor creature insane by giving him all sorts of stimuli all at once. Of course the Dexamyl was responsible for some of my calmness, but for the most part I felt that the mescaline had prepared me for any number of strange events. I had had my mind grabbed and shaken—the way a dog shakes a rabbit—and my little world had been opened wide enough that I was able to contemplate insanity with a fair amount of equanimity.

But then, from what I could remember of articles I'd read, "split personality" wasn't considered one of the more disastrous insanities. The two personalities might have completely different sets of values, different ways of thinking of themselves, but each could be sane and healthy in its own way.

Also I seemed to remember that the first step toward

a cure for the disease was the recognition of one personality by the other. I had already taken that step. I knew about Rob, and it was seeming more and more probable that he knew about me. Maybe he wouldn't come out again. Maybe now that "Robber" was dead, he'd be content to be absorbed into "the new me"—whatever that might be.

Probably the best thing would be to stop thinking about him. I didn't know that much about psychology, and I didn't want to give myself any false hopes or illusions—or to frighten myself with unreal worries. I'd wait until I could talk it all out with Bill; then together we could decide what to do about Rob.

I turned on the radio and found KSL. They were playing a classical piece that I recognized vaguely; a lovely melodic thing that went very well with the night and the little VW scooting through the darkness.

I stopped for gas at Wendover, the little half-Mormon, half-casino town on the Utah-Nevada border. I set my watch back an hour to 1:30; I'd made excellent time, averaging sixty miles an hour. If I could keep the rate up, I'd be in San Francisco well before three in the afternoon.

And I was feeling great! Not even a hint of a letdown. Even so I picked up two coffees to go at the little cafe next to the gas station, just to play it safe.

I made even better time once inside Nevada, with its wide new freeway and no speed limit. The highway was practically empty—just me and a few trucks. It was 2:45 when I got to the tiny town of Wells, where I stopped again, this time taking a few minutes to sit in the bright cafe (the only thing open in town) and relax from the driving. I chatted and laughed with the waitress about the "nuts" who came in this time of the morning (wondering if she could guess how well I fitted into the category). I decided I didn't need another cup to go; I'd be in Elko in less than an hour. The way I felt, I was sure I could make it.

I caught myself yawning about half an hour later, but that didn't worry me. I didn't feel tired; I just felt like yawning. Now the road was almost totally empty; I passed only one lumbering truck. With nothing besides driving to distract my thoughts, I allowed them to wander back over the events of the last few weeks—back to the time I'd received the first note in the mail. More and more I could remember Rob's secretive activities. I could remember "dreams" I had had, long before the notes started arriving—terrifying erotic dreams, dreams of mutilation, degradation—all of them (I realized now) grossly homosexual in content. After seeing those drawings and doodlings of Rob's, I could begin to understand where the dreams had originated. They were like fantasies of fantasies, dreams twice-removed. I doubted that Rob had ever *done* anything, had ever put his fantasies into practice, otherwise I'd have "awakened" on somebody's doorstep, or out in the car.

There was one dream that seemed more vivid than the others—a night in San Francisco. That one had surely come on the night I'd arrived for the AGDA conference, when I'd gone to bed early, anticipating a long session the next day: I remembered "dreaming" I was out on the streets, bewildered and excited by the cars and the lights and the strange people, frightened and yet fascinated by the "worldly" people wandering around, allowing my imagination to construct elaborate sexual fantasies about them. I remembered a store with a sign that read *Adults Only, Books, Films, Novelties.* Men were continually going into and coming out of the place, and I'd decided I wanted to know what was so interesting inside. The windows had been blocked off with a pegboard display of paperback books that had titles like *Queer Passions* and *Queens on Parade, Boy Watchers, Leather Lovers—Queer* this and *Queer* that, *Gay* this and *Gay* that—all with photographs and drawings of naked men on the covers, their private parts covered with paste-on stars. I'd gone past the store several times, strolling "casually" until I got up the courage to go inside. I remembered the terror and excitement I'd felt as the door closed behind me and I'd looked around, seeing my fantasies explode into life on the walls in huge pictures, high up, above row upon row of magazines and paperbacks—of naked men, with huge cocks half-erect, slick-looking. There were hundreds and hundreds of magazines andd paperback books—*cocks everywhere!*

I'd been amazed to see all those men standing around, so casually leafing through books and magazines, some with obvious erections.

And then I had seen the rack of photographs! Thousands of photographs—naked bodies, hard cocks, men masturbating, men fucking each other, men sucking other men's cocks. Those pictures had seemed almost real to me then. Actual pictures of men doing the things I had only dreamed about.

I remembered thinking how it would upset "old Robber" to see such "sinful" things, and I'd bought a set of them, and then sneaked back into the hotel—up the back stairs like a criminal—with a brown envelope clutched under my coat. The same envelope that was now in my glove compartment.

Remembering those photographs, a sweet tingling began in my groin, and my cock struggled to inch down my pantleg. I squeezed it and delicious shivers spread out through my body. I unbuttoned my fly, reached inside to feel the firm warmth.

In a way it was too bad I wasn't still in Salt Lake. I could go to that steamroom now, knowing what to expect. Lie back and let somebody soap me down and massage me—and this time let him go ahead and suck my cock! God! It would feel so *good* to have it sucked right now!

I started to be shocked by the idea, but quickly

reminded myself that was part of my past; I couldn't allow myself to be shocked by such things—that would be like resurrecting old Robber. I had to keep an open mind, adjust myself to the changes in the world. Chuck had assured me that the world was indeed changing and that sex was "no big deal".

I eased my cock out, tugged my balls to hang out through my fly. What harm would it do to take out those pictures and look at them? I could study them now with a new perspective.

I started to look for a place to turn off, but there were signs that said *Emergency Parking Only.* I didn't want a Highway Patrolman to come by and catch me looking at dirty pictures. But then again, wouldn't he be surprised to come over to the car and shine his light in and see me jacking off? I could show him the pictures and watch him get a hard-on, and then...

I brought myself up short, abruptly dismissing the fantasy. That was something Rob would think about!

A sign came into view: *Rest Stop—2 miles.*

Perfect! All that coffee had worked its way down to my bladder, and I needed to pee anyway. *Piss,* I corrected myself. Only kids said *pee*—kids and self-righteous adults. Old Robber wouldd have said *pee*— or worse: *urinate!* The word seemed ridiculous: *urinate! Piss* was a much better word; you could almost feel the relief.

I saw the lights ahead, lonely and dim, shining down on a building with bright yellow windows. The place looked completely deserted. It seemed so strange, all those lights blazing away, here in the middle of nowhere.

I followed the side road off and parked in front of the rest rooms. My cock had gone limber, and I started to tuck it away—but then on a crazy impulse I opened the door with it still hanging out. I felt brash and daring, even though I knew there was no one within miles to see me.

I walked casually up the sidewalk, my cock and my balls flopping around in the cool tingling air. It was crazy, but very exciting.

The small room was empty. I stepped to the urinal and stood there shuddering deliciously as the hot stream gushed out and went gurgling down the drain. Then I noticed some writing on the wall of the toilet stall:

Hi there, truckdriver! You missed a great blowjob. I stayed here an hour and two drivers stopped. Both of them had big dirty cocks and I sucked them off right here. They said I was better than fucking a cunt. If you have a big cock and a hot load of cum, stop at the next place like this. I'll be waiting for you with my hot mouth.

My cock started getting hard instantly! I could picture the guy, kneeling on the floor of this strange little room, sucking some big burly truckdriver's cock. I remembered John Adams groping me in that rest room—then kneeling before me on his kitchen floor, his face buried hard in my pubic hair, swallowing, clutching my ass.... I put the two memories together and imagined him kneeling here now, reaching out for me, pulling me closer, sucking my cock into his warm foggy mouth....

I leaned back against the toilet wall, closing my eyes, massaging my cock with one hand, my stomach and chest with the other, whispering aloud: "Suck me, John Adams! Suck my cock!" Sweet flushing sensations began swirling in my belly; I spat into my hand, slickly milking my cock, imagining it inside John Adams' throat—until I shuddered and arched my hips forward and shot thick white gobs onto the dusty tile floor.

I fell back against the wall, gasping, suddenly realizing what an idiotic thing I had done! I should have known that a sexual climax would sap my energy!

I staggered to the washbasin, feeling as limp as my cock. I splashed icy water over my face, taking deep gulps of air into my lungs. That revived me a little, but I felt certain that even if I could make it to the car, I'd collapse there and fall asleep instantly. I *had* to take another half of that dexamyl!

I knew it would take twenty or thirty minutes to get into my bloodstream, but I had to stay awake! I couldn't let Rob come out! Not here in the desert! God knew what kind of crazy thing he might try to do.

I swallowed the pill, then wiped off my dripping cock with a paper towel, stuffed it away—then staggered out to the car. For a long time I stood looking inside at the empty front seat, groggily wondering where the other person had gone. Then I realized there had been no other person—only me. The other one was *inside* my head—and I had to keep him there for as long as possible.

I got the car onto the freeway, with the windows wide open, cold wind swirling through the car. There were signs now along the road, announcing *ELKO—15 miles...12 miles,* but I wasn't sure I could hold out that long. If I could get coffee in Elko, that might make the pill work faster....

I yawned.

A voice whispered: "*Relax, Robert. Let go.*"

No!

"*Come on, relax. You're so tense. Why are you so tense?*"

"Shut up!" I yelled.

The voice chuckled. "*You'll never get rid of me that way. Be nice. I like you. You're not like him.*"

"Please," I begged. "Please be quiet, Rob."

"*Relax....relax....relax....*"

"Rob, I'm frightened!"

"*No! Don't do that! That's a bad thing. Mustn't get frightened. Just let me take over, man. I'll take care of you!*"

"You can't drive."

"*Sure I can. I been watching how you do it. It's easy. I drove before, anyway, remember, before old Robber put me away in that room?*"

Suddenly I was out, sitting there at the steering wheel, listening to him tell me: "Got to get gas....in Elko....use credit card....so sleepy...."

"Just go to sleep, man," I told him.

....sleepy....

"Go to sleep, Robert."

I felt good. I felt strong. I felt free!

Robber *was dead! In the morning they'd find him scattered all over Salt Lake City. And now I was getting stronger and stronger. I was growing up! I could feel it!*

I didn't really understand everything that was going on, how two guys like Robert and me could have the same body–but it seemed to make sense. At least, Robert believed it, and, for the time being, Robert was smarter than me. He'd said, "That ought to make you happy"–about old Robber being dead–and it sure did!

Robert had figured it out. I was glad that he did, because I still didn't like to think much. We could get along good, Robert and me.

But he'd made one mistake that kind of made me mad. He kept calling me Rob *and that wasn't my name. I was* Bobby!

I decided to leave him a note when I woke him up. It would say, My name is Bobby, stupid!

There were a few other things that I had to change too. Robert still didn't like me, not really. He still wanted to keep me locked up. But that was because he was scared of me. Maybe I could do things to let him know that he didn't need to be scared of me, like being careful of the car.

Anyway, it wasn't as bad as those terrible names old Robber kept calling me.

But Robber was dead! Dead-dead-dead!

And now I could do all the things that I wanted!

I just had to be careful, like Robert said. I couldn't do anything really bad–even if I could slip back to my room and let him take the blame–because somebody might hurt him, and that would hurt me.

Yes, sir, I was getting smarter and smarter all the time. And it was getting easier and easier to know what was going on, even when I was stuck away in that dark room.

But lately that room hadn't been so damn dark. It was getting to where I could see things and feel things. Not clearly. Not yet. Things were still kind of hazy. But some of the time I could listen in to what Robert was thinking. And I always could hear him whenever he talked to me, either out loud or in his head.

I saw lights ahead, and at first I thought it was another one of those Rest Stops, but it turned out to be much bigger than it looked, and I guessed it was that town Robert wanted me to stop at–Elko. (I couldn't remember where we were going.) Maybe I ought to wake him up and let him do all the things, then take over again when we got out of town.

But not yet. I wanted to have some fun! I wanted to do something wild and exciting.

It scared me a little, thinking about driving through a town–but I figured maybe if I went real easy and slowed down to what it said on the signs, maybe no one would bother me.

It surprised me to see so many lights blazing away. It was four o'clock in the morning. Back home in the morning everybody was sound asleep. But then, I was awake, so it sort of made sense for a few others to be awake too. Maybe they were all going where we were–wherever that was. Maybe we were all going to have a party and all run around the house naked and suck each other's cocks.

I started to look for a place I could park Robert's car without banging it. I drove all the way through the town–real slow, and keeping my eye on the mirror in case somebody started to chase me, ready to wake Robert up the minute anything happened–but nothing at all happened, and I got all the way through town without having to wake him up. Finally I saw a place with its own little parking lot, just off the road. It was called Fred's, *and its lights were all on, with a sign that said* Cocktails *in blue in the window, but without any cars in the lot, so I pulled in. The car jumped and made funny noises when I put on the brakes, but I managed to get it stopped. That ought to make Robert proud of me! It sure made me proud of myself. It made me feel even stronger, knowing I could drive a car all the way through a town, and then stop it and park it without banging it or anyone chasing me! I even remembered to take the keys out and put them in my pocket.*

I really was growing up fast!

There was one guy inside the place, sitting down at the end of this little bar. (For the first time in my life I was inside a real bar! Just the idea made me tingle all over.) He looked up and smiled, like he was real glad to see me. "Hi there," he said, and stood up to watch where I'd sit down. "What'll it be?"

For a minute I almost panicked. I couldn't remember what Robert drank. Old Robber drank vodka, and I wasn't about to have that! I saw a sign back behind the bar that said Hamms, *so I said, "I'll have a Hamms, please."*

"Right!"

It made me feel so good, the way he seemed happy to see me. I wondered if maybe I'd seen him before, but I didn't think so. That damn Robber had never let me have any friends.

He brought me a glass and a bottle and poured the glass full and put it down in front of me. The first sip of the stuff tasted awful, but the second was better.

I looked up and noticed the bartender was standing there watching me, and I wondered if maybe I'd done something wrong. I said, "Thank you very much."

"That'll be fifty cents."

"Oh! Oh, sure!" I stood up and searched through my

pockets and found Robert's money, a wad of paper bills, and some small change. I gave him two quarters and watched him as he took it to put in the cash register. He had on real tight pants and it looked almost like he was naked with that color just painted on him. That got me excited, thinking about him being naked there behind the bar. I could feel my cock getting hard.

When he turned around to come back, I looked hard to see if his cock would show in those tight pants—and it sure did! It looked big! Maybe it would be as big as Billy's.

I wondered how I could get him to take it out and show me. Would he get mad if I just came out and asked him? Probably. You just didn't go up to someone and ask to look at his cock. It would be great if you could, though!

"Something wrong?"

"What?"

"You were staring at me like I had something on me."

"Oh no, I was just..." I looked up at him and he was watching me funny, with his head sort of tipped.

"I wasn't looking at anything."

He stood for a minute looking at me. Then it looked like he made up his mind about something. He got a beer out of the case and opened it for himself and took a long swallow. Then he leaned back on the cabinet, with his legs apart, and scratched himself.

"Oh, man," he said, "this place is so fucking dead tonight. You're my first fucking customer since like two o'clock." He leaned toward me, on his elbow against the bar. "Been uptown?"

"I drove through."

"Yeah, well, I guess things are hurtin' all over, with this fucking inflation, but shit, I get sick of just sitting here, you know? Shit, I could fuck some broad right there...." He pointed to the top of the bar, and then

laughed. "Come to think of it, that's a great idea. Right? Right there on the fucking bar! Now all I need is some chick to walk in."

"Yeah...." I could imagine him taking his clothes off, with this girl laying spread out on the bar. He would look good with his clothes off, I though, with his cock sticking up, hard as a rock. I wished he would go on talking, saying fucking all the time, talking about fucking a broad on the counter.

"You had any action tonight?" he asked.

"Any what?"

"Any ass, you know?"

"Oh–no, we've been driving all night."

"Oh, yeah, well, me neither. It's a fucking drag, you know? Who's we?"

"What?"

"You said we been driving. Your old lady with you?"

"Oh, no, me and Robert. He let me drive some of the way."

He tilted his head and looked at me funny. "Did he? Well, that was nice of him, wasn't it? Where's he?"

"Oh, he's asleep. Don't worry, he won't wake up."

"Why should I worry? Is he dangerous?"

"Him? Hell no! I just couldn't stay if he woke up, that's all."

He laughed again–and he reached deep in his pocket. I could see his fingers moving as he played with himself.

"He don't like you out fucking around by yourself, huh? You, uh...looking for something specific?"

"Something what?"

"Besides pussy, man! A little of the straight stuff, maybe."

It was easy enough to figure out what he meant, the way he was playing with himself–playing with his "straight stuff"! "Maybe," I said.

"Yeah...I kinda figured." He grinned and took his hand out of his pocket. I could see that his cock was *hard. "Don't get me wrong, it don't bother me. What the fuck? Right?"*

I laughed. "Right. What the fuck!"

He started playing with himself again, this time on the outside, sort of squeezing it, pulling it up where it showed better. My stomach got to feeling very funny–the way it did when I started to jack off.

"I mean, everybody's entitled to play his own game, right?"

"Right."

"So...what's your game?"

I shrugged my shoulders. I still wasn't completely sure what he wanted to hear. I knew he was interested in getting his cock sucked, just like I was. But it didn't seem like he was offering to suck mine–not by showing me his, he wasn't.

For a minute it scared me, thinking about actually doing *it–but then I thought what the hell? I wanted some excitement, didn't I?*

It might be kind of fun to suck his cock.

"Well?" he said.

"What?"

"Aw, come on, buddy. Are you interested or ain't you?"

"Maybe," I said. "Are you?"

"Well, shit, mac, I wouldn't be standin' here with a fuckin' hard-on if I wasn't."

"Let me see it."

"How much is it worth, buddy?"

I tried to remember how much money Robert had brought. I hadn't expected to have to pay anything, but what the hell? "It can't be too much," I told him. "We didn't bring much cash." I took Robert's money out and counted it. Eleven dollars...and seven cents. I spread it out on the counter. "Is that enough?"

He scooped it up. "Well," he said. "If that's all you got, that's all I get." He put it into his pocket. Then he came around the bar. "Hang on." He went to the door and looked out, then he propped the door partly open with a chair. "It's okay," he said. "This way I can hear if somebody drives up. That's one good thing about this dump, can't nobody sneak up on you. What about your buddy? Will he wake up, you think?"

I smiled and shook my head. "No. He won't wake up till I want him to."

"Okay," he said. "Let's go back by the cans."

I got off the stool and followed him. Near the back of the room, where the bar curved around and there was a little trap door for him to go through, he leaned back on the bar and unzipped his pants and pulled his cock out. It wasn't stiff now, just sort of half-hard, drooping down. It excited me, just seeing it out. I felt I wanted to touch it. It seemed so strange to be reaching out for another guy's cock, but then I remembered that night with Billy and I told myself, Just do what you done then. So I touched it. It jerked up and got harder. The guy was just leaning there, his elbows on the bar, watching what I was doing. I closed my hand around it and squeezed, and he hunched it toward me. "Suck it, baby," he whispered. "C'mon, suck ol' Jessie's cock. Make it feel good."

I got down on my knees and leaned my head forward, watching it get closer and closer. I felt dizzy and funny all over. My own cock felt like it would go off any minute!

Suddenly he reached down and grabbed hold of my head and jammed his cock into my lips. It scraped my teeth and he jerked back. "Don't you bite me, you sonofabitch!"

"I'm sorry! But you...I wasn't ready."

"Well, you get yourself ready, cause I'm gonna fuck your face! And don't bite!"

"I prommfff!" He shoved it into my mouth again. It tasted funny, sort of salty and bitter, but it felt good. It *felt warm and thick and tight and it filled my whole mouth! I clamped my lips over my teeth, so they wouldn't scrape, and then just let him go ahead and fuck, while I reached down and fumbled to get my cock out.*

"Oh, yeah," he was saying. "Oh, yeah, baby, suck it! Oh, man, am I glad you came in here, oh suck it!"

I was pumping my own cock, tingling all over, as he put his hands over my ears and held my head tight and fucked harder and harder....

"Gonna give you my cum, baby! Hot sticky cum! Shoot my load in your fuckin' throat! Fuckin' mouth! Oh, Jee-zuss! Oh, mannnn! Oh...my...God!"

Suddenly he held my head tight and shoved! And the head of his cock went right down my throat, and I felt his hot stuff shooting into me. My own cock went off like a geyser, and I tried to pull back, but he held my head tight, with his cock down my throat, still shooting, and I couldn't breathe! Then I knew what he was going to do to me! He was going to choke me to death with his cock! He was just going to leave his cock down there and just keep shooting and shooting until I was dead!

I didn't want to die!

I was kneeling—with something warm and hard in my mouth, blocking my throat—and my cock was shooting wildly! Hands clasped the back of my head and my face was buried in thick scratchy hair.

"Ohhhhh....*Shit!* Mannnnnnn!"

The thing started softening, inching out of my throat. The hands on my head relaxed, then fell away. I jerked backward and looked up.

A man stood over me, his head tilted backward, his mouth open. His cock was still dripping, white semen oozing out, dropping onto the floor. My own cock was in my hand and my own semen was sticky through my fingers.

I stumbled to my feet, terrified, dizzy, totally disoriented, my body still churning.

A few seconds ago I'd been driving the car on the highway—and then suddenly I was in a strange room with a strange man—with his semen in my mouth! I felt I was going to be sick. I looked for a place to spit, but there wasn't any. I closed my eyes and swallowed. I had to get out of there! But my body was still uncontrollable.

"Oh, man!"

The sound of his voice jolted me into action. I saw what I thought was the door, and stumbled toward it, stuffing my cock in my pants as I went.

"Hey!"

There was a chair propping the door open. I jerked at the door and kicked the chair aside.

"What the fuck? Hey!"

Outside the cold air chilled me, helped wake me up. I looked for the car, spotted it, then ran to it. I heard him laughing behind me. I fumbled to get the key into the lock, and saw that the door wasn't even completely closed! As I backed in a circle, gravel clattering, I saw the man leaning in the doorway. It looked as though his cock was still hanging out. He was laughing and waving to me.

I could only guess which direction to go in. In the "dream" it seemed I'd already driven through town. I turned left, away from the center of lights, then shoved the gas all the way down to the floor. The Volks bucked and then shot away.

I was furious with Rob! The idiot could have got me killed! Or arrested! It was insane, taking chances like that! Right there in the bar! With the door propped open!

"*Imbecile!*" I yelled. "Grow up! You do that again and you'll get us both strangled, and what the hell good will I be to you dead? Or arrested? You get us inside a jail, and I can't get us out!"

I felt a slight "cringing"—like a dog being scolded—but nothing else; no retort.

I tried to calm myself down—but damn him! It was so fucking frustrating, being angry with someone you couldn't see! Couldn't touch! Someone you only *dreamed* about! Not someone sitting here where I could see him, get hold of him, shake hell out of him! I had to *feel* it. I had to *guess* what he was thinking. I didn't even know when he was listening and when he wasn't! I was sick and tired of him!

I felt a kind of whimpering fear—a fear that I might do something—feel for something....

I slapped my hand on my pocket, reached inside....

There wasn't a penny!

I was trying to think of something else to yell at him, when I suddenly noticed the gas gauge: the needle was hovering about a hair's breadth *below* the empty mark! And this car didn't have a reserve tank.

I couldn't get angrier.

Now each new stupidity that piled on the others seemed simply pathetically humorous. It was cruel to yell at him. I could imagine him curled inside his "dark room" frightened and confused and ashamed.

Realistically, I couldn't be angry with Rob. It wasn't his fault he was still a child—it was Robber's. And Robber would never be completely dead until Rob was grown up. They were both parts of each other. One counterbalanced the other—and I was a strange kind of offspring of the two of them. Ultimately I had to take the responsibilities for Robber's mistakes until they were corrected.

And for Rob's.

Even if we ran out of gas, I couldn't blame him. He had only wanted a little excitement. He was still just a child. Well, he'd had his excitement, and I hoped it had taught him a lesson. The sooner he learned, the better off we'd both be.

"But please," I said softly. "Please don't get us into trouble. I'm not blaming you. It's not your fault. But, *please*, let *me* do the thinking. We'll have our fun."

The engine started bucking just as I passed a sign reading *Carlin–1 mile*, and I managed to coast to within half a mile of the little town. By then I was definitely feeling the pill taking over again, restoring my energy and my good humor. And the sky was beginning to go grey; I could see the desert landscape now, and it was beautifully empty. I almost felt good, walking into town. There was only one tiny gas station open, and it wasn't one that would take any of my credit cards. It took fifteen minutes to talk the attendant into taking a check, but he finally agreed, and took down my driver's licence number and the number of every single one of my credit cards; even then he would only go ten dollars. By the time I walked back to my car, the eastern sky was bright, getting ready for sunrise. The air was pleasantly cool, and it felt good.

It was six o'clock when I finally drove out of that gas station, and the sun was a blinding glare in my outside mirror. But it was too late to worry about being late; I'd just have to call Bill from Sacramento or someplace and tell him I'd be late. The important thing was that nothing really bad had happened; I was still in one piece, still alive and reasonably well in spite of everything.

I stopped in Winnemucka and bought a thermos bottle, and for the rest of the trip I kept it beside me, constantly ready to uncork it and gulp down more coffee the minute I felt the slightest indication that Rob might be trying to get out again.

I reached Reno at ten-forty-five. I'd been making good time, but I knew there was no way possible for me to get to San Francisco before three. I wasn't at all hungry, but I decided I ought to have something to eat, and from the cafe I called the office.

Virginia told me that Ed had called just a few minutes before, saying he wouldn't be in either. He was in Ogden. I started to get angry, knowing we had no accounts in Ogden, knowing that Ed's only possible reason for being there was to be with Kate—but then I asked myself *why not?* What right had I to be angry with Ed for wanting to be with the woman he loved—and their children?

"When he gets back, Virginia," I told her, "if you will, tell Ed I want Gary to go over the books. Oh, no—no problem. I just want to know what we're worth. Tell Ed I'll call him later in the week, okay?"

And that—as I hung up the phone—seemed to be one of the last remaining doors to be closed. I felt much better about everything as I started up over Donner Summit. At one point I looked back and saw the stark, empty black hills and desert stretching behind me—like my life; and just after one o'clock, I passed over the summit and started down into the lush green valleys of California. It seemed to me to be beautifully symbolic: I was leaving a dead vacant past, moving into something fresh and new—a rebirth, a coming alive after a long-long empty winter.

I had stopped for gas at a station just west of Sacramento, and was wandering around, feeling on top of the world, filled with a beautiful new optimism—the fields and the trees were so green, and the sky was so bright and blue—when I glanced into the station's office and saw the clock. It was 3:09!

I had completely forgotten about calling Bill!

I raced to the phone booth, but by the time I'd got Bill's number from Information, then change from the station attendant, ten more minutes had passed. I placed the call, angrily castigating myself for not calling earlier as I'd promised. I was assuming he'd asked me to call before three because that was when he went to work.

Three-thirty or four would be about the right time for a second shift someplace. Now I would probably have to wait another eight hours to talk to him.

To my surprise, a deep voice answered the call on the second ring. "Hello?"

For a moment my bright spirits revived: "Bill?"

"No, this is Warren."

I hesitated unsurely; it had never occurred to me that Bill might have a roommate. A woman answering the the phone wouldn't have surprised me, but a man?

"Is Bill there?" I asked.

"No, he left about, oh, twenty minutes ago."

"I see. Is there any way I can call him at work? It's sort of important."

"He won't be at work. It's his day off. Hang on just a minute." Faintly I heard him call, "Hey, do you know where Bill went?" There was a pause. "Will he be at the bar later?" Then: "Still there?"

"Yes?"

"I'm sorry, but we don't have any idea where he might be. You could try calling the bar later on—around ten or so—usually he comes in, but you never can tell."

"What bar is that?"

"The Phoenix," he said, sounding puzzled, as though he'd expected me to know which bar he was talking about. "If he does come in, should I give him a message?"

"Yes," I said despondently. "Tell him his brother called. Thanks."

I was starting to hang up when I heard him say, "Bob?"

"Yes?"

For a moment there was silence, and I thought maybe he'd hung up, but then I heard something that sounded like, "Oh, shit!" and a long sigh. "Bob, I'm sorry. You should have told me who you were. Listen, Bill was expecting your call earlier."

"I know," I said. "I...didn't get a chance."

"Listen, Bob, don't bother about calling that bar I mentioned. I mean, there's no guarantee he'd be there. I'm sure he'll be home by midnight, though. Why don't you call then—or tomorrow."

"All right."

"I'll tell him you called if I see him. He'll be sorry he missed you."

"Yes," I said flatly. "I'm sure he will be. Well, thanks."

I hung up the receiver, then stared at it. I knew I had no right to be angry with Bill; he'd asked me to call before three, and I hadn't. Maybe he'd had an appointment, or maybe a date—although that seemed unlikely at this time of day—but, damn him, if it was his day off, why the hell hadn't he waited just another twenty minutes?

I knew I was being irrational, that missing him had been entirely my own fault, but I couldn't help myself: I remembered the disappointment last night when he hadn't been willing to talk to me, and I couldn't stop thinking that the same thing had happened again. It was the way Robber would have thought and I knew it, but knowing it didn't stop the dark ideas from forming. I shoved the door open and left the booth, feeling weary and disgusted. What the hell was I doing in California anyway? How had I convinced myself that Bill would be happy to see me?

Now the fields were just ordinary fields, the sky was just sky; the filling station was ugly and cluttered—and the attendant was glaring at me, waiting for me to pay him for the gas. I'd been a romantic fool, dreaming about a happy reunion with my brother. The Prodigal Son had returned, filled with Sunday School fantasies about parties and fatted calves, only to discover that no one really gave a damn whether he came back or not.

I was very tempted to turn the car around and go back the way I had come—go back to living in the nightmare. But I knew that I couldn't. I'd been so foolishly confident that the answer to all of my problems would be finding Bill, I'd burned most of my bridges behind me. Even if I got back in time to destroy the note I'd left for Chuck, I'd still be stuck with the promise I'd made him: to give Kate the divorce. I'd already failed in one promise today; I couldn't let myself go back on another one.

There was nothing to do but keep going. On the plane I had wished that I hadn't left San Francisco; well, now I was on my way back and I might just as well finish the trip—although what I would do when I got there was anyone's guess.

I finished the drive in a mood of sullen emptiness. The pill I had taken in Elko was still functioning to keep me awake, but that bright optimism had left me completely. Several times I tried to convince myself that Bill's roommate had been telling the truth, that Bill had waited all day for my call, and would indeed be sorry he'd missed it—but the effort was too much. Old Robber had risen up from his grave and was reestablishing himself, and I didn't have enough confidence left to resist him.

The weather and traffic seemed determined to aid and abet my mood. About thirty miles out of Sacramento, a strong wind began blowing from the west, wintery cold, and just about that same time all four lanes of the freeway began filling. Leaving the Sacramento valley, going down into Vallejo, I left the bright springtime behind me. Foggy clouds scuttled over the sun and finally obscured it completely. The chilling wind blew stronger and stronger from the dark bay. And the traffic grew thicker and thicker. The speedometer needle dropped from sixty to fifty to forty to thirty.... By the time I started across the Bay Bridge, and entered the fogbank, the car was barely creeping along.

And once in the city itself, the traffic was hopelessly

snarled, backed up for blocks behind every entrance and exit to the freeway. It took half an hour just to get from the Fifth Street exit across town to Van Ness, and by then I was thoroughly miserable and exhausted, asking myself why I had ever wanted to come back to such a cold, dreary, grossly overpopulated, inhospitable city? After five or ten minutes creeping up to an intersection, drivers behind me would start honking the instant the light changed, then dart into other lanes to go racing past, glowering out of their streaked, steamy windows; pedestrians would walk calmly against the light, or dart out in the middle of a block, yelling and shaking their fists at me if I didn't see them and stop instantly.

Trembling from fatigue and frustration, I finally managed to find the hotel I'd stayed at before. I parked in the lot and took my suitcase inside, not giving a damn that I looked (and felt) like a tramp in my levis and workshirt, with a two-day black stubble of beard.

Once inside a room, I collapsed on the bed without bothering to unpack or clean up. I was tired and disgusted and I couldn't have cared less what happened if I went to sleep. Let Rob come out; let him get me into any kind of mess he wanted to. What possible difference could it make at this point anyway?

Chapter 2

"You sonofabitch!"

I jumped up off the bed, shaking and mad as hell! That damn Robert had lied to me! He'd promised that Robber was dead. Cut up and scattered all over Salt Lake. And then he'd just sat there and let him wake up and take over again.

That sonofabitch fucking bastard!

So he expected me to get him in a mess, did he? Well, damn him, I'd show him what a mess really was! I didn't even have to think what to do: I'd take off my fucking clothes and just march right out of here and down in that elevator and out through that fucking lobby and on to the street. Right out in the middle of fucking San Francisco!

And he'd wake up stark naked in jail!

The lying, rotten sonofabitch!

I sat on the bed and took off my shoes and socks. Then I stood up and took off my shirt and my pants. I'd fix them both! I'd teach them both lessons they'd never forget.

I could picture some fat lady starting to get on the elevator, then seeing me there without one fucking stitch on, and her running down the hall, and me yelling, "Fuck you, Fat Lady!" and her calling the manager to call the police. "There's a naked man in your elevator!" But by the time the cops got there, I'd be out on the street, dancing and yelling, with my cock and balls flopping around, and everyone stopping and staring.

And then I'd wake up Robert!

Let him try to get out of that kind of a mess!

My body was tingling and my heart pounding like hell, just thinking about it. I went to the door, opened it and stepped out into the hallway. The hall was empty, and that made me feel disappointed, but I thought what the hell, there'll be people to see me downstairs.

I started to close the door, but for some reason it just wouldn't close all the way. It was like I had suddenly got weak and couldn't even close a goddamn stupid door. Fuck it! *Leave it open. Let Robert sit there naked in jail and worry about whether some crook had got in and stolen his clothes.*

My damn heart was pounding like a fucking drum as I started down the hall. I knew I was getting scared, but this time I wasn't going to let that stop me. Once I got on that elevator, that's all it would take. Once an elevator started down, you couldn't make it stop. It had to go all the way to where you had punched it, and even if I passed out and Robert woke up, he'd have to go all the way down to the lobby, and someone *would see him and call the cops!*

But damn it, I felt like I was walking through soup! He was fighting me! I could feel *him. He was trying to wake up.*

But then I saw somebody coming. Way down at the end of the hall.

Too late now, Robert! Too fucking late now!

It was a man, coming toward me. I stopped for a minute, waiting for him to spot me and go yelling back down the hall for the cops. He stopped too, but he didn't yell. He just stared at me.

Then I saw that he was undressed too!

What the hell was he doing? If someone else did it, that spoiled it!

I felt dizzy. My head felt all fuzzy inside. I seemed to remember the man. Did he recognize me? Was that why he had stopped? Maybe he knew me. Maybe he wanted to suck my cock. He seemed like a damn good-looking bastard from all I could see. He was older than me—old enough to be my old man, almost—but what the fuck? That would make it all the more interesting.

That would be even better than going downstairs. We'd do it right here in the hallway! Let that fat lady see him just kneeling there sucking away at my cock!

I started toward him—and he started toward me—but the closer I got, the more dizzy I felt. The way he was watching me was the same way someone else used to watch me....

And then suddenly I knew who he was!

"Good God!" I whispered.

I whirled away from the mirror and raced back down the hall and into my room. I slammed the door, bolted it, then leaned back against it, so frightened and furious I couldn't even think. My mind was a maelstrom of savage abuse and recriminations, enraged even more by the utter futility of self-castigation. Vividly I began to see fragments of stories and movies about madmen going berserk, howling and breaking things, tearing at everything including themselves—and I knew I was not very far from that point. How easy it would have been at that moment to start crashing my head into the wall, to scream at the top of my lungs and start pulling my hair out, to rip down those goddamned insipid drapes, throw over the bed, rip the sheets into tatters, hurl chairs out the windows. Just give up and go insane!

That would fix Rob! That would stop him. If I went insane, then he probably wouldn't even exist any longer!

One thing stopped me: an almost comically mundane realization that someone would have to pay for it. And not simply money for damages. They might lock me away in a padded cell, and I might never again remember my real name—let alone Rob's or Robber's—but someone would suffer for what I had done, and I knew that most likely it would be Chuck. ("Hey, Chuck, I hear your old man's in the looney-bin. Like father, like son, right Chuck?")

It would have been such a fantastic release just to let

go—to break everything in sight, and then, in one grand final gesture of triumphant failure, to rip myself open with the shreds and the pieces of the havoc. But I couldn't. And finally I slipped down until I was sitting on the floor, and put my head into my hands and wept—at first with frustration, and then with self-pity, but at last with a purely instinctive need for purgation.

And when it was over, I got up and went into the bathroom and washed my face. Then I went out and sat on the bed, feeling totally empty, but cleansed. I sat for a long time just staring ahead, seeing nothing, thinking nothing, allowing my body to gather its strength mindlessly.

Out beyond my windows, the grey daylight faded; lights came on in unseen buildings, waxing and waning in eddies of fog. In the hallway people came and went, chattering, laughing, sometimes quarreling, sometimes with no more than a soft swish of footsteps on carpeting. And slowly my mind started functioning again. One of my first clear thoughts was that life would go on, with or without me; my suicide or insanity might cause a momentary excitement among the hotel guests, or the people on the street as they hauled me away in a police car or ambulance, but the people would quickly go back to their ordinary lives and I would become nothing more to them than "that nut in the hotel", or "that loony who killed himself", an anecdote to tell the folks back home, then forget. I did not want to become an event in someone else's vacation—not at that price.

I knew that my life had contributed very little to the world as a whole; only a small handful of people even knew I existed; my death or insanity would take away no more than the little I'd put in. Still, that "little" was important to me and I couldn't allow myself to negate it. I had a son—and I had my own life. And, when I considered it, not many people could honestly claim more: a few major prophets, perhaps, and a few Nobel Prizewinners. But not many more.

So why should I be so unforgiving of myself because of my failures? I had tried to live the way I'd been taught to live. I had refused to give Kate a divorce because I'd been taught that divorce was a sin. I had tried to fit myself into a pattern, and it hadn't worked—but how could I be sure which was at fault, myself or the pattern? Maybe I was "different", maybe I had been born "queer"—and not necessarily in the homosexual sense of that word: maybe I'd never be able to make the rules work for me, no matter how hard I tried. But that didn't set me apart from the entire world. There were thousands of people, maybe millions, who were screaming and yelling that the rules didn't work for them either—but they blamed the rules, not themselves. Maybe I wasn't so different after all.

Was I any worse off than my own father? Bishop Matthew T. Thorne, the epitome of American middle-class Godfearing normalcy—a man so respected in Glen Falls by people who would never really know him that his name had become almost holy: *Bishop Thorne!* He had two sons who hated him and a wife who had stopped loving him long ago. He and Mom lived together simply out of habit now, sleeping in different rooms, living separate lives, paying as little attention to each other as possible, simply putting up a "good front" for the relatives and neighbors.

Had Kate and I done worse? Chuck had been no more neglected than Bill and I had been—nor for that matter had Cindy and Dorene. Our lives had become habit too; but by breaking the habit—even though it had involved having my nose rubbed in it—I was giving us all a fresh chance at some kind of happiness, or success, or, if nothing more, at least a more comfortable failure. I'd also regained something I'd thought lost forever: the beginnings of love and respect from my son. I could not throw that away—not by killing myself, nor by running naked through hotel lobbies.

I might not have contributed much to the world, but

by killing myself or going insane I'd ruin any even remote chance I might have of someday doing something that might make a ripple in history. If I did no more than prevent Chuck's being ashamed of me, I'd be doing something worthwhile. There was no sense at all in continuing to punish myself, either through Robber's gloom and self-deprecation or through Rob's childish temper-tantrums.

But I couldn't, in good conscience, blame Rob for his anger with me: I had indeed allowed myself to backslide into becoming Robber again. But the mistake had not been in letting Robber come back from the grave and take over—it had been in believing he was dead in the first place. I hadn't lied to Rob; I'd believed he was dead myself. But Robber was no more dead than Rob was, than I was; as violently dissimilar as we were, still we all had to live in the same body together. I understood now that I couldn't get rid of either of them by ignoring them, pretending they were dead, or by pushing them back into a "dark room" in my mind.

I knew what that felt like now.

I hadn't been "asleep" one second of the time during Rob's angry undressing and stomping out into the hallway. In a way it had been like dreaming: dreaming about being sucked back into a cage in my mind, becoming a prisoner within my own body, screaming without voice, pounding without fists, helplessly hearing my own thoughts turning against me. It had been the most desperate and exhausting effort of my life just to keep him from closing that door—with no hope at all that I'd ever be able to get back to it. Only circumstance had saved me—the lucky fact that some unknown decorator had decided to put mirrors at the ends of the hallways.

For a while I was baffled by Rob's non-recognition of his own mirror-image. Surely he'd looked into mirrors before. But then I remembered his thinking that Robber "hid in mirrors". That too had bewildered me at the time, but now, when I put the two together, I began to understand: Rob had been "put away" into his dark room during those few feverish days back in Glen Falls. I hadn't "changed places" with Bill, then; in effect, I had truly become a new person, almost without memory, because I'd shut out all of my memories of Bill. By suppressing and denying and negating myself, I'd rid myself of the guilt, but I'd also rid myself of the person I'd been—both good and bad. I'd even gone to the extent of suddenly refusing to answer to *Bobby*, insisting on being called *Robert.* Only *Robert* was proper enough for the good, clean, righteous boy I'd suddenly become. But Bobby had not been destroyed by the conversion; he had only been put out of mind, out of consciousness—and there he had lain, a perpetual child, sulking about being locked up by a robber—until Robert had grown unwary enough, or weary enough, for Bobby to come out again. No wonder he behaved like a petulant child. And no wonder he didn't recognize himself. He probably expected to see himself as a sixteen-year-old kid, not a thirty-five-year-old man.

Somehow I had to find a way to make him understand that he wasn't a child any more, that he *was* a thirty-five-year-old man. I could see now that he looked upon me with the same kind of unquestioning acceptance as a child would an adult. It had never occurred to him that *he* would be in jail, right along with me. Somehow we had to make a pact not to endanger our communal body—not to hurt it or get it arrested or have it wrapped up in a strait-jacket. The problem was, how could I convince him? How could I even make contact with him?

On an impulse, I stood up from the bed. In an alcove between bedroom and bathroom was a combination dressing-room/closet with an old-fashioned ladies' vanity and a huge oval mirror. I switched on the overhead light and stood there regarding myself. "That's *you*, Bobby," I said softly. "That's *your* body. You're that damn good-looking bastard you saw in the hallway. You're me, buddy. And you're Robber too. We're all three the same guy, and we've got to face it and live with it. If one of us goes to jail, or kills himself, or goes crazy, that's it for all three of us!"

I began to feel foolish, standing there naked talking to myself. I almost gave in to the impulse to laugh derisively, turn off the light, and try to forget the whole crazy business. *Treat it as an unpleasant nightmare—like everything else!* But that was the old Robber talking.

I told myself: *Yes, it is crazy. That's precisely what it is—it's insane. But that doesn't make it unreal. It won't go away by pretending it doesn't exist or by treating it all as a bad dream. It is not a bad dream; it is real.*

Trying to make it unreal was like constantly closing the doors that I wanted to be opened. I had to deliberately open those doors and then leave them that way. I had to start learning to live with both Robber and Rob, learn to cope with them as parts of my personality, not as two evil spirits who took control of my body. And *I* had to realize that we were the same thing, before either of them could. I had to prove to *myself*, not just them, that it wasn't so bad being me. *All* of me.

I chuckled, thinking about the old song "Why not take all of me?" Another song popped into my mind, from one of those albums Chuck had played for me: "Come together...right now....over me!"

Yes, I thought, it had to be done *right now*. I couldn't put it off till tomorrow, or until after I'd talked to Bill. I had been very childlike myself, thinking I could run back to Bill with my problems, wanting him to say some magic word to make all the bad things go away. I had created the problems myself, however childish or ill-advised I had been, and now I had to solve those problems myself.

I was trembling with apprehension as I let my eyes close, then whispered, "Come out, Rob."

Nothing happened.

"Rob?..."

Bobby! The name snapped into my thoughts like a sharp rebuke. *Bobby, Bobby, BOBBY!*

I nodded. *I'm sorry. I meant Bobby.*

I felt a sullen smugness which quickly became a kind of curious expectancy.

Slowly I opened my eyes.

I looked at myself in the mirror, seeing myself as I had just a moment ago, but now with a new sense of awe and excitement. That was *me* in the mirror! *Me!* The excitement brought out gooseflesh all over my body—and I touched it, feeling the delicious tingle—watched myself touching myself.

I felt sad! Something very precious had suddenly gone from my life. As worrisome and frightening as it had been, still it had been an escape to be able to think of myself as a child again, without all the restraints and restrictions an adult has to live with—without that maddening sense of *responsibility.*

But the sadness passed as I thought about all the nice new things I could do with my adult body. I let my hand run down over my stomach, watching it, feeling it, and down to my cock. At first it felt numb, almost cold, withered in my hand like a little dead animal. That's the way Robber liked to keep it, all of the time—but it didn't feel good that way! I wanted it to feel good. It was my cock, and it was special, and it was beautiful!

It started to get warm, and to grow, and a soft, sweet fluttering began in my stomach.

I wanted to go out and find someone to touch me the way I was touching myself! Someone I could touch the same way. Someone who would touch my cock, and let me touch his, and then suck it! I wanted to find out what this "new" body of mine could feel like when I wasn't all bottled up—when I had all my doors wide open! Right now!

I laughed at my own impatience. *No, not yet.*

I gasped and staggered back as a sudden stunning pain erupted in my head.

Stop it!

The pain seemed to falter.

Bobby! Stop it!

Reluctantly the pain went away. I hadn't realized what a frightening power this childish part of me had developed; I should have known—remembering the headaches and the dizziness and trembling. I took a deep breath, then looked into my eyes in the mirror. "Bobby...don't *you* feel that, when you hurt me? Don't you feel the pain too? I can't let you stay out if you keep hurting me."

For a moment it seemed that the pain would flare again, but then, with a sullen acceptance, it faded—and with it, that feeling of newness. Bobby had gone back into his room to sulk and consider things.

"We'll go out," I promised my reflection. "As soon as we shower and shave and get dressed."

Not just out, I thought, but out to find someone—someone I could touch, someone who would touch me. I wanted that as much as *he* did.

Another thought came into my mind like a dark voice of doom: *You're a queer.*

I cringed, almost turned away; then I looked at myself, from my head to my toes, half-expecting to see myself as a monster, twisted and ugly—but my body hadn't changed in the slightest. I smiled. "All right," I said aloud. "I'm a queer. I'm a cocksucking homosexual and probably have been my entire life, only I just didn't have the good sense to know it. Is your way any better?

Making other people miserable. Is that what you want? To hate yourself for the rest of your life?"

The dark voice grumbled like thunder clouds roiling in my mind, but eventually it too subsided as Robber went back to his room, to ponder my questions.

But I had to stop calling him *Robber.* That wasn't his true name any more than *Rob* had been Bobby's. He was *Robert* the "clean-living", "clean-thinking", "morally-straight", uptight Robert.

Robert and Bobby. The "new" names made them seem much more a part of me—and I'd already discovered that knowing their true names was like having a kind of power over them.

Feeling an almost giddy sense of triumph, I turned from the mirror and went into the front room to get my shaving supplies.

Robert and Bobby...and Bob.

Last night, at the end of my mescaline trip, I'd announced to Bill: "This is Bob." That's who I wanted to be—the collective me, when I managed to pull myself together—that man who had called himself Bob, with all of his fantastic self-confidence and insight and self-assurance, with that wonderful feeling of "everything's all right". That's who I wanted to become.

And I couldn't help feeling that I'd just taken a giant step toward finally becoming him.

I shaved and showered quickly, feeling as impatient as Bobby to get out and start to discover what this new life of mine had in store for me. At the same time, like Robert, I couldn't help being concerned about that new life's being "queer". I knew very little about homosexuals, but for the most part, I didn't like what I knew. The image I had in my mind was of what Ed called "fags"—slim, giggling girl-boys, sashaying around like prepubescent girls pretending to be Ladies, lisping, calling each other "my dear" like a bunch of Edwardian fops transplanted into the twentieth century.

But John Adams had not been like that.

Nor had Chuck.

Chuck had said, "Dad, the world's changing."

Maybe it was. Maybe I could find a place to go where I could meet someone like John Adams. I remembered him telling me what a fine time he'd had in the city, how he'd hated to leave. "Anything you want, just reach out and grab it."

I started to put on my new jacket and bellbottoms, then stopped myself. John Adams had been wearing levis and a T-shirt; I felt I could be reasonably sure that he hadn't dressed that way especially for the flight home. My levis were lying right there by the bed—and my old blue workshirt didn't smell too badly.

As I watched myself dressing in the old-fashioned mirror, it seemed I had made a complete circle these last three days. This room was enough like the one I'd had then as to be practically identical; it would have been very easy to believe that only a few moments had passed—that I'd started to put on the new clothes and thought: *Wait! What's going to happen to me if I do?* And I'd been absorbed by a fantasy, about going home, dying, being reborn, and returning to decide: *No, I'll skip the new clothes and put on some old ones.*

I felt something in my shirt pocket and fished it out: the last half-tablet of Dexamyl. I decided to take it. Right now I was running on pure nervous energy, and that might fail me at any time. I didn't want to depend on a drug, but at the same time I didn't want Bobby or Robert taking over if my energy failed me.

And I still wanted to call Bill later. That had been Robert reacting when I'd ignored what his roommate had told me, deciding instead that he didn't want to talk to me. I might even try calling that bar the roommate had mentioned.

The Phoenix.

I might even enjoy going there personally to look for him; the name sounded very apropos of all that had been happening to me.

Chapter 3

Surprisingly, most of the fog had lifted by the time I came out of the hotel; now it hung like a dark but glimmering blanket over the city, obscuring only the tops of the highest buildings, leaving the streets looking freshly washed and shining. I hurried away from the hotel feeling much the same way, with a new sense of direction and purpose. The last three days had been like a passage through Purgatory, a cleansing, a baptism-by-fire; but this was the real beginning.

Trying to decide where to go, I began to remember the night Bobby had sneaked out to buy those pictures. I seemed to remember the name *Polk Street.* If nothing else, I could go to that store and ask someone where to go. I hated the idea of approaching a stranger to ask, "Where's a queer bar I can go to?" but I couldn't think of any other alternative.

Polk Street was only two blocks up the hill from the hotel. I stood on a corner, trying to remember which way I had turned to go to the bookstore, but I couldn't concentrate on the decision; the atmosphere along the street was almost one of carnival, with costumes ranging from ragged-hippie to tailored suits with ruffled shirts. I began to realize that there was an extremely high percentage of men wandering around, and very few women (and looking more closely at those "women" made me begin to wonder about the true nature of the sexual equipment under their dresses). There seemed to be a feeling of expectancy in everyone I saw—and the way some of them looked at me as they passed, I began to feel that they would like to make me the thing they'd been expecting.

It was not an altogether unpleasant feeling.

One young man hitched his trousers around so that his cock made an even more obvious bulge in the tight fabric, smiling brightly as he walked past. He wasn't a John Adams, but then he wasn't unattractive, and his actions had clearly shown that he wouldn't reject me if I knew how to approach him.

I turned, slowly and casually, to look after him as he walked up the street—then paused to look back before going into a doorway. I looked up at the sign above the door: *The Primrose Path.*

I hesitated only a few moments before going into the bar (pausing as I listened to a conversation in my head: *Turn around, you fool, before it's too late. Keep going. It's a gay bar. They'll all be gay inside. That's what you've decided you are, isn't it? You step inside that door and you're declaring yourself. You'll be telling everyone "Look at me! I'm a queer!" Fuck off! Who cares? Who really gives a fuck if I'm queer or not? Chuck. He's queer too! He'd approve of my going in. "You've just taken your first giant step, Dad." Go ahead. You've got to do it sometime.)* Then I pushed the door open and went in.

For a moment—just as I stepped through the door, as the music and the conversation seemed to pause, as faces turned to look at me—I might have believed I had stepped into an average American semi-high-class neighborhood cocktail lounge, where, for some reason—such as a PTA meeting or a grade-school recital—the young men of the neighborhood had gathered for a drink without their wives. But only for a moment: the atmosphere of carnival I'd felt on the street here became a feeling almost of frenzy. The music was so loud that it rattled my eardrums, but the din of voices was even louder, and there was a stridency in some of those voices which was painful to listen to. The room was not particularly crowded, but it seemed like an anthill—constant movement. In and out the front door, from one booth to another, back and forth to the rest rooms—and I stared, unbelieving, when I saw that the far end of the room was a dance floor, and that the couples there dancing were all males.

I saw the young man who had smiled at me sitting on the second stool down at the bar; the last stool was empty. I tried to look very nonchalant as I wandered to the bar. He turned as I sat down, and I thought he would start a conversation, but then he turned quickly away as though suddenly remembering that he was "shy".

I knew that I couldn't stay here very long; I'd never be able to relax and enjoy myself in this constant racket. There was a feeling of desperation in the room that made me want to hunch my shoulders against it.

The bartender, an otherwise very normal-looking blond young man, was moving around behind the bar in a way that reminded me of an old Fred Astaire movie. When he finally noticed me and came dancing over, he smiled like a toothpaste ad and said, "Hi there, Sweetie, what'll it be?"

I cringed and ordered a beer, deciding not to have any hard liquor until I had found a place much less frenetic than this—and preferably one where the bartender wouldn't call me Sweetie.

I was beginning to wonder if my bright optimism back at the hotel might have been shortsighted: I wasn't even sure that I wanted to talk to the young man I'd followed in—not if he turned out anything like Twinkletoes behind the bar.

"Hi there," said a husky voice behind me. "Do you mind if I scrunch in here?"

I turned to see a man, in his thirties, I guessed, standing with his hands on his hips, his head tipped slightly to the side, smiling at me. He was not unattractive physically; he had on a sweater, but I could see that he wasn't fat, and his tight pants revealed fairly muscular legs—plus an obviously small cock. "Were you talking to me?" I asked.

"Yes, I was. I asked if I could scrunch in beside you, but what I really wanted was to say hello. My name's Tony, but my *friends* call me Sophia. What's your name?"

"Robert," I said automatically. I started to correct myself and tell him "Bob", but decided against it.

"Robert," he said dreamily. "I had a lover named Robert once. Of course, we called her 'Bobette' because she wasn't quite as butch as you are, poor dear. What are you doing way down here by yourself?"

He put his hand on my arm, and I twisted away, pretending I had something in my eye. "It just seemed like a good place to sit," I muttered.

"The smoke in this place is just awful. I keep telling Dennice that she ought to keep Murine on the bar—or gas masks."

The young man on the next stool had been glaring at "Sophia", and now turned away in disgust; he took his drink and went back toward the dance floor. "Sophia" called, "Thank you, darling! You'll be rewarded in heaven." He sat down, leaning to the man on the third stool, grasping his arm. "Hello, Love, listen, I've got something to tell you you just won't believe, so don't go away." Then he turned to me and crossed his legs like a chorus girl. "Well, Robert, may I buy you another beer—or something?"

"No, thank you. I'm only going to have this one."

"What a pity! The girls are just dying to meet you, and I'm supposed to lure you back to the booth and introduce you—but fuck them! Let them suffer. They're evil cunts anyway. They haven't got the courage to come up and talk to you, but once *I* got you back there, my dear, they'd be raping you right on the table! *Some* people are *so* tacky! Where were you planning to go when you leave here?"

"I hadn't decided."

"Are you new in the neighborhood or just slumming tonight?"

"Neither. I'm from out of town."

"Oh! What do you do?" he demanded. "For a living, I mean."

I felt like telling him it was none of his fucking business--but I was so annoyed with him that I was getting intrigued: I wanted to see just how obnoxious he would get before I told him I wasn't the least bit interested in him. "Nothing at the moment," I said.

"Are you an actor or something? I keep getting these flashes that I know you from somewhere. Do you know Kenny Peterson in Hollywood?"

I laughed. "No, I'm afraid not."

"*Are* you an actor?"

"No."

"Well, you certainly should be, my dear. If you ever go to Hollywood, let me know and I'll give you Kenny's smart address. She knows every queen in the industry, and, honey, with your looks, you could fuck your way right up there to become the new Cary Grant or somebody. I see you as a detective, you know? One of those two-fisted he-men that gets the shit kicked out of him, but always wins in the end. My dear, those movie theatres would be *dripping* with cum! *Do* you fuck?"

I almost started to laugh. "When I feel like it," I said, trying to keep my voice from cracking.

"Well, what does it take to get you feeling like it? If you'll pardon my French, I would just *love* to get my asshole stretched to a fare-thee-well tonight. Jesus, I'll bet you're built like a Mack truck! Listen, fuck this shit, let's go home and make babies!"

"I'm sorry," I said quickly, "but I'd rather not."

That stopped him, but only for a moment. "What does that mean? 'I'd rather not.' I'm not good enough for you?"

"You're...not exactly my type."

"Type, shmipe, what's the difference in the dark? An asshole's an asshole, baby, and mine is one of the most educated in town."

"Sorry."

He almost started to glare at me; then he shrugged carelessly and said, "Cheat yourself," and twisted around on the seat to face away from me. "Hello, darling, listen, I'm sorry I ignored you, but I was trying to make time with this supposedly butch number behind me. Listen, you'll never believe what happened to Edwina and I. Well...we got our smart asses kicked out of the Ganymede last night. I am so *sick* of those fucking hippie-queens, I can't tell you. This one really obnoxious fairy with his T-shirt and muscles actually stood there while I got dressed, and then *pushed* me to the office. I was so furious I couldn't even talk! And you *know* how upset I have to get before *that* happens."

I turned away, shuddering, trying to shut his voice out of my mind; but I couldn't get away from it. Even the earsplitting music didn't drown it out:

"We didn't do *anything!*" He giggled. "Well...that's not exactly true. You know Edwina and me when we get together. That poor girl. She's not exactly a charmer in her birthday suit. But she tries. Well, we were both stoned to the tits when we decided to go, and both of us got on a laughing jag, and we just couldn't stop. I mean, we'd go into that steamroom, and there would be all these *intense* fairies just *looking* at each other, and if you even *thought* about groping somebody, she'd jerk away like it was some kind of, I don't know, stevedore convention instead of the nelliest whorehouse this side of the Bronx. Well, to us, it was hysterical! All those big butch numbers who looked like they'd shit if you so much as spoke to them—sucking each other's dicks like it was going out of style. Mary, it was like watching the gay Last Supper—even with You-Know-Who up there on the top shelf, blessing everyone with his big peter! All we had to do was just look at each other, and bust up. Well, you can take that shit seriously just so long, my dear. It was just as well they threw us out, because I was almost ready to puke, it was so *masculine!* At least we got our money back."

I couldn't resist it. I leaned toward him and touched his shoulder. "Excuse me."

He turned slowly to look at me, as though he had never seen me before in his life. "Yes?"

"I couldn't help overhearing your conversation...."

"How unfortunate for you. Perhaps you should see a doctor."

"This place you were talking about—what's it called?"

"Surely you're not planning to take up your sword and go charging off to defend a girl's honor?"

"Not exactly," I said. "I just thought that if you disliked it so much, maybe I'd like it."

Rather than looking insulted, he smiled with an expression of intense relief. "Well, of course! How *gauche* of me not to have known it! I *am* sorry, my dear, but I simply did not realize who you were—with your clothes on and so...*hairless.* But you're one of the *perfect* ones, aren't you? One of the Archangels! Well, darling, the Temple is known as the Ganymede Baths, and it's right at the bottom of Broadway, you can't possibly miss it. I'm sure you'll fit in like a pea in a pod. They can worship you and you can worship them, and I'm sure you'll all be just divinely happy. I don't know the address, but I'm sure you can find it in the Yellow Pages...under *S* for *Shithouse.* Tell them Sophia sent you, won't you? Ta!"

He slipped off the barstool and turned to his friend: "Pardon me, darling, but I must tell my hungry sisters that their Handsome Prince just turned into a Frog."

The Ganymede was indeed listed in the Yellow Pages (under *B*—for *Baths).* I hurried back to the hotel and got my car, hearing "Sophia's" hostile voice in my head like a yippy little dog chasing me, nipping at my heels. I couldn't feel put down by his tirade because I couldn't relate it to myself; I was sure he'd have done the same thing with anyone he'd chosen to pounce on. His very first words to me had been like a challenge: "Like me in spite of my rudeness", as though his ultimate victory would be to submit himself sexually to someone who despised him. I could understand how such a conquest would be food for a downtrodden ego—but I could not understand why someone would go to such lengths to insure that hatred. The whole psychology of victory through submission baffled me, convincing me more than ever that if I couldn't find more homosexuals like John Adams, I'd be much better off going back to Idaho and buying that little farm, miles away from anyplace, getting a dog, and, as well as I could, ignoring completely the rest of the world. After all the trouble I'd been through, making the changes I had so far, I didn't want to go through even more to become someone like Sophia—and start calling myself "Roberta"!

Still, I was pleased with myself for having gone into the bar and stayed long enough to find out the name of an alternative place, without letting the atmosphere, or "Sophia's" glib put-down depress me, as it certainly would have a few hours ago.

I found the address easily—a dimly-lit recessed doorway in a large, apparently deserted office building down near the waterfront. There was no sign on the building, no name on the door, only a small insignia—a line-drawing of an eagle with outstretched wings, with a naked male body clutched in its talons: Zeus carrying Ganymede up to Olympus. A stranger in town would have to know a little classical mythology to be sure he had found the right place.

A few minutes later I found myself walking down a low-ceilinged, softly lighted corridor, carrying a key to room 111 ("To your left and upstairs. Have a nice evening."). Earlier I'd wondered if it would be like the Uintah Plunge, with its peeling plaster and burned-out lights, but once through that second door from the street, I'd realized that this was not going to be anything like that place; both called themselves "steambaths", but there the similarity ended. Here the atmosphere was thoroughly relaxing. Soft pleasant music seemed to be all around me. Here there were dozens of men wandering around, most of them young, and many of them very attractive, manly-looking, well-muscled, with white towels narrowly wrapped around trim tanned waists. One or two I saw were clean-shaven and short-haired, but most of them had long hair, moustaches, sideburns, many with full luxuriant beards.

I went up a wide stairway, then turned down another long hall, passing open rooms where men lay on their small beds, some on their stomachs, with firmly-rounded white asses contrasting with the tans on their legs and backs; others were propped up on pillows against the back wall, legs spread, casually fondling themselves. Men were wandering along in the hallway, moving in and out of soft pools of light, pausing to look into open doors. There could be no doubt whatever that everyone there was looking for sex—but their complete openness, plus their young virile bodies, gave me more of a feeling of wholesomeness than degeneration. It didn't make sense according to all I had once believed about homosexuals, but I couldn't deny the very healthy atmosphere I felt. That frenetic desperation I'd felt in the bar was totally lacking here. Here there was no posturing, no scurrying, no loud strident voices—in fact for a long time I heard no voices at all, only music.

My room was small, but not like those wretched little toilet-stalls at the other place, with their half-walls and narrow bench; this was completely enclosed, painted a deep restful blue. Near the door, at the end of a bunk-sized bed, was a framed mirror, tilted toward the bed, and above that was a light fixture controlled by a dimmer. On the wall alongside the bed was a colored-charcoal mural depicting two large winged cocks, flying bodiless, each wildly ejaculating into the dark blue, their opalescent semen merging between them to cascade downward toward the bed, becoming beautifully intricate paisley designs which surrounded a legend: *To Fuck Is Human, but a Good Cocksucker Is Divine!*

I sat several minutes on the edge of the bed, staring at myself in the mirror, listening to an argument between Robert and Bobby. I realized that I could sit here all night, and the argument would go on and on endlessly with no hope of finding a realistic answer—the answer lay *out there.* So finally I stood up and undressed (here, they even had clothes-hangers, and a notched rod to hang them on).

Back in the hallway, with my towel wrapped around my waist, the elasticized band of the keys around my arm, I searched for the steam room, following signs that led downstairs and into a long narrow room where two men were towelling themselves. Both of them looked up as I came in. They studied me openly, making no attempt to disguise the fact that they were appraising me sexually.

I had the feeling that I was moving into, becoming part of, some kind of almost-real fantasy. A part of Reality existed here—I was real and my body was real, the men watching me were real—and yet there was a dreamlike quality about everything; a dream just on the verge of awakening.

But for the first time in my life, I began to enjoy being looked at.

There were several long railings attached to the walls, with towels wrapped around them. I hesitated, unsure that I wanted to take off my final defense, my last vestige of "modesty", but I guessed that no one wore their towels into the steam room, and I knew I'd stand out like a sore thumb if I did, so I wrapped it around one of the railings and went around a corner and into a circular shower. I hesitated again in the doorway, seeing three men under the showers, one of them with an erection. I had never before seen, nor imagined I ever would see, grown men nonchalantly exposing their hard cocks to each other—or to anyone else who happened to walk by. But no one seemed the least bit concerned about it, so I decided I shouldn't be either, telling myself it was simply a part of this strange new reality I was experiencing.

I showered, then went into what I guessed was the steam room—except there wasn't any steam. In the middle of four knee-high tiled tiers was the wildest gleaming jumble of naked bodies I could possibly imagine. Six or seven men, sucking each other, masturbating each other, caressing each other. Slightly apart from the jumble, two long-haired men twisted into an embrace, kissing passionately, apparently oblivious to the two others who knelt before them, both faces buried in their crotches, heads bobbing in unison.

My first impulse was to be shocked and outraged—to spin around and race back upstairs—but I thrust that completely out of my mind and stood there, leaning back on a warm slick wall, watching them, feeling my own cock beginning to rise. The drama was beautiful—there was no other word to describe it. It had a freedom and openness that transcended anything I had ever imagined.

The door to the showers opened and I glanced sideways—and felt my heart suddenly pause, and then crash into my throat. The man who stood in the doorway, staring back at me, was tall, broadshouldered, darkly tanned, with wet-curled black hair matted over his muscular belly and chest. His long black hair almost brushed his shoulders, and he wore a thick, shining black beard.

A voice in my head boomed: "Hello, Bobby-o!"

For a moment, the room disappeared, and the two of us stood in a green field, naked, smiling at each other.

Then, without a word or warning gesture, the man stepped into the room and grasped my hand to lead me through still another door, where steam billowed out around us as we entered. The room seemed not to be a room at all, but a boundless space of swirling darkness. I could make out more tiled steps, and more bodies—these dim, dark and ghostly, wavering as the steam curled around them—but I had neither the time nor inclination to study them, to react to them in any way; clutching my hand, the man led me up the steps, higher and higher into hotter and darker and thicker steam. And it felt as though a sweet surging energy was rushing into me through his hand.

My heart was pounding insanely as the man tugged me into a dark corner, then turned to face me. By then I could feel the hot steam collecting all over my body, my pores opening, sweat seeping out, merging with the hot droplets of steam, beginning to inch downward in trickling rivulets. His hands took my arms and pulled me toward him, our bodies pressed together, slick and warm. He reached for my face, held it cupped in his hands as he brought his lips down to mine, pressing his tongue gently between them. I shuddered deliciously, feeling that fantastic energy flushing through my entire body. I opened my mouth, clasped him to me, meeting his tongue with my own.

I could not see them, but I sensed people slowly gathering around us—touching us, watching us. I felt hands on my leg, creeping upward like little animals; fingers found my balls; other fingers wrapped themselves around my cock, tugging it, stretching it, kneading it. I could feel the man's cock hard against my stomach—and it felt huge! A mouth took the head of my cock in, sucked itself upward, swallowing, tugging my cock into sweet flushing heat! Hands worked over my stomach and back, down my spine, gripped the cheeks of my ass. My body became pure sensation—no longer merely a body, but a mass of exquisite tinglings and shimmerings.

Hands on my shoulders were urging me downward—and I lowered myself slowly, twisting as I did, so the mouth on my cock could stay all the way down; I pressed my face against the man's wet muscular body, slipping down his slick hairy chest, and his stomach, until I could feel the thick head of his cock touching my cheek. Somewhere, distantly, I heard music throbbing, as I grasped his tight buttocks and turned my head slowly until the head of his cock rested warmly against my lips. His cock seemed incredibly long! As I took it into my mouth, it seemed to relax suddenly, to become firm without being totally hard—just limber enough to bend and accommodate itself to each curve of my lips and mouth and tongue. Drums pounded in my veins! His cock became more than a cock; it became the most personal extension of his fantastic body, the instrument for an ultimate communion between us—and I wanted to make love to him, through it, in a way I had never made love to anyone, ever. I wanted to make him feel the same dizzying rapture I was feeling. I wanted to take him into me, to make that part of his body also a part of my own. I urged my head closer and closer toward his groin, and his supple cock inched over the back of my throat—and went down! Wild explosions of color and sound and sensation engulfed me. He was moaning above me, his hands clutching my shoulders, his hips starting a gentle tentative thrusting.

With each slow drive that sweet churning within me surged higher and higher, until it seemed that my body could not hope to contain it—and still it grew! He lifted me up and kissed me again, pressing his tongue into my mouth where his cock had been. His hands slipped down my back to my ass. One slick finger sneaked down into the crack and touched the tight opening there. He twisted me slowly, running his tongue down my neck, over my shoulder, and then down my spine. A shaggy head rose up in front of my crotch, and I watched my cock disappear under a thick moustache...just as I felt fingers spreading the cheeks of my ass...and a face pressing between them...and a hot tongue slickly bathing my asshole!

With his hands clutching my hips, he eased upward again; I could feel his hard cock creeping up the inside of my leg, lifting my balls. As the head of it touched the hole, I tensed fearfully; but suddenly the one kneeling before me took my cock all the way down, and his throat started constricting around it, and my body seemed to melt! In that moment I felt a sharp pain—and then an incredible *rush* up inside my guts! And suddenly his body was pressed hard to mine, and I was filled with him! I had never felt anything like it! My body dissolved then and there! I felt nothing except an astonishing fever to have every inch, every particle, of his stunning cock inside me! His hairy arms tightened around my chest as I sank down, felt his cock go in deeper. He eased back, then urged it in harder, even deeper! And the throat on my own cock was milking it, swallowing it!

I felt his body tighten, his arms tense: "Come," he whispered. "Now!"

I felt him explode into me—and the heat of his orgasm surged through my own body and exploded again to go gushing out through my own cock—and into a throat that kept swallowing and swallowing....

Both of us slipped down until we were leaning against the back wall. With one of his hairy arms draped wearily over my shoulder, we leaned against one another, gasping and chuckling, watching the cluster of bodies around us still writhing.

A few minutes later we helped one another to stand, then made our way down and out the door.

There were only two in the outer room now, up on the top shelf, one on his stomach, the other fucking him, oblivious to us or the rest of the world.

We watched one another as we showered, smiling whenever our eyes met, then went out to dry off. My mind was a jumble of things that I wanted to say to the man, but words seemed so foolish at this point. I wasn't sure why, but I sensed that he knew what I wanted to tell him: how good I felt; how deliciously empty and clean; how fantastically *sane* it seemed to stand there face to face with a man I'd just had sex with, and feel no guilt, no shame, no need to withdraw into myself! It was something I'd been waiting for all my life. And it had happened—with him! With a man I had dreamed about—throwing off his black overcoat, standing naked in the sun, calling "Follow me!"

I felt a momentary disappointment when the man tossed his towel over his shoulder, gripped my arm and said, "See you later," and walked out—but it quickly passed. There was no need to run after him and find out his name and address. Either I'd see him again or I wouldn't. I couldn't let myself worry that the "love-of-my-life" might be walking away from me. For the time being my dream-man had performed his function, and I was much more excited about all that had happened to me as a result:

I wasn't hearing voices in my head any more!

No chattering, no scolding, no arguing. Something had happened to Robert and Bobby. They weren't there any more.

I tossed the towel over my shoulder and walked out into the hallway, feeling almost radiant. I didn't even flinch when a man came around the corner and stopped short, staring at my nakedness. He grinned brightly and muttered, "Right on"—but it wouldn't have bothered me even if he'd glowered at me. I wouldn't have cared. I had found something and it didn't really matter who approved or disapproved. The thing I had found was vastly more important to me than a stranger's disapproval; I had found myself—and fuck the world! I was happy.

Chapter 4

For a few minutes I lay on my bunk upstairs, watching the men who went by. I could well understand why "Sophia" had been so uncomfortable here. Among these men, in this atmosphere, naked, there would be no way for such a person to call attention to himself—to make such a desperate *point* of the fact that he was different-by-god-GAY! His sort of posturing and "cleverness" would be totally invalid here, not only unnecessary, but undesirable. An alien from another world would have been no more out of place. All the formalities and socializations had been stripped away; "personalities" had to be hung up with the clothes, left behind in a locked room. He'd been lost, maskless, stripped of his identification. Getting himself kicked out would have been his only means of reassuring himself that he was still as obnoxious as ever. I was sure he'd be telling the story to everyone he knew for as long as they'd listen.

I'd undoubtedly done him a favor by turning him down; he probably thrived on rejection. In a way, "Sophia" was the gay equivalent of Robert, who became disoriented and helpless when something good happened to him, and no matter how much he thought he wanted something good, he had to twist it and torture it until it became bad. Such people were miserable, because misery was their only identification.

What would have happened, I wondered, if, instead of shutting it out of my mind, I'd allowed that night with Bill to make me believe I was homosexual? It was beginning to seem very likely that my desire for him that night had not been merely the result of my frustration with Jenny Lou. I could remember other nights now, nights when I'd lain awake, thinking about Bill just across the room, unable to get the image of his beautiful young naked body out of my mind—feeling my cock getting hard as I thought about his cock—and hating myself for such "dirty" thoughts.

It was possible, even probable that I'd started whoring around with girls like Jenny Lou because of my sexual fantasies about Bill—because homosexuality was to Mormons "an abomination in the sight of God". It was better to spill your seed in the belly of a whore than to jack off, and as sinful as that was, jacking off was infinitely preferable to being an abomination.

"Sophia" had probably made it his life work living up to being an abomination. However wretched and misspent my own life had been, at least I'd been spared that fate.

"Want some company?"

I glanced up to see a man standing in my doorway.

He wasn't at all unattractive, and I certainly did not mean to reject him when I groaned and said, "Not right now," but he pulled himself back from the door, glaring furiously.

"If you're just resting, you should close your fucking door!" he snapped, then marched away angrily.

I stared at the empty doorway, shaking my head. Apparently there were others besides "Sophia" who thrived on rejection—even if it wasn't real—and apparently not all of them were stereotype "fags".

But I supposed he was right, in a way. In this place, an open door would amount to an open invitation. I didn't want to close the door and just lie there in my booth, but I certainly didn't feel up to having sex again. I was reluctant to leave, knowing that once outside the Ganymede doors, I'd be back in "Reality", but I also knew I'd have to face it sooner or later.

Now might be a very good time to go to that bar and try to find Bill. Feeling as good as I did, it wouldn't hurt all that much if it turned out he didn't want to see me. But the more I considered it, the more likely it seemed that, like the man who had just marched so angrily away, I had blindly assumed a rejection where none had been intended. Instead of believing Bill when he'd insisted he did want to talk to me—or his roommate when he'd said Bill *had* waited for my call—I'd allowed Robert's habit of feeling rejected to start operating again.

I dressed quickly and took the key downstairs, where they gave me my own keys and wallet. I asked the attendant if they had a telephone book where I could check for an address. "Sure thing," he said pleasantly, and hauled out a massive volume and pushed it across the counter to me.

I found the address and copied it onto the back of a Ganymede business card. As he put the directory away, I asked, "How do I get to Folsom Street from here?"

"Miracle Mile?" He grinned, as though we shared a clever secret. "It's easy. You just follow Broadway to where it connects with The Embarcadero, then make a right, and go along under the freeway for about eight, maybe nine blocks."

"Thanks."

He nodded and smiled, then buzzed the lock on the door. As I went out, he called, "Have fun. Come back soon."

"Thank you," I called back. "I will."

I felt great as I drove along Folsom. I felt I'd accomplished something tremendous in the last few hours. Looking back, with the benefit of hindsight, I could see that, however slowly, however painfully, I'd been climbing up out of that pit I had dug for myself, bit by bit removing the "garbage" of my life—and now I felt cleansed and free! I couldn't help remembering how I'd raced away from the Uintah Plunge, feeling so wretched and dirty. Now I felt like I'd passed some kind of mysterious test—and had just graduated with honors!

I had no trouble at all finding the bar, but locating a

place to park was another matter; I drove around the block three times before someone pulled out of a space just a few doors away from a large blue sign whereon a golden Phoenix rose out of curling red flames.

As I got out and locked the car, I noticed another car parking across the street. The driver hopped out, looked both ways along the street, then trotted across—and I had a dizzying impression of *deja vu:* I could have sworn it was John Adams! He was dressed almost exactly the way Adams had been in the airport—faded blue denims, low-waisted, flared at the bottoms, a T-shirt and a levi jacket. Then I saw that his hair was much longer than John's had been, and he had a full beard; still I could not shake the feeling that I knew the man.

He was headed for The Phoenix. My heart started beating a bit faster as he paused in the doorway and glanced back at me, as though he shared the feeling that we knew one another. For a moment I thought that it might be Bill, but dismissed the idea as preposterous. My brother with long hair? Impossible!

Or was it? I had dreamed of a man with long hair and a full black beard, and a voice saying: "Where is thy brother?" At first I'd decided that the man had been Bill—but because of the notes and my encounter with John Adams, I'd jumped to the conclusion that Adams was Bill. And when that had proved incorrect, I'd forgotten about the dream—until a black-bearded man had come into that room at the baths to lead me into the steam room. But maybe the dream had been about Bill after all, not John Adams—nor the man at the baths. Considering all that had happened to me in the last few days, why should I find it so difficult to believe that my dream had been prophetic? Such a notion fell into the catagory of "occult nonsense" or pure science fiction—but what difference did it make what sort of "unreal" classification it fitted into? In the last three days my world had been turned upside-down; I'd been discovering that most of what I knew about the world—or *believed* that I knew—was wrong in one way or another. At the same time I'd discovered that many of the things I had previously called "nonsense" or "superstition" had very real germs of truth in them. My "premonition of disaster" had come true—why not my beautiful dream?

But before I could think of something to say to him, the man turned and went into the bar. Music and voices rushed out into the street, then faded as the double blue doors swung closed behind him. I recognized the song that was playing—it was one I remembered from one of Chuck's albums: "All you need is love...."

I hesitated, taking a deep breath, and then pushed the doors open.

In spite of the loud music, just stepping inside the bar gave me a "hushed" almost "reverent" feeling. It was like stepping from a busy, bustling city into an unworldly rustic retreat somewhere deep in the woods. The walls of the long room were covered with weathered wood slabs, lit by dozens of flickering candles; candles were everywhere—big thick ones with several wicks, tall skinny ones, votive candles in sparkling ruby and blue holders.

Back in one corner were ivy-planters, hanging from the ceiling, with candles flickering behind them. Looking at the ivy and the dancing shadows the trailing vines cast on the ceilings and walls gave me the feeling that I'd been here before—a long-ago feeling. I suddenly remembered my Grandmother, a beautiful, gentle, little white-haired lady whose entire life had been one of love. I could almost smell sugar-cookies baking. I could almost see twilit banks of yellow roses growing along Grandfather's front fence. I could almost see hollyhocks and nasturtiums and lilacs and dewy blue morning-glories—and that dark mysterious arbor, covered with ivy, where Bill and I had played "cars" long ago.

The bar itself—the long counter and the cabinet behind it—looked as though it had come straight out of an Old West saloon. High on the wall above the bar, lit by candles in what looked like a church altarpiece, was a large golden design on a blue background; it looked like an *A* and an *O* fused together. Although I was fairly certain I'd never seen the design before, I had an uneasy feeling that I ought to know precisely what it represented—but before I could reason it out, another uneasiness started, deep in my stomach, and I looked around the long room again: every single person in the place was a male.

Forty or fifty long-haired, bearded, mustachioed men stood around casually, laughing, talking—some with their arms around other men's shoulders or waists. Others stood quietly, their eyes closed, swaying and moving with the music. Still others were leaning along the wall, seeming totally lost in contemplation, their faces almost saintly in the flickering candlelight.

Either The Phoenix was a retreat for a very unorthodox monastic order—or it was a gay bar. These men could have been the same ones I had seen at the baths, now dressed in the strangest assortment of costumes I'd ever seen: faded, patched, tattered levis, overalls, underwear tops, worn denim jackets—rawhide vests with no shirts under them—buckskin pants—moccasins—sandals—beaded headbands; one man wore an Indian blanket over his shoulders; another had on a blue workshirt like mine, with a huge red and gold butterfly embroidered on the back. It was a gay bar; it had to be—even though it was the complete antithesis of The Primrose Path.

I began to understand why Bill's roommate—his male roommate!—had sounded so nervous when he'd told me not to bother calling "that bar" he had mentioned. A part of my mind wanted to be shocked or revolted by the possibility that Bill might be gay, too—but all I could do was smile at the idea. I wasn't shocked at all; I was delighted!

I saw the black-bearded man now, leaning against the bar, talking to a blond, long-haired bartender. On the wall directly behind them was a framed oval mirror; written on it were the words: *Love Is An Organic High!*

The man stepped away from the bar and started toward the back of the room, and I started after him.

As I moved through the crowd, another impression of *deja vu* flooded over me. Again it seemed I had been here before—but not in this lifetime; in some other, the memory of which seemed to hover just out of the reach of my consciousness. It was like *coming home*—back to a forgotten beginning—returning from a thousand-year pilgrimage into strange and unwelcoming lands.

It was like being on another mescaline trip! I truly felt *high!* Men smiled at me and I found myself smiling back almost radiantly. There was a buoyant energy in this room that I could feel as surely as though I had touched an electrical wire—the same energy I'd felt at the baths, between myself and the man who had led me into the steam room. Only here it seemed amplified a hundred times!

The music seemed to twist and curl around me, as a husky voice chanted, "Here comes the sun...here comes the sun..."

I followed the man through an archway at the end of the bar, into another long room—then stopped short, suddenly overwhelmed by a painting that took up the full length of one wall: against a panorama of vast blue sky, with just the tops of mountain peaks showing at the base, stood a naked man, larger than life, fantastically beautiful, spreading his arms just for me, smiling with profound welcome.

It was an effort to tear my attention away from the

mural and look around this second room. Apparently others felt equally overwhelmed by the painting; a dozen men were sitting along a low bench against the wall, gazing raptly at the beautiful figure.

There was a small bar in the corner, and the man I wanted to talk to was sitting near the end of it, facing slightly away from me, listening intently to another long-haired bartender—this one with bushy red sideburns and a walrus moustache.

"...Didn't know who the hell it was...." the bartender was saying. "I just assumed it was one of your tricks."

I remembered that voice. ("Bob? You should have told me who you were. Bill was expecting your call earlier.")

"...Got to worrying, so I called Scotty, at the Phone Company, and asked if he could check. Well, he called back just before we left. The call had come from a phone booth in West Sacramento. He's probably in the city right now. I'm sorry, Bill, but I didn't know who it was."

"Dammit! I knew I should have waited. Well...I guess he has to know sometime. Don't worry about it."

I stepped up behind him and put my hand on his shoulder. "Bill?"

He turned to look up at me—then grinned brightly. "Well, hello again. I thought that was you, coming in, but I wasn't sure." He chuckled and patted my ass. "Didn't recognize you with your clothes on—as the saying goes."

I stared at him, my mouth gaping open. "Oh, Lord!" I leaned weakly against the bar and started to laugh—not loudly; it sounded more like a whimpering chuckle. I felt as though I'd just heard the punch line of an incredibly long and involved shaggy dog story!

"What's so funny?" Bill asked.

I took a deep breath, then let it out slowly. "You didn't even recognize me with them off."

He frowned. "Should I have?"

I laughed again. Suddenly I had become the teller of the shaggy dog story; I was still the only one who knew the outrageous punch line. "Not really," I said. "I didn't recognize you either."

"Do I know you?"

I nodded. "Once upon a time," I said. "Long, long ago."

He smiled unsurely, studying me. I could almost *feel* the first piece of the puzzle slip into place: *Click!* His smile slowly faded: *Click...click...click!*

"Bob?"

"Yes."

He closed his eyes and whispered, "No...no...I don't believe it...." He shook his head slowly back and forth, repeating, "No...no...it's just too damned impossible!" He looked up at me. "*You?*" For a moment I thought I saw a flicker of fear in his eyes, but then he started to laugh. He stood up and grabbed me, jerking me to him, and both of us stood there hugging each other, laughing like fools. He stepped back, holding tightly to my arms. "Well...I knew something was going to happen...but I sure as hell didn't expect to meet you...." He turned, grinning, to the bartender. "You can stop worrying, Warren," he said. "He's here." He looked at me again. "Is this what you wanted to tell me last night?"

I shrugged. "More or less. It's a long, crazy story."

"You don't know the half of it! God, it's good to see you, Bob! Hey! What do you think of my bar?"

"Your bar?"

"Well...a third of it." He jerked his thumb toward Warren. "That blabbermouth there is one of my partners. The other one's out on the other bar."

Warren was leaning over the bar, looking thoroughly confused. I put my hand out. "I think we've already met—on the phone."

He shook my hand, muttering, "Will someone please tell me what's going on?"

Bill laughed. "What is it you keep telling me? 'It will all be revealed in due time.' I'll tell you when I find out." He took my arm. "Come on and meet Brad—and then let's go out to the house, where we can really get to know one another."

"What exactly does that mean?" I asked, grinning.

He squeezed my arm tightly. "You know damn well what that means, Bobby-o. We've got a lot of lost time to make up for. Only this time we'll each know who the other one is!"

Chapter 5

It was still fairly early, around ten o'clock, when we left the bar, arranging for Warren to drive Bill's car home after closing time so that Bill could go with me and direct me out to their house on Fourteenth. On the way, as briefly as possible, I told him what had happened; by the time I had finished, it was almost one o'clock, and we were sitting on the floor in the front room of his house, watching the dying flames in the fireplace.

"...But it wasn't until you dragged me into that steam room that things finally started coming together."

He chuckled. "In more ways than one, I would say." He turned from the fireplace to study me. "Well...all I can say is...I'm proud of you, Bob. A lot of guys would have freaked out completely. I'd say you had the makings of a very good head."

I laughed. "I'm glad I have the makings of something."

"Don't sell yourself short. That's Robert talking."

"Sorry," I said. "It's a habit that's hard to break."

"Just stick around for a while. We'll help you break it."

"We?"

"Brad and Warren and me—and a few others. The Family. We've all been through it, one way or another, Bob. Maybe not as dramatically, but we've been through it."

"What was it like for you?" I asked.

He shook his head. "Don't get me started on that or we'll be here all night. Tomorrow maybe." He turned to stare into the fire. "But there is something....Do you feel up to hearing the other half of your story?"

"The other half?"

He nodded. "You only know part of it."

"Oh?"

"Don't look so worried. It's not bad. Scoot over here where I can lie on you."

I moved closer leaning back against the front of the sofa and Bill sprawled out on the floor, resting his head on my thigh. "You know what you said about coming together? Well, that's exactly what's happening, Bob. All sorts of things are coming together. Sometimes it scares me, how fast things are happening—and then other times it seems it's taking forever.

"Bob..." he said softly. "I don't mean to belittle what you've been through. I know guys who would give their left nut to have a mescaline trip like the one you went on. But it isn't unique. I've been there. So have Warren and Brad. So have most of those guys you saw in the bar tonight. And the baths. That's why we opened The Phoenix. That's not a gay bar, Bob. I don't know what to call it, but it sure as hell isn't a gay bar. I keep wanting to call it religious, but that's not what it is. That's a sick word, and this thing that's happening isn't sick at all. It's *more* than a religion. It's *living*, you know? And it's something that's happening right now all over the world. I don't mean it's *going* to happen. It's already happened. And the people who know that it's happened are the ones who are going to be part of it. The others will just sit back and wonder what the hell is going on—like that queen in The Primrose Path you told me about. Dylan says it: 'You don't know what's happening, do you, Mr. Jones?' There are hundreds of rock songs, Bob, maybe thousands.... Sometimes in the bar, I'll be tripping on the music...something I've heard maybe a hundred times, and suddenly I hear something I've never heard before...."

"Messages..." I said softly.

"Exactly! I don't know, Bob. I know what it *seems*

like but I'm afraid to let myself believe it. But it's happening, no matter what you call it. And it's something poor old Bishop Thorne won't understand in a thousand years, because he's waiting for the heavens to open and white doves to fly down—and that's not going to happen. No, you've got to go *inside* for this—inside yourself and inside other people. You've got to get past all the shit on the outside. It may sound corny as hell, Bob, but you know that sign on the mirror in the bar: 'Love is an organic high'? That's not just a clever saying by somebody like Timothy Leary. It's the God's honest truth. The drugs are just a substitute—they grease the way, maybe—they open our heads so we can start to understand what the real high is. I can't knock them, but they're not the real thing, as the Coke people say."

I smiled. "I suppose that's what Chuck was talking about."

"Probably," Bill said. "The kids knew what was happening long before the rest of us ever dreamed of it. Because they had less shit to scrape off than we do." He reached up to take my hand. "Well, anyway...something happened to me yesterday, too. You see, when you called last night, the reason I couldn't talk to you was...I was tripping...just like you were. I *wanted* to talk, but the things in my head were too insane. You see, Warren and Brad and I are buying this piece of property, up above Santa Rosa, and Saturday night after the bar closed, about a dozen of us got together and drove up there. It's really a beautiful place, Bob...twenty acres up at the end of this fantastic green valley...just a couple of farms besides us...foothills and big trees, and this wild little stream going through. We took sleeping bags..." He chuckled. "Nobody got much sleep, but we had them to sit on. Anyway, just before sunrise, about half of us dropped psilocybin—which is pretty much like mescaline and acid. And, Bob, don't laugh—we had the most beautiful Easter Services you can possibly imagine.

"You know what you were telling me...about watching the sunset, and the stars, with your boy? Well, there's a kind of...*multiplying* effect with dope when more than one of you takes the stuff. It was like what you went through, only a dozen times stronger. And we've discovered that we don't all need to drop; if we're really in tune, everybody trips. So, anyway, the point is—when you called last night, I was still so fucking high that I couldn't talk straight. Also, I was scared. Because...call it ESP, call it occult, call it crazy...but I think you were *with* us, yesterday. I thought about you all day long. It was like...like you were there but I couldn't see you. But I knew you were on my trip with me. And then when the telephone rang...I swear to you, Bob, I knew it was you. I knew it, but I wouldn't believe it, you know? Even when you said, 'This is Bob,' and that's exactly what I expected you to say, I still wouldn't believe it. I thought, hell, I've been talking about him all day, and this is just one of the guys pulling my leg. Only it wasn't. It was you. And today...I knew you were coming. I really did. I sat by that fucking telephone all day, just waiting for you to say 'I'm here!' "

"I'm sorry...."

"Hell, don't be. As you see, it all worked out just fine in the end."

"Things have a way of working out..."

"Yes, they do. Do you see, Bob? It all fits together. Something happened to both of us yesterday. Like your dream about somebody calling you Bobby-o. Don't you remember? It wasn't Dad who started calling you that. It was me. That was our 'secret call' when we played hide-and-seek and stuff. Remember?"

"Yes..." I remembered it clearly now.

"Well," he continued, "you had that dream when you got back from that god-awful steam bath, right? Okay, I'll bet we could check the time and it would end up the same damn time we were all sitting around on our sleeping bags, passing joints before we dropped. Because I can remember going off on a whole trip, remembering the farm and the fields and the whole thing, just like you described it. We were all bare-ass naked, sitting around the fire like a bunch of Indians passing the peace-pipe—and that's the same time you dreamed about a naked man with a beard calling you *Bobby-o.* Coincidence my fine ass! And this whole business of 'Where is thy brother?'—and you thinking that lawyer was me—and figuring out I was gay. Coincidence? Sure."

"All right," I said. "It wasn't coincidence. But what was it, Bill? What did we...tune in on?"

"Who knows? He sat up and turned to look at me. "I don't know. When you try to explain it, you end up using all the old words—and they don't work. No," he said, "this is either something brand new, or something very very old. But a whole lot of people are feeling it. Read the magazines. Listen to the rock songs...." He stood up. "Speaking of which...Hang on just a minute, I'm going to punch a button."

A moment later, music poured out through speakers hung high in the corners of the fireplace wall:

"We were born before the wind...."

Bill came back into the room, now pulling his T-shirt over his head. "This is our 'mystical' bar-tape," he said, "for 'high-holidays'—if you'll pardon the expression."

He tossed his shirt onto the sofa, then leaned over me, gripping my shoulders. "It is also very good music for getting up the courage to say something important." His hands slipped down my arms as he knelt beside me; he gripped my hands tightly. "A long time ago, Bob, there was something very special between us. I'm sure now that we both knew it, we just didn't know how to handle it. Bob, I wanted so much not be afraid that night. I wanted so much to do what you asked me to.

Well...it looks as though we've both learned a few things since then—and I'm not afraid now. I love you, Bob. I've loved you all of my life. And, by God, I'm not the least little bit ashamed of it!"

I looked into his eyes, feeling a wonderful, breathless emotion beginning to rise, pushing tears into my eyes. "That's what it's all about, isn't it?"

He nodded. "That's it."

"I love you too," I said softly. "And I'm not ashamed of it either."

Slowly we undressed each other, watching each movement, relishing each touch. There was no rush, no frantic fumbling, no words. I was filled with the most exquisite peacefulness I'd ever known—and words would have demeaned it. Bill and I touched each other, and kissed, and held one another close, our bodies pressed together, our hearts beating like one in a single body. And then he twisted around and we lay side by side on the soft carpet, easing each other's cock into our mouths—and the feelings were vastly beyond anything "sexual". His long supple cock slipped easily into my throat, as though it had always been meant to fit there—and my cock felt exactly the same inside him. We fitted perfectly. And that beautiful energy cascaded between us, until finally it seemed that our bodies and minds had become one thing—incredibly beautiful and open and free. The moment for climax came and went many times, each time lifting us higher and higher into an exquisite luxury—and then, slowly, sweetly, we came at the same time, and his life seemed to pour into me as mine spilled into him. And then we lay quietly, still joined both physically and mentally, long after that last luxurious tremor had faded...just drifting together in the music:

"...Here comes the sun...here comes the sun...it's all right...."

PART 3

Dear Son:

It seems so strange, writing a letter to you. What a shock it is for a father to realize he has never exchanged letters with his own son. But always before, when you were away at camp, etc., it was your mother's job to write the letters. And whenever I was away, it was less trouble to call and say, "Tell Chuck Hello."

But this change goes along with everything else I've been going through (and we'll have to get used to corresponding if we're to know anything about one another from summer to summer). So much has been happening—so many changes, Chuck. But I think you would understand them. I'm sure you would. And I'm beginning to understand your reference to "something" that, when I saw it clearly, would "blow my head wide open". Lately I've got into the habit of listening—are you ready?—to a certain FM "Rock" station, and the songs I've been hearing have a way of making me stop whatever I'm doing and stare at the radio, wondering where I have been all my life! I've been finding a whole new world, Chuck. The one you introduced me to, that night.

I hope you appreciate, even a little, how difficult it is for a man of my generation to admit mistakes to anyone, let alone to his own child. I was raised to believe implicitly in the "rightness" of adults—and I did believe it; I had no choice, because the only alternative available to me was to believe I was "wrong". I was constantly reminded that my father knew more than I did, and since he was in control of almost everything that happened to me, I took it for granted that he knew what he was talking about. I tried to raise you the same way—without even thinking about it—just as my own father never thought about it. That isn't an apology or cop-out, simply an explanation. It's frightening when I think about how much we accept as "gospel" when we are children—and afterward never think to question it.

But there's something that gives me a great deal of hope: Recently I've been meeting people of my own age who are going through the same sort of mind-blowing discoveries I've been making. And we're all involved in a process of sorting through our lives, separating the good stuff from the garbage. The thing which sustains me, keeps me from feeling that I've totally wasted thirty-five years of my life, is the fact that there is good, and quite a lot of it—once you start getting rid of the garbage.

As you know (I assume your mother has discussed some of this with you) I've been living here with my brother, Bill. You know very little about him because I rarely mentioned him—and the reasons for that are too complicated to go into now. But he's really a great guy, Chuck. You can imagine my surprise when I discovered that he is very deeply involved in all of the things we discussed that night—particularly the thing we talked about as I drove you over to Jerry's—if you remember that conversation. (How could either of us forget it?) And he has taken the same kind of approach you have taken. (We'll talk much more about that when I come home to sign all the papers, etc., etc., probably in a couple of weeks. Bill will be with me, incidentally, so you'll have a chance to get acquainted with your "long-lost" uncle. I have an idea you'll like him.) At any rate, through Bill, I've begun meeting some really fascinating and "beautiful" people—my own age. That night in Mother Earth, I felt so sorry that I couldn't be your age, discovering the "New World" through more innocent eyes. Now I understand that that wouldn't be right; I don't need to be a dewy-eyed Innocent to appreciate what's happening. My life-experiences, both good and bad, lend a solidity, provide a foundation, to the discoveries I'm making, which wouldn't be there were I sixteen or twenty-one.

One hears and reads so much about how the young people have matured so much faster than their parents—because of mass-communication, etc. But no one seems to have realized that those same parents have been affected by the same forces. At my age, now, I know more about the world—about "Life" as it is actually lived, than my own parents do, even now—and I'm only beginning to learn! No doubt you are very rapidly catching up with us, but meanwhile, we of my generation, who are waking up to all that is happening, make up what Bill calls "The ELDERS of the Tribe." (All Tribes need Elders!)

*I don't really know what the point of this letter is—I just felt like writing, I guess. Yesterday, Saturday, some of us went up to this property Bill and his friends (*my *friends also, now) are buying—and all day I felt so close to you—as I again renewed my acquaintance with mountains and trees and water and fresh air. I kept remembering what you said about "things having a way of working out right."*

I'm beginning to hope—to believe—that the world is indeed changing for the better. In fact I've had a very strange feeling that we're slowly moving backward *into a better time, as though we'd reached some sort of critical point, and are now very slowly and very carefully backing away from destruction. The changes won't happen overnight, nor without a lot of hard work—but it no longer seems as impossible as it did just a few short weeks ago. Now I can see it happening–and hear it happening–and now I feel I can be part of it. I feel I'll find a way to help build it, make it grow. And how great it is, Chuck, to feel part of something again–especially* this *something. Sometimes when I go out shopping, or whatever, I look around and see the difference between the "New People" and the Old, and I wonder why things can be so obvious to some and so totally unmeaningful to others. But then I remind myself of how deaf, dumb, and blind I was. It takes one hell of a jolt to get yourself out of the habit of believing you know what is going on.*

I'm tremendously excited about the whole thing! And that's a beautiful feeling!

By the way, you probably won't recognize me when I arrive. There are a few additions to my face. I'm afraid your mother will be outraged–even more when she sees your uncle's long hair–but you should appreciate it.

Well, I'd better finish this and get it into the mail. I'm supposed to be helping Bill cut a new "trip-tape" for the place he works at. Every Sunday evening we have a kind of "Celebration" and listen to a new tape of the "Be-Happy" rock songs. Right now he's recording the one I heard for the first time, the night I came home and found you and Jerry so "peacefully" listening in the living room. (Which reminds me: Please give my best regards to Jerry. I'm hoping I'll have time to get to know him better–along with some of your other friends.) Strangely enough–or is it strange at all?–the lyrics to that song provide a very appropriate end to this first letter to you:

"Everything's all right–everything's fine."
Perhaps we can make it come true.
I'll be seeing you soon.

All My Love–
Dad